Resolution

A Novel

by

MARK ELLOTT

Resolution

A novel by Mark Ellott

First published in 2019 by Leg Iron Books

ISBN 9781081148775

LEG IRON BOOKS

Prologue

June, 1987

DAILY NEWS

Sunday 7th June, 1987

Koh-I-Noor Stolen.

In a daring raid last night, the Koh-I-Noor diamond - the largest cut diamond in the world - was stolen from the Crown Jewels.

During the [...] day morni[...] that the ga[...] the Tower [...] stone from [...] away with [...] ted.

The police [...] ing enquiri[...] to have so f[...]

Detective Constable Radfield stated this morning that the police are following several lines of enquiry. When asked if this was the work of notorious international jewel thief, Fábián Rousseau, he declined to elaborate.

Joey Dunlop Wins Senior TT

Joey Dunlop won the senior TT yesterday after the race was postponed from Friday due to bad [...]

The Evening Journal

Monday 8th June, 1987

Hunt for Fábián Rousseau Continues

Police are still hunting for Fábián Rousseau, suspected of masterminding the audacious theft of the Koh-I-Noor diamond from the [...] the

Detective constable Radfield issued a statement that they are currently liasing with Interpol and the French Surèté Nationale in what has become an international manhunt.

When questioned about whether they suspected Fábián Rousseau, Rad- [...] to be

Tories Lead In Polls

Margaret Thatcher is set to return to Number 10 according to the latest polling.

With only two days before the election, Labour are falling behind and the Conservatives look set to win a third consecutive term in

THE MORNING STANDARD

YOUR NUMBER ONE SOURCE FOR HEADLINES   Thursday, 11th June, 1987

Tories Set to Win Election

As the country goes to the polls today, Margaret Thatcher is set to make history and secure a third term in power, with MORI currently predicting a 43% share of the vote

Labour are lagging 11 points behind and the SDP/Liberal Alliance are at 24% with hopes of building on their suc[...]

Koh-I-Noor Recovered.

Following an intensive investigation since the theft of the Koh-I-Noor last weekend, police have recovered the missing diamond.

Three men, aged between 22 and 40 are currently helping the police with their inquiries. The men are believed to be French nationals.

Detective Sergeant Radfield - recently promoted - issued the following statement:

"Following a thorough investigation, the Koh-I-Noor diamond has been recovered and restored to its rightful place in the crown jewels.

However, our enquiries are ongoing as we have still to apprehend the suspected mastermind behind this audacious theft. I am working closely [...] colleagues to

Pascale Hervé felt the cold dark waters of the Douro drawing her down. The current below the surface dragged her deeper and deeper and the weeds wrapped themselves around her legs like the demons of Hades trying to draw her into their dark, cold world, squeezing the last breath of air out. She desperately clung on as her brain, starved of oxygen, wanted to let go. She tried to shake her head, but it felt sluggish. She tried to breathe but her lungs filled with water and she coughed it up and her head felt light, stars flashing before her eyes.

She looked up as her lungs felt like bursting. The sun was little more than a lightening of the murky water above her head.

Swim! Swim damn you! Don't drown in this godforsaken river!

She pushed down with her leaden arms, fighting her way to the surface. Slowly, surely, the water grew brighter as the surface came down to meet her.

***

Death materialised on the shore of the River Douro. He looked along the sandy beach. Something wasn't right. He fished in the folds of his cape and pulled out a smartphone. He looked at the screen and frowned. He tapped it with a bony finger, but to no avail. It told him nothing new. Still it displayed the obtuse error message.

"Bloody technology," he complained to himself. *"Nothing's been right since the IT guys took over. If they didn't spend all their time trying to be clever and playing computer games, this damned gadget might actually do what it is supposed to do."*

He turned to his horse who was busily munching on a bush, so no one was listening. *No one ever does,* he thought morosely.

Tapping the app again, stabbing ever more irritably at the screen with a bony digit, he got the same display as before.

"It still says there is an error message," He muttered to no one in particular. *"Why are these messages so unhelpful?"* He frowned at the phone, which was pretty good going, given that he had neither flesh on his forehead nor eyebrows to frown with, but he managed it nonetheless.

"What is an out of memory error supposed to be anyway? Why don't they tell you in plain English what they mean? Bloody technology!"

Death looked back on the old days with some fondness—when he had a room full of hourglasses to work with. Nice wooden frames with elegant, classic glass interiors with the silver sand of life slipping through the tiny waist and each had the owner's name etched on a brass plate. Elegant, yes that was the word—elegant and simple. Less, thought Death, was definitely more. They were things of beauty in their own right. Sure, he thought to himself, it might be crude from a technology point of view, but it worked and was reliable—not like this modern stuff and its vague "out of memory" messages, which could mean anything.

Ever since the smartarse IT guys arrived and changed everything for the better he had been struggling with this problem—wrong place, wrong time, sometimes both. Besides, he thought darkly to himself, "better" is a subjective term. "Better" for him was a room full of nice comforting hourglasses in tactile wood and glass that you could touch and look at and worked as they were supposed to, not like this technology stuff that worked in ways mysterious to the mind of supernatural beings, lost in electrons and opaque gadgetry. Once he had a library full of lives that stretched into infinity. Now he had a small featureless office, a desk, PC and a smartphone. He did not consider this to be better.

He snorted to himself as he looked about him at the empty river flowing indolently to the sea somewhere to the west. Something wasn't in tune here and he didn't like it. There was supposed to be an accident and folk to collect. They were noticeable only by their absence.

"Bugger! Right place, wrong time. Again! This is another mess that I suppose I'll have to fix."

***

Le Havre, May 1987.

The steely grey light of dawn heralded the start of a new day. As the sun lifted its head slowly in the eastern sky, the docks of Le Havre took form and the cranes loomed ominously in the morning mist still hanging languidly over the water. It would be another hour before the final tendrils of vapour cleared completely, but the calm still air promised a fine day. So, incidentally, did the broadcast on the car radio, but the occupants of the Peugeot 205 remained sceptical, preferring proof to belief.

Geneviève Sophie Duval was not a happy woman. At thirty years old, she would have passed for five years younger. Petite and fair skinned she wore her blonde hair cropped in a short bob which she habitually flicked back, despite it coming nowhere near her eyes. Sighing from time to time, she glanced irritably at her watch before returning her gaze to the tranquil waters of the docks.

Her companion sat silently drawing the last gasps of smoke from her cigarette before reaching for the button on the door. The window hissed down allowing the cool morning air to push aside the smoky fug. Pascale Hervé flicked the dog end out into the morning before raising the window, trapping the smoky atmosphere inside once more. Where her companion was fair, Pascale was dark with the olive complexion of the Mediterranean. Curtains of black, lank hair fell about her sombre face as she stared aimlessly at the empty docks. Where Geneviève chose a smart jacket and skirt suit with matching suede boots, Pascale opted for the more casual leather jacket and jeans. "I do casual," she once explained. "I avoid smart."

"I noticed," Geneviève replied flatly.

The ferry they were waiting for was an hour late and they had been dozing fitfully in the car. Geneviève stretched awkwardly and yawned, glancing across at the P&O vessel nosing into the dock. Her gaze moved across to the dashboard clock that glowed a luminous seven fifteen. Sighing, she shifted her attention to the faxed photographs lying on the dashboard, taken the previous evening in Portsmouth.

As the first vehicles emerged from the ferry, Geneviève drummed her fingers impatiently on the steering wheel and flicked her hair away from her forehead again. Pascale stared ahead, hands thrust firmly into her jacket pockets, saying nothing.

Several motorcyclists emerged from the ship and descended the ramp. They appeared to be travelling in a group as the first riders waited for the others to emerge before the gaggle rode together to the customs post.

Then Geneviève saw what she was looking for. Two matching Honda VF1000s emerged and joined the others. The riders presented themselves at the disinterested customs post and were waved straight through before they had time to retrieve their passports from their tank bags. Neither saw the Peugeot as the group left the port and turned their bikes onto the *Route Industrielle*. Geneviève perked up as they emerged from the *Douanes* and turned the Peugeot's ignition key. As the little flotilla of bikes entered the crazy congestion of the French rush hour, Geneviève engaged first gear.

Pascale broke her silence. "That's them."

"The VF1000s." Geneviève checked that the road was clear.

"Ok. Now we move, eh?"

She reached for the radio and confirmed the sighting.

"Roger. Just follow. Do not engage."

"Understood."

Geneviève smiled and followed the bikes into the rush hour traffic heading for the *AutoRoute* as Pascale replaced the radio back on the dashboard.

Chapter 1

Lodève, Christmas Eve 2017, thirty years later.

Pascale Hervé waved her badge and the gendarme lifted the tape and allowed her past the cordon with a salute. *"Lieutenant."*

The narrow street was quiet now as much of the small market town had shut down for the festivities. Evening was descending with a light drizzle swept in from the Mediterranean some fifty kilometres south. The old walls of the buildings were illuminated by the silent blue flashing lights of the emergency vehicles and the Christmas lights suspended from the streetlamps. Pascale cast experienced eyes across the scene. *A suicide*, she sighed. What a time to end it all. What, she wondered briefly, drove someone to such despair that they felt there was no alternative but to end it all?

Ordinarily, a suicide wouldn't be something she would be troubled with. However, there was always the possibility that it was foul play, so she needed to rule it out before handing over to the local police. *Brigadier* Patrice Laurent was crouching over the body.

"Patrice," she said.

Patrice stood. *"Madame,"* he said, watching his superior as she surveyed the scene as they had done so many times before.

Retirement loomed and she was unhappy about the prospect. He took in the slim figure dressed in leather jacket and Kevlar jeans she'd worn for riding the motorcycle from Montpellier. Despite being in her fifties now, her dark hair pulled back in a low ponytail showed few signs of grey and her olive skin was lined about her dark eyes, but was otherwise fresh and smooth. Pascale had aged well, yet in her demeanour there was an underlying unhappiness as age brought with it its own reward; the end of her career. This was her last Christmas with the department and by New Year she would be gone with nothing left to do. No purpose to her life.

"What do we have?"

Patrice looked up at the building deep in the Arab quarter of the town where the streets were narrow and dark, such that the buildings were clustered together shutting out much of the light during the day. Now in the early evening, the artificial light caught the drizzle and held it up for examination before it drifted off into the shadows. "Fell from that window," he said, gesturing to an open window three storeys up. He looked down at the corpse, spread-eagled on the flagstones.

"Come, look."

Pascale knelt down and looked at the crushed and broken body. Immediately she saw what was troubling Patrice. The man was alive.

"Impossible," she breathed.

"Indeed," he said, kneeling down beside her to examine the body once more. "This is not the first one lately. The back of the skull is shattered and yet there is life in the eyes. Third one of these undead corpses in the past twenty-four hours."

She looked in the eyes that stared back at her. There was life, yet no reaction. The pupils were dilated and they moved to look at her, drilling into her soul, and occasionally the eyelids blinked, so, yes, there was indeed life, but this shouldn't be happening, she assured herself.

"This man should be dead. Have the paramedics taken a look?"

Patrice nodded. "They are as baffled as we are. Everything about the body is dead except the eyes." He stood. "If you have seen enough, they will take him back to Montpellier."

She stood. "And the others?"

He sighed. "Exactly the same. The body is dead to all appearances, but there is something still there. Tests show that the brain is dead, but the eyes remain alive. It makes no sense. It's as if..." He paused, considering the absurdity of what was going through his mind.

"As if?" she prompted.

"As if... As if the soul cannot depart the body, as if there is some link keeping them there. I'm not making any sense, I think."

"No less than what we are looking at." She glanced at her watch. Guillaume would be wondering where she was. Again, she was out late working when they were supposed to be having a quiet night in. She should have been home an hour ago. He wanted to celebrate the coming of Christmas with her and once more she was allowing dead bodies to come between them. He would understand. He always understood and sometimes that irritated her to distraction. Maybe if he got good and angry, she would feel better about letting her work absorb her life to the exclusion of everything else, including her marriage.

"Any sign of foul play?" she asked with little expectation of a positive answer.

Patrice shook his head. "He left a note. Even so, we will do a complete search of the crime scene."

"What a time to do it, eh?"

Pascale spent a short time looking about the man's flat and perused the suicide note held out for her by the CSI, sealed in its plastic bag. The usual thing, she mused, looking at the final pathetic communication from a desolate soul. Life was just too much for some. Loneliness and despair while everyone else was celebrating togetherness and family. Christmas was, for the lost souls, a dark, lonely place full of anguish and pain. Season of good cheer indeed. Goodwill to all men, except those who lived alone; lonely, lost and without the touch of human kindness - even in the throng of the crowd. And in that moment, she recalled another Christmas. One full of loss and heartache. The dead man on the pavement was not alone in his desolation.

Melancholy followed her as she walked back to the bike. The Harley Springer Softail loitered menacingly on its sidestand. The American beast was a brutal thing; ugly to the eye and designed for the long, straight highways of the American west. The twisting, narrow European roads were not its ideal terrain and every time she rode it, it reminded her of its heritage. Roundabouts were a particular bane as the long wheelbase and wide rake made counter steering difficult at best, so the bike had to be wrestled against its will into tight turns. Pascale, being perennially stubborn, persisted with the bike rather than buy a European or Japanese machine more suited to the roads around the Cevennes Mountains. She relished the challenge. The battle of wills betwixt rider and mount made for an interesting ride.

She pulled on her helmet, fastened it and as she straddled the machine she started the engine. Her hunter bag full of the necessities of life dangled from her shoulder. She shifted it behind, so that it nestled comfortably in the small of her back as she sat.

The rumble from the exhaust echoed down the constricted streets, bringing a smile to her lips. Pulling in the clutch, she engaged first gear with a clunk and edged her way out of the winding thoroughfare past the *Super U* supermarket and towards the junction with the A75. She negotiated the roundabout, hauling the bike reluctantly through the necessary turns, musing on the heavy steering and low ground clearance of the machine and inwardly questioning her choice of bike. She loved it on the one hand and yet the critics who complained that these bikes really didn't handle well at all were correct in their assessment. Her dogged determination to tame the beast amused her, she supposed, knowing full well that she never would.

Once on the *AutoRoute*, the bends were less extreme, becoming more sweeping as the road descended to the plain and the shores of the Mediterranean. She accelerated through the tunnel south of the town and settled the machine at a steady 80kph, feeling the wind pressure on her chest and enjoying the sensory feedback of the bike at this speed. Here, the bike's lazy handling became more pleasurable as she moved into the left hand lane to overtake a gaggle of cars with a tanker truck at the head of the queue.

The road started to gently climb again as she drew alongside the truck. It was at this moment, the vehicle signalled left to move out and overtake a slow moving Citroën Picasso in the right hand lane. As soon as the signal blinked on, the heavy vehicle swung out into the left lane. Pascale glanced in her mirror. The car she had just overtaken was already out in the lane behind her, planning to follow past the tanker. To her right, a silver Renault Clio was in the process of undertaking. Inexorably, the tanker moved out and the triangle of available tarmac diminished. There was nowhere to go.

***

The house looked ancient. Centuries old. A rambling higgledy-piggledy collection of granite and mortar that had evolved rather than been built—with each century adding its own distinct architectural flavour—sitting in the middle of a clearing. Gnarled old oak trees, bereft of leaves at this time of the year, poked their naked branches like bony fingers into the moonlit sky. Above, the occasional cloud scudded across the pale-faced moon that grinned down like a toothless old vagrant at the blue planet below.

Pascale breathed out and her breath caught like a miniature cloud in the chill air. The gravelled driveway scrunched under her booted feet as she walked. The large oaken door was open and outside a red Ducati sports bike lounged with latent vitality on its sidestand. Even stationary it looked as if it was travelling at eye-watering speed. She paused briefly to look at the machine; her natural curiosity was aroused as it always was when she saw a motorcycle.

How did I get here? she wondered. Then, almost immediately, *Where is here anyway?*

As the door was open, she walked through it into the house. Somewhere inside, she could hear music. Someone was playing that godawful Christmas album that gets dusted off and played *ad nauseam* every December. Although, as she reflected sourly, more like every October onwards in the shops and on the radio. It really was the most tacky, dire, drivel she thought to herself, so who on earth was so lacking in taste that they would play this dreck voluntarily?

Her curiosity aroused, she followed the sound, walking along the semi-dark corridors into the interior of the rambling house. *No,* she thought irritably, *I am not having a wonderful Christmas time, thank you very much.* The sound grew louder as she walked until she found the source. The room was warm and cosy. A fire roared in the grate and sitting in one of two expansive leather wingback armchairs puffing on a huge cigar, a shadowy figure awaited his visitor.

Pascale stared at the vision before her. The room was a mixture of the comforting and the bizarre. Around the walls, mounted on boards fixed to them with upside down L-shaped wooden brackets, ran a miniature landscape, carefully constructed to scale with a train trundling along tiny tracks. It wound through the model mountains and valleys of a place far away that she had never seen.

She shifted her gaze to the fire and the armchairs separated by a low coffee table. Against the fireplace rested a scythe. In one of the chairs sat Death. He was leaning back with his hood slung over his shoulders, revealing the fleshless skull with the luminous eye sockets that watched her every move. On his bony dome, he wore a red and white Santa hat. As the train ran past his seat, he reached out and plucked a glass of single malt from one of the wagons and lifted it towards her.

"Salut."

Pascale stood, transfixed. She couldn't make up her mind whether she should be looking at the incongruous sight of the Grim Reaper with a Santa hat on his head, sipping whisky and smoking a cigar, or at the method of the drink's delivery.

"A toy train…" She said eventually, struggling for something coherent to say. It was the best she could manage.

"A model railway!" He retorted haughtily. *"That is a scale model, I'll have you know. It's OO9."*

Pascale raised an eyebrow that said something like "I have no idea what you are talking about and really couldn't care less anyway." Rapidly followed by "You've got to be kidding me, right?" It's amazing what a raised eyebrow can say when you put your mind to it and Pascale Hervé had perfected the art. Everyone in the department had become used to translating it as most of them had, at one point or another, been on the receiving end. Today it was Death's turn.

Death continued, blithely ignoring the visual cues she was giving out like a full sized steam locomotive travelling at line speed directly towards him that said "who gives a fuck anyway?"

"It's OO scale," he said. *"4 millimetres to the foot, but narrow gauge. I've modelled it on the railway at Ffestiniog. That's in Wales,"* he explained. *"They used the railway to move the slate after it was quarried. These days, it's used by tourists. A beautiful spot and certainly worth a visit. I can recommend it."*

"I don't care what it is," she replied with the realisation dawning on her that what she had been recently witnessing was connected to the sight before her. "You've been lounging about here drinking and smoking when you should have been collecting souls, haven't you? That's why I've been investigating undead bodies."

Death had the grace to look mildly guilty, which is quite an achievement when all you have is a fleshless skull for a face.

"I felt like a break. Everyone else does at this time of the year."

"I don't. People don't stop dying just because it's Christmas. Someone still has to clear up the mess and that someone is me. I have to work, so why shouldn't you?" she scolded.

"Not for much longer," Death pointed out, ignoring the rebuke. *"As I understand it, you are supposed to be retiring on New Year's Eve. It all finishes for you, doesn't it?"*

She said nothing. Tears fought to well up at the corners of her eyes and she blinked them back, angry with herself for the emotion. Death gestured to the empty armchair. Compliantly, she sat and as she did so, the floor moved much like the deck of a ship at sea. She looked about with mild alarm.

Death waved a bony hand dismissively. *"Oh, that's nothing. It's just time getting impatient."*

Again, the raised eyebrow.

"I can do pretty much what I like with time. How else do you imagine I manage to collect all those dead souls? Every so often, the continuum ripples in response. It's just showing off because I'm overdue. As you noticed," he added. *"That's the thing with time. There's plenty of it, so we can enjoy a drink and a chat."*

He reached down and lifted a bottle of dark red wine that had been sitting by his feet. *"Pegiorolles,"* he said. *"I believe you are partial?"* He poured a glass and proffered it.

Pascale took it and sipped at the fruity, aromatic liquid, tasting the warmth of the summer sun trickling across her taste buds and the gentle glow as it slid effortlessly down her throat. The flavour of the south of France; the foothills of the Cevennes where the grapes had ripened and been pressed before fermenting. The foothills with their micro climate of long, warm summers and harsh, cold winters and the gentle slopes that led down to the mild Mediterranean. The Languedoc Roussillon—her home—the land she loved with a passion and this red encapsulated it all in one fruity flavour. She smiled as the liquid warmed her throat and oesophagus as it went down. All the time, Death watched his guest as she drank. This self-assured woman at the peak of her abilities was now facing change and she didn't like it one little bit.

"What will you do?" he asked.

Pascale blinked. "Do?"

"When you retire?"

Puzzled she put the glass onto the low table that sat between them. "Do? What do you mean, do? I'm dead. I won't *do* anything."

"Are you? Do you think that you are ready to come with me? You see, I do not think that you are, so, please, humour me."

Puzzled by this line of questioning, she thought for a moment. "I really don't know. I've spent my adult life in the police. It's all my life and now it will be gone. I am redundant, useless, cast out to pasture as it were. I have no meaning to my life anymore."

"Really? That's it? You are your work? Nothing else?"

She reached for the wine and took another sip, savouring the flavour. "It seems that way. I've spent so many years doing it, I cannot imagine doing anything else and…and I really hate the idea of handing over to others."

Death smiled. She thought it odd how he could do that, but nonetheless, he was definitely smiling. He took a puff at the cigar and blew out a plume of smoke that drifted up to the ceiling.

"You are more than your work, you know. You have been told that often enough, but you don't listen, which is surprising for someone who is usually a good listener."

Pascale was startled. "You know an awful lot…"

"I know everything. About everything and everyone. It's my job, you know. I like my job. I'm good at it."

"So I see," she said drily. "Yes, people nag me. They see retirement as an opportunity not an end. Yet my career was so important. I am a police officer. I will always be a police officer. It seems but a moment ago, I was a twenty-year-old recruit with my life and career ahead of me and now... Well, now here I am at the end with no future and nothing to show for it but the past and no one will remember."

"Everyone you have touched will remember. Every life saved..."

"Saved?"

"When you solved crimes and put murderers behind bars, did you not save innocent lives? What you did touched many, many lives. Take my word for it. You leave behind a legacy that cannot be measured. But it is the past now and you must look to what lies ahead."

"But I am dead. There is nothing ahead."

"I told you, this is not the time. So indulge me. Imagine that you are not dead. Imagine that you have your life ahead."

He paused for a moment and watched the miniature train as it traversed the tiny mountains of North Wales, wending around the equally tiny slate tips and through miniscule tunnels. He reached across to the mantelpiece and turned a switch on the controller, bringing the train to a gentle stop in the station. *"Need to pick up the passengers,"* he explained. *"What about that thought you once had?"*

"Thought? What thought?"

"About teaching people to ride bikes?"

"Good God! That was decades ago! I was in my twenties or early thirties I think. It was a passing fancy, nothing more."

"But you did teach, though. At the academy."

"Yes. I spent a few years there, after Geneviève died." Ah, Geneviève Duval. Her partner. Her partner who ignored protocol and paid the ultimate price. She missed her friend of so many years. Long gone now.

"And you liked it, didn't you?" Death's questioning brought her sharply back to the present.

"I suppose so." She reflected for a moment. "Yes, I think I did."

"More than that, I believe. You discovered that you are naturally didactic and you were in your element. That would be closer to the truth now, wouldn't it?"

He was right and she knew it. Guillaume had been happier then, too, as her hours were more regular and his finely cooked meals tended to be eaten rather than thrown away. But the lure of promotion and crime detection had been too great a draw and she returned to front line policing.

"I couldn't do it on the Harley," she remarked, returning to the subject of motorcycle training.

"No, I suppose not."

"The handling would make it hard work."

"Tell me about it."

15

Pascale raised an inquisitive eyebrow again and Death noted how attractive she looked when she did that. She should smile more, too, he observed.

"I had a Harley once. I thought I ought to look like something from a Meatloaf album cover. Well, you get these fancies, don't you? The image, you know. Well, I do have to say it looked the part. Unfortunately, they don't respond well to counter steering. As I discovered when I came to my first roundabout. Harleys aren't designed for roundabouts."

"What happened?" she asked, knowing full well what happened.

"Nothing. I leaned on the handlebars and the bloody thing kept going. I went straight across the roundabout for some impromptu off-roading. Just as well it was an empty road. Piss-poor ground clearance, too. Not to mention off-roading on road tyres. Undignified doesn't start to cover it. Meatloaf wouldn't have wanted that on the front of his albums."

She laughed then. Genuine laughter that engulfed her and lit up her face. He looked at her and thought that this was the first time in a long time that she expressed mirth. Happiness had eluded her for so long yet now, in this room, at the end of time, she was relaxed and happy, such that she could laugh at a humorous anecdote.

She stopped then, gasping for breath. "That's why I like them," she explained. "They are cussed brutes."

"I got the Ducati after that. It goes round corners."

"I noticed."

"So?"

"Maybe. I would have to get another bike though."

"Use your pension pot. A decent European or Japanese middleweight would do the job nicely. Think about it. All day out on the bike getting paid for it. And home in time for one of Guillaume's delicious dinners."

She nodded. "Nice idea, but it's all moot. I'm dead, remember?"

"Ah…"

"Ah? What's that supposed to mean?"

He furrowed his non-existent brow and scratched his head. *"Well, things aren't quite what they seem. You see, normally I go to my clients. Yet you are visiting me at home. Don't you think that a little odd? Now is not your time."*

She looked about her at the room. The armchair with a skeletal mythical entity wearing an absurd Christmas hat, surrounded by a model railway that ran around the room delivering tumblers of whisky and the fact that she was *here* was the odd thing?

"You are at a crisis point. A moment in time when two possible outcomes can arise. You have to make a choice. I can take you of course, if that is what you want. Or you can choose another course. It is entirely up to you. I do not believe that you are ready for me yet. Besides, you have unfinished business."

16

She looked at him—eyeball to luminous eye-socket—for what seemed an eternity. *"You have work yet to do,"* he said, taking another drag at the cigar, *"so a choice to make. You have ghosts to lay to rest. And an injustice to resolve. You have a choice,* Madame—*come with me now if you must, or seek resolution."*

A choice.

It really was as simple as that.

***

She squeezed hard on the front brake and the long fork springs dived. She kept squeezing harder, harder, harder as the momentum of the bike shifted its weight over the front wheel pressing the tortured tyre onto the tarmac as the rubber compressed in protest. Yet the rubber gripped and slowly, inexorably, almost imperceptibly at first, the triangle of road between her front wheel and the truck opened up. She released the brakes and pressed firmly on the right handlebar. A combination of adrenaline and sheer bloody-mindedness forced the recalcitrant bike to change its line. The sliver Clio was braking hard, giving her just enough room to swerve into the hard shoulder where she brought the brutal beast to a shuddering halt. Shaking, she put her feet to the ground and placed the machine on its sidestand before her knees gave out. Gasping for breath she waited for her heart rate to return to normal.

"Resolution," she said to herself. "I chose resolution." At no one in particular. "I fucking chose life! Do you hear me?" Then she pondered *I wonder what he meant by that?*

***

The office was illuminated as it usually was by the flickering green-blue of florescent tubes. Desultory bunting spelling out *"Joyeux Noel"* and *"Bon Fêtes"* were the department's limpid attempt to give an air of festivity to the austere room. It seemed to Pascale that rather than an air of festivity it gave it a tired, slightly pathetic aura. She placed her hunter bag on the desk and looked across at Patrice who had arrived before her. She made no mention of the near miss. "How is our attempted suicide?"

"Attempted?"

"Is he still alive?"

"What are you talking about Pascale? He was stone dead as you saw."

"But, there was evidence of life?"

Commandant Daniel Viala looked out of his side office and shook his head. "I think you need a break. You have been working too hard."

"What about the others?"

"What others?"

I can do pretty much what I like with time. How else do you imagine I manage to collect all those dead souls? Of course, she thought. It made sense.

"*D'accord.* If there's nothing else, then," she said. "I'll get off home."

"You do that and have a good Christmas." Daniel winked at her. "And I reckon that retirement next week can't come a day too soon."

He lifted a hand and waved as she walked out of the office. Maybe he was right, she thought to herself.

As she turned the key in the lock, pushing open the door to the apartment, the smell of cooking swept across her senses. Guillaume was busy cooking. "*Boeuf bourguignon*," he said as if to himself. "So, shall it be rice or buttered potatoes?"

"Rice," she said.

"Rice it is. Good day?" he asked, glancing at his watch, unsurprised by the lateness of the hour.

"As good as they usually are."

"Which is why I wonder about you, my darling. You claim to love the job, yet come in here depressed and tired. That retirement…"

"Couldn't come a day too soon. I know, I know."

He turned back to the cooking and fussed about for a moment. "Can you lay the table, *Cherie?*"

She set about preparing the table and opened a bottle of *Pegiorolles*, placing it in the centre. "I've been thinking."

"Go on."

"When I retire, I plan to retrain to teach people to ride *motos*."

Guillaume stopped for a moment and looked at her. Surprise blended with relief crossed his face. "Really? *Seriously?*"

"You don't think it's a good idea?"

"I think it's an excellent idea. At last! You are naturally didactic after all."

"That's the second time someone had said that in the past twenty-four hours."

"Anyone I know?"

She shook her head. "No. No one you have met."

"Well, you do it. You'd be good at it, I know. Spending all day on the bike and getting paid for it. What could be better? Retirement isn't about stopping everything. It's about changing direction and a slower pace. You aren't just waiting for God, you know."

"I know. You've said." She poured two glasses of the red and handed him one. Taking a sip and savouring the dark liquid she said, "I think we should take a road trip on the bikes sometime."

"Anywhere in particular?"

"*Royaume Uni.*"

Guillaume turned his attention away from the beef to look at her. "Any particular reason?"

"I would like to go to Wales. There is a place there called Ffestiniog. They have a railway, I believe."

Guillaume turned back to the cooking and stirred the pot.

"Perhaps," she said, moving closer and wrapping her arms around his waist, "you could put that on a low heat and we can go into the bedroom. Make me feel alive! I need to feel alive! The *bourguignon* will wait."

***

New Year's Eve 2017, Montpellier.

The party was a convivial affair, but for Pascale, one tinged with regret for this was her final farewell. Colleagues joked about the past and there was the predicted send-off with speeches and old war stories along with the obligatory presentation. But the one person missing was the one person she wanted to be there: Geneviève Duval. The one person who would never be there.

It was strange, she sometimes thought, how one could be alone in the crowd. A natural introvert, Pascale eschewed crowds and parties, giving way on this occasion as it was, in part, being thrown for her benefit—the New Year being a convenient excuse for a double celebration. So she endured the small talk and tried her best to create a jovial façade while inside she grieved the loss of what had gone before. Despite her newfound plans, there was regret and sadness. Where did those decades go?

She looked across the room, scanning familiar faces when she caught sight of a shadow lurking in a corner, a drink in one hand and a cigar in the other. She frowned as he placed the cigar between his teeth and raised a hand to his forehead in a mock salute. She looked about to see if anyone else had noticed, but the party continued as people danced and talked, oblivious to their gate crasher. She looked back and blinked, but the mirage had gone. *I must have imagined it.* Much like, she thought, she had imagined the episode the previous week. *All in the mind.*

"You have unfinished business. Ghosts that must be laid to rest."

Perhaps retirement was really not too badly timed after all.

Chapter 2

Already the day was warm with the gentle Mediterranean sun. The assassin waited and glanced at his watch. He was on time. He drummed his fingers absently on the steering wheel, his mind drifting to another place, another time. *We were younger then,* he observed to himself. He looked up at his reflection in the rear view mirror. The years had taken their toll, but hadn't wrought too much havoc, he was happy to note. A few lines around the eyes, but they remained clear and sharp. A tinge of grey at the temples, but otherwise his hair remained dark and full. He looked after himself, so was fit and supple. Age, he told himself, was all in the mind.

The time had come. The prison door opened and a man stepped out into the sunlight, blinking as his eyes adjusted. How long had it been? Fifteen years? Time off for good behaviour. It seemed like a lifetime now, although his victims for whom it had really been a lifetime, entered neither his thoughts nor those of the man come to meet him.

The assassin stepped out of the car. For a moment they stopped and looked at each other before embracing.

"It's been too long," the assassin said. "I have everything ready for your homecoming."

He picked up the other man's bag and led the way to the car, noting that despite the prison pallor, the years hadn't done too much damage. Like himself, he had worn well. The dark hair was still intact with a few grey flecks and the close-cropped beard was greying now, but otherwise, he seemed fit and healthy.

"There are things we need to discuss," he continued, striding easily.

"What?"

He stopped for a moment and turned to the other man. "It was a fake. They all were."

The other man frowned. "The ones we stole? We knew that thirty years ago."

"No, not the ones we stole. The ones they recovered."

It took barely a moment for the significance to sink in. "So where are the real ones?"

"Ah, now, isn't that the question? I have an idea how we may find out."

And Death sat on his horse and watched. He looked at his smartphone, but there was still an error message.

"Fascinating."

***

The assassin watched. He was a patient man, so he would wait. Much of his life was spent waiting and he was used to it.

He flew in from France the previous evening and made his way across London to Paddington, catching the last train to Bristol. Once he met with his two accomplices, they made their way to the expected haunts of their prey. Eventually they found him soaking himself with drink. The assassin sighed. An abstainer, he wondered at the lack of control he was observing, but said nothing. His two companions likewise sat in the car, remaining silent as they watched and waited much as a cat will watch silent and still for hours before pouncing.

The years had not been kind to Frank Cotter. Once a short, powerful man, his belly now sagged where the muscles had given up in their decades-long attempts to contain the beer he poured down his throat. His hair was receding and unwashed, what remained hung lank about his neck and the stubble on his chin was white these days. His jacket and tee shirt were stained and worn and his jeans fitted his waist only with the help of a belt that struggled gainfully to hold on below the sagging belly; also he smelled of sour sweat.

He supped his beer alone. How many had it been that evening? He had long since stopped wondering, preferring the haze the alcohol induced to the harsh reality of a life littered with failure. Periods of time incarcerated were interrupted by excess and wallowing in self-pity over what might have been. Since his wife died of cancer the previous year, he had spiralled into a pit of despair and drink.

The barman glanced across at him as he sat staring into the beer glass seeing no redemption, only temporary release.

"Enough, tonight, Frank, old son."

Frank looked up as if seeing him for the first time "Eh?"

"I think you've had enough, Mate. Time to go home."

Home? Home to what? he wondered. An empty house that echoed with ghosts of the past and regrets for what might have been had he been a better man. A past that he had thrown away on a life of petty crime. Always chasing the big job and always ending up on the wrong side of the law— usually through incompetence and poor planning, but Frank put it down to bad luck. Always bad luck. Each time promising her that this would be the last time, this time he would be going straight. And each time, more years wasted inside. And eventually it was the last time, for when he came out, she was gone forever.

The barman came over and took the near empty glass away as Frank gazed into the past. He lifted his rheumy eyes to look at the younger man.

"Home, yeah... I know, I know."

He slid from the bar stool and staggered as his feet hit the floor, swaying as he regained his balance.

Outside the night air was cool. Summer was nearly a month away and the chill air sliced through his tee shirt causing him to shiver momentarily. He looked about him for his car. Seeing the battered old Focus, he trod unsteadily towards it, fumbling in his pockets for the keys. The door unlocked with the blipper and he clambered into the driver's seat. He tried to place the key in the slot but missed. *Fuck!*

The assassin slipped out of his car and started to walk across the car park, but a movement made him stop. A police Range Rover drew into the car park and pulled up alongside Frank's car. Silently the assassin made his way back to his own vehicle, entered it and watched events unfold.

While Frank was struggling to line up the key with the ignition switch with no success, he heard a tap on the window.

"Planning on driving, were we, Sir?"

Frank turned abruptly. *What is it with pigs these days? All seem to be cocky teenagers!*

"Step out of the vehicle, please, sir," the young man said.

Frank angrily swung the door open as the police officer stepped back. The officer took the keys from Frank's hand. "Step away from the vehicle please, sir."

For a moment in Frank's muddled mind, resistance blossomed then died like April snow. There was a time, but not now, he hadn't the ability and even in his inebriated state, he had sufficient self-awareness to realise this. The police officer's companion held out a breathalyser and asked Frank to blow. She took it back and read the digits on the display, raising an eyebrow.

"I'd like you to accompany us to the station, sir."

The assassin turned to his companion who sat mute in the driving seat. "We'll pay Frank a visit at home, I think. Wait for him there."

"Okay," the man put the car into gear and drove off.

The following morning, Frank woke on the hard bed in the cell. His head pounded, but that was nothing new. His mouth felt rough and tasted like something he had vomited. A glance at the bucket in the corner confirmed it. He sat up and held his aching head in his hands.

Fuck it! Why? Why can't I just not wake up? Every fucking day another torment, another hurdle, another fucking day to get through. For fuck's sake, just let me go! I've had enough.

He heard the peep-hole slide back. An eye appeared then the door swung open. The custody sergeant walked into the cell.

"How are we this morning?"

"How the fuck do you think?"

The sergeant was unabashed by the colourful response. He'd seen and heard it all before. This was nothing compared to some of the abuse he received. Besides, Frank had collapsed and slept soundly so had been no trouble once he had been processed.

"We're releasing you on police bail," he said. "Pending a magistrate's hearing."

"Okay," Frank stood up and walked toward the door that the sergeant held open for him. Like the sergeant, he was an old hand and they played the parts they had both learned to play so well.

It was a bright morning and Frank took the bus home. He would have to collect the car later.

The door to his house swung open when he put the key to the lock. His hackles rose. Looking more closely, he could see that the door had been jemmied open. Pushing it quietly aside, he stepped into the hallway. He stood still and listened. Nothing. Slowly, silently and with a catlike movement that belied his otherwise ungainly manner, he moved through the house.

He found them in the kitchen. Waiting. As he entered he was aware of a movement behind him. Turning, he saw the heavy step into the doorway, blocking it. The bulge in his jacket showed he meant business should Frank try to make a run for it.

But it wasn't the heavy in the doorway that transfixed Frank's attention. Nor was it the other hood who blocked the doorway to the garden. It was the man who was sitting at the table, nonchalantly eating one of Frank's bananas as he watched a pan boiling on the hob.

My God!

It must have been thirty years or so. Sure, the hair was shorter now and flecked with grey, but the years hadn't thickened his lithe body and the eyes were still as black as sin. They still sent a shiver down Frank's spine.

"Hello, Frank. Long time."

"You! What are you doing here?"

"Where is it?"

"What? I've no idea what you are talking about."

The assassin smiled and stood. He nodded to his accomplices who grabbed Frank roughly and pinned him to a chair, taping him in place with duct tape.

The assassin walked over to Frank and leaned forward close, so that Frank could feel his breath on his face.

"You know full well what I'm talking about, Frank. Now are we going to make this easy or messy?"

"I don't know what you are talking about!"

By now, fear was seeping into Frank's consciousness. His eyes widened as the other man walked across to the hob. Satisfied that the water was bubbling nicely, he looked across at the man who had taped Frank to the chair.

The man reached down and ripped Frank's tee shirt away from his chest. Frank's breathing increased as he realised what was going to happen. His sweat smelled of sour alcohol and spittle dribbled from his mouth. *"Please!* I don't fucking know…" His cry for mercy was punctuated by an ear-splitting scream as the assassin lifted the pan and threw the contents across Frank's chest.

"Now, where is it?"

"I don't know what you're talking about! I tell you!" The words were punctuated with sobs of pain, fear and self-pity.

Calmly, the assassin refilled the pan from the tap and set it back on the hob. He watched as it came to the boil.

"I have plenty of time," he said. "I am a patient man. The diamonds. Where are they?"

Again, the piercing scream as the next pan of boiling water landed on Frank's chest. As if this was an everyday chore, the assassin refilled the pan and brought it to the boil, ignoring the sobs of pain coming from his victim.

Then he walked up to Frank and slowly poured the contents of the pan into Frank's lap. By this time, Frank was insensible with the pain, his body shuddering with shock. "I don't fucking know," he sobbed. "I don't fucking know."

And finally, the assassin believed him. Turning away from his sobbing victim, he picked up his phone and dialled.

"Hello, no, he doesn't know. Yes, I believe him. Sure. Just have to tidy up here."

He terminated the call and reached for the silenced pistol in the shoulder holster under his jacket. Lifting the weapon, he smiled briefly at his victim then pulled the trigger and Frank fell back dead with a bullet hole in the middle of his forehead. With barely a blink of the eye, he turned the gun on his accomplices and shot both dead before leaving the house and closing the door.

"Sorry guys, no witnesses."

And Death watched. And waited. He swept his scythe and the three shades lifted themselves up before vanishing. Death looked at the assassin as he left.

"Fascinating. I would never have believed it if I hadn't seen it for myself."

***

Lodève, August, 2018.

The F800GT was a surprisingly underrated machine. Pascale mused upon her switch from the cumbersome Harley to the nimble BMW as she led her two successful students from the test centre back to the training school offices in Lodève.

What she wasn't expecting when she arrived back was a ghost from the past.

"You have unfinished business. Ghosts that must be laid to rest."

He was sitting there relaxed as he read a magazine as if waiting for an appointment. Étienne, the office manager, nodded towards him as Pascale walked through the door, removing her helmet.

"He's here for you," he explained.

Thirty years or more it must have been. *He has hardly aged* she thought to herself. The hair was cut shorter and there was a hint of salt and pepper, but the eyes were as clear blue as they were when she last saw him. His face was relatively unlined and he could pass for a decade younger than his age. *He must be nearly sixty now*, she concluded.

Mike Jenner stood as she walked across the room, his eyes clouded with something akin to accusation.

"You're supposed to be dead," he said by way of introduction.

Ah, yes, that...

***

September 1987

Pascale climbed over the broken parapet and edged along to the cab where she carefully clambered onto the fuel tank. The side window was open, so she reached for it with her right hand, following with her right foot to the cab step.

"Careful, Pascale," Geneviève said nervously.

"Never mind me," Pascale replied. "Get back from that car, it could go up anytime."

Geneviève stepped back warily, never taking her eyes from Pascale while Mike looked on as he helped Freddie to his feet.

With her left hand gripping the window opening, Pascale let go with her right hand and reached for the door handle. The truck lurched with a sickening scraping sound, causing her to lose her footing. As she grabbed the handle, the door swung open and she swung with it, crashing into the front of the cab as it reached the limit of its swing. For a moment she swung by her hands above the river. "Zut!"

"Pascale!" Geneviève cried out reaching for the parapet.

"No," Mike left Freddie to his own devices and placed a restraining hand on her shoulder.

"I'm okay, I'm okay," Pascale panted. Hanging from the door by her fingertips. She looked down at her feet, swaying in space, high above the Rio

Douro. She groaned. Straining, she hauled herself up and wrapped her left arm around the door pillar, swinging her feet in an attempt to close the door. Exhausted, she hung there.

The truck driver peered cautiously at her through the open doorway. "Senhora?"

Gasping for breath, Pascale asked, "You are okay?"

The driver nodded, clutching a handkerchief over a cut above his left eye. "Yes. I knocked my head, I think."

"Well, don't look down."

The driver looked down. The man's eyes widened in panic as he scrabbled away from the door opening.

The truck lurched, sending Pascale once more into the void above the river. Scrabbling with her feet she maintained a tenuous grasp on the door. "Stay still! This thing's unstable enough as it is."

"Senhora, Senhora, I . . ."

"It's okay, just don't do anything sudden."

"There was nothing I could do, Senhora."

"I know," Pascale panted in reply, the fatigue draining her dark complexion. "It doesn't matter, not now, anyway."

"Pascale," Geneviève called out. Pascale looked across at her. Flames were licking around the Peugeot. "The car . . ."

The Peugeot erupted into a fireball, singeing their skin and cremating its occupants. The wave of hot air blasted the truck's door outwards on its hinges and once more Pascale was thrown against the front of the cab. Freddie and Mike joined Geneviève as she ran away from the conflagration and towards the southern bank. "Pascale, jump," she called out.

Pascale lifted her head and stared at the driver. "The way I see it, Monsieur, we have two choices."

"Senhora?"

"We can stay here and get fried..."

"Or?"

"Or we can jump and get drowned."

The driver hesitated, the fear naked in his eyes.

"Driver?"

"Yes?"

"What does this tanker carry?"

"Aviation fuel."

Pascale's eyes widened in alarm. "Merde."

She reached into the cab and grasped the driver's shoulder hauling him out of the cab launching him into space and down to the cold clutches of the Douro. For a brief moment she hung there looking across to the bridge where the others stood. "Geneviève I..." The rest was lost in the dull whump of the conflagration on the bridge as it flung the cab far out across *the river. Showers of flaming debris fell about them as they dived to the ground.*

***

"So you survived," Mike said, stating the obvious.

"Has anyone offered you a coffee?" she asked lightly, avoiding the question. He shook his head, so she went to the pot on the hob and poured two cups of strong black liquid, handing one to Mike and keeping the other for herself. She sipped at it silently, before answering.

"It was complicated," she said eventually.

"What was? That you were a bent cop? Undercover? I never could make any sense of it all. Or that you weren't killed?"

She shook her head. "You were supposed to think that."

"Even Geneviève?"

"Yes, even Geneviève."

He stared at her, awaiting an explanation.

"I was undercover, that much was true. No one could know. Fábián Rousseau was… is… a dangerous man. That is why he is in gaol."

"Not anymore."

She raised her eyebrows, mentally calculating the years. "He was convicted in 2003, so has only been inside for fifteen years. For murder, such a short time for a life."

Mike's face twisted with anguish at the reminder.

"I know," she said. Changing the subject briefly, "would you like to get something to eat? It's been a long day and I'm hungry."

He nodded and they went out into the street. At this latitude, the sun was still strong in August and the heat hit them as they stepped onto the pavement. Following Pascale's lead, Mike walked with her to a café opposite. She took a table on the pavement under the shelter of an awning. She ordered cold drinks and perused the menu before selecting omelette. "I'll have the same," Mike said.

They sipped their drinks for a while, engaging in little more than small talk before their food arrived. They ate mostly in silence—the reason for the conversation hovering in the background awaiting its moment.

When the plates were cleared and the coffee placed on the table, he broached it.

"Radfield has been in contact."

She raised an eyebrow. "Sergeant Radfield, eh? How is he these days?"

"DCI now. Although not for much longer he tells me as he is due to retire early next year."

"Ah, yes, retirement," her eyes clouded briefly as she recalled her own struggle with the concept. "Comes to us all."

"Indeed. Well, Fábián Rousseau…"

"Yes? What of him?"

"As I said, Radfield has been in contact. He'd like to speak to you."

Pascale didn't answer immediately. He watched her as her eyes moved to the people walking along the main street, her mind somewhere else— another time, another place and long forgotten memories drifting to the surface. *People and places,* he reflected.

"What is there to discuss?" she asked eventually.

"I cannot answer that. All I can say is that he wants to see you fairly urgently."

She arched an eyebrow.

"I have a plane ticket booked for tomorrow from Beziers."

-"That was presumptuous."

"Maybe, but he was insistent. We need your passport details, though."

Pascale sipped her coffee. "So why isn't he here?"

"Busy man, I guess."

"I see. And why you?"

"I volunteered. Least I could do. Guess I wanted to see a ghost from the past. That you were really alive."

They lapsed into silence. Pascale was watching the passers-by and Mike was watching her.

"What has happened that you are not telling me?" she asked.

Mike looked at her, his eyes betraying nothing. He had anticipated the question and knew it would have to be answered. "I cannot say. Radfield will explain. Suffice to say, it's all got pretty urgent."

She nodded and rose. He watched as she walked into the dark interior of the café to pay the bill, returning a few moments later. "Where are you staying tonight?"

"The hotel across the river. *La Croix Blanche.*"

"*D'Accord.* And the flight?"

"Sixteen twenty."

"Okay, I'll come with you. It will be nice to see *Monsieur* Radfield again, I guess. Tomorrow, then."

She fished in her hunter bag and withdrew her passport. "Here, take a picture on your phone."

As she said goodbye, a movement across the street caught her eye. A shadowy figure standing in a doorway, half concealed by the shade. He lifted a bony finger. She shook her head. Mike frowned as he caught the movement.

"It's nothing," she said. "I will see you tomorrow."

Chapter 3

Bristol, July, 1987

It is probable that if Mike Jenner hadn't been hospitalised with appendicitis, Stephanie Ross' sister Karen would never have had her accident.

Stephanie was calling at her sister's house when Detective Sergeant Radfield waylaid her. Karen lived in a converted Victorian house in the Bishopston area of Bristol. At that time of the year, high summer, the bright sunlight enhanced its shabby exterior. Bleached stucco reflected a bygone age. On her ride across Bristol she'd noticed gold and brown tingeing the foliage lining the roads. Already the leaves were starting to turn. As each day faded into history it took a little of the summer with it. Already it seemed the year was degenerating into old age and she mourned the passing of that stillborn summer, and recalled the incessant wet weather—especially that first week in June on the Isle of Man when the racing was postponed each day, with the Senior race being run on the Saturday and shortened to four laps from the usual six.

Standing at signpost corner in rain that was coming at them sideways, she along with Dave Fry, Karen and Mike all wondered why they bothered to make a trip that had turned into an endurance event and they were only spectating.

The remains of the dying season's warmth fed the rapidly growing lawn with rich nutrients. Karen was never one to rush about with a lawn mower and her lack of horticultural skills was reflected in a patch of lawn that resembled a wildlife park.

Faded and tired with cracks in the stonework and guttering that oozed moss and haphazard roof slates in need of replacement, the building concealed the secrets of a hundred or so years of Bristol's history—at least the little bit that passed within its walls. Fortunately the Victorians were generous with their room dimensions. The conversion had left Karen with a spacious three-room apartment—well, two and a bit, the bathroom was little more than a functional box.

Radfield seemed uncertain as he stepped out of his car and intercepted her on the steps leading to the rambling garden. He paused to wipe his receding brow with a grubby handkerchief and ran an appraising eye over the roses running amok along the borders, their sweet odour heavy in the sultry air. The warm sun concealed a gathering storm in its coat tails. For a moment he stood, saying nothing. Anything but the unpleasant task in hand. He walked up to Stephanie as she crossed the garden.

"Excuse me…"

She stopped and turned to face him. A youngish man, she supposed, yet showing signs of aging before his time.

"Yes?"

"Excuse me," He held out his warrant card. "Detective Sergeant Radfield, Metropolitan police." He turned to his colleague who likewise held out a warrant card. "WPC Morgan from the local police. I'm looking for relatives of Miss Ross... And you are?"

"Miss Ross," She replied. "Can I help?"

Radfield shuffled awkwardly. "Er... So, you are related to Miss Karen Ross?"

"My sister. She is away on holiday. I'm feeding the cat and generally keeping an eye on the place."

"May we go inside?"

"What's up?" she asked, leading the small procession of Radfield and Morgan towards the house and pushing the door open against the sea of junk mail.

"It's about your sister..."

"Karen?"

"Um, yes, Karen."

He turned briefly to exchange eye contact with Morgan who followed him through the door. "Put the kettle on."

She nodded and walked past Stephanie to the kitchen at the end of the hall. Stephanie's senses were screaming like feedback from an electric guitar jarring her nerves, yet she maintained a calm face and presented it to Radfield.

"What's up?" she repeated, her voice growing brittle despite her attempt to retain an outward façade of calm.

"Miss Ross, please, sit down," Radfield led her into the front room and she followed waiting for him to tell her his news *and why the Met?* She asked herself, wanting to shriek at him—*for God's sake, spit it out*. She sat.

"It's about your sister..."

"What about her?"

"There's been an accident..."

***

Mike Jenner was not a planner by nature. A free spirit twenty years too late, he preferred to live life as it presented itself to him. While some people attempt to steer themselves through the tempestuous seas of life, Mike accepted the inevitable and rode the storm. "Life happens," he once said. "Then..."

"Then what?" Stephanie had asked him.

"Who knows," he grinned, blue eyes flashing amusement. "Ain't that the rub?"

32

Stephanie and Karen's mother once accused him of fecklessness and she was probably right. Unmanageable was a word Stephanie preferred to use. Educated, witty and intelligent, he preferred to bide his time despatch riding rather than seek what others might call a meaningful career.

A loose collection of friends, Stephanie, Dave, Karen and Mike shared their love of travel and motorcycling whenever the opportunity presented itself. Dave, burly, brusque and reserved, tended to be the placid and stable part of the brotherhood that existed between him and Mike, who tended to be flighty and, as Stephanie's mother had pointed out, feckless.

Karen was probably the softer side of herself, Stephanie reflected. While she would take charge because it is what she did, Karen would only intrude when she deemed it absolutely necessary. For several years the four of them spent their summer breaks touring the continent aimlessly, finding themselves wherever the road took them. Until Karen saw a leaflet.

Maguire Motorcycle Tours offered what Mike's impromptu trips lacked—organisation. Stephanie was unable to make the trip and Dave was starting a new job, so he declined, leaving Karen and Mike to go.

They arranged to travel to Portugal on a guided riding trip. That is, Karen decided and Mike agreed because he knew what was good for him. By the late eighties, motorcycling was already moving away from cheap transport to becoming a leisure pursuit and there were the beginnings of a market. You take a bike, either yours or one you've hired, pay the tour company for a courier, along with an itinerary. All accommodation is booked ahead and away you go to wherever the destination is. It's a bit like touring alone but with the backup that only a dedicated company can provide; things like pre-planned stops and accommodation. Karen wanted to try it and Mike gave in, like he usually did. Then, two days before the off, he started complaining of abdominal pains. They grew worse until eventually, doubled-up with the pain, he called out his GP who promptly rushed him into hospital for emergency surgery. The upshot was that he was booked on a ferry with Karen and had no way of going.

"You go," he said, sleepy from the anaesthetic.

"Karen didn't want to go at first," Stephanie told Radfield. "Until I butted in, like I usually do, and backed Mike. I figured she would be fine. Besides, what was originally planned for four of us didn't mean that she couldn't do the tour on her own and, as it was organised with other people making the trip, she might make new friends. So while he's in hospital and she's away, I could see to his flat and hers and the cat. After all, I was going to do that anyway while they were away."

The WPC came in with steaming mugs and placed them on the coffee table. They ignored them. There's something very British about mugs of tea in a crisis, Stephanie thought. No one cared whether they were drunk or not but someone must see to the kettle. Radfield listened patiently, slipping his glasses off to polish them before replacing them on his round pink face.

"Then what?"

"So we agreed," Stephanie said, "Karen under our combined pressure should go to Portugal so that only one ticket would be wasted. Mike could claim on the insurance for the lost ticket. Anyway, she'd been working a lot lately and I figured she needed the rest."

"You figured…"

"Yes," she replied, inwardly smiling at the memory. Karen played at her own game. After all, it was usually she who knew best.

"So she went and I've been looking after his flat, this place and the cat."

***

For a while, she did nothing as the news of her sister's accident sank in. Radfield had assured her that Karen was alive, but couldn't say much more than that. Eventually, they left, promising to keep in contact.

The cat flap flipped and a huge tabby cat trundled across the room and wrapped himself around her legs imploring her to feed him, which she did. She smiled as she reached down to stroke the animal's back before wandering into the other room of the flat which served as the kitchen diner and living room. This spacious room was divided into two by the kitchen units arranged across the space separating the dilapidated kitchen from the rest of the room.

Shelves full of books, records and tapes lined the walls. A midi stereo system nestled on one of them, somewhere between Milton and Shakespeare. Photographs and fantasy posters adorned the areas of wall not already obscured by shelving.

Karen was a tidy person by nature and the flat, while full with her books and art deco lamps and ornaments, was neat in a cluttered sort of way.

Turning to the fridge and selecting an opened tin of cat food, she forked a portion into the bowl on the floor and the cat promptly dived into the food, devouring it hungrily, gurgling on his incessant purring. Stephanie waited patiently for the coffee machine to boil, switched on the radio and listened idly as she watched the cat chew through his tinned mush.

Meatloaf's *Bat out Of Hell* faded into silence and the presenter started her patter.

"This is the new GWR, Bristol and Bath's better music mix, on a Tuesday morning, and we'll be back after the news at nine with Elton John, Tina Turner and UB40. From the Mendips to the Cotswolds, this is the new GWR FM, your better music mix."

After a suitably tacky jingle the news started. "Good morning it's ten o'clock and this is Carolyn Lewis…"

She went on to tell her listeners that three people had been killed in a motorway pile up on the M5, a lorry went out of control at services near Birmingham, crossed the central barrier and burst into flames spilling diesel all over the motorway. It then hit three cars heading in the opposite direction. When, Stephanie wondered, will people learn to keep a decent distance? Dismissing the thought as it occurred, she wasted no time in idle conjecture about the vagaries of human nature, or that new phenomenon, road rage.

The news continued with a story of record compensation being paid to a man who was wrongfully dismissed from a local printing firm. Samuel Parry told the interviewer that the payment of thirty thousand pounds was a just end to his year long fight against Portman's. The company was unavailable for comment, unsurprisingly.

Soccer hooligans had been arrested in Denmark, after a night of riots with rival fans. Local Conservative MP, Piers Beauchamp, condemned the behaviour and recommended joint action with the Danish authorities, including the confiscation of passports and stiff gaol sentences.

As Stephanie slopped more cat food into the pile the cat was already devouring, Miss Lewis continued her tale of woe with a story about a gruesome discovery in the south of the city. Forensic experts were contemplating how to remove a concrete slab found in a house at Brislington thought to contain a body. Police investigators suspected that the remains were those of Grant Wellsway who disappeared twelve years ago.

After Grant Wellsway the story about a jewellery blag was almost mild in comparison. Police were hunting two gunmen who raided a Hatton Garden Jewellers during the previous afternoon. They had issued descriptions obtained from video shots taken during the raid and were warning the public that these men were dangerous and not to approach them. *The usual stuff*, she mused, sweeping the bowl into the sink and rinsing it with luke-warm water.

Finally, the Metropolitan Police were still hunting for the thieves who stole the Koh-I-Noor in a daring raid the previous month.

"This is Carolyn Lewis on the New GWR at five past ten."

The morning show presenter returned. "Thank you Carolyn and now the weather and travel. Generally sunny this morning after yesterday's torrent but with high winds, possibly clouding over this afternoon. Tomorrow is going to be windy with heavy rain and on Thursday more rain. Pretty naff out there, all in all, best stay in if you don't have to go out. The A37, Yeovil to Ilchester road, is closed, as is the ford at Yate rocks, it's like the river Severn out there at the moment. Trains are being diverted to Temple Meads as Chipping Sodbury Tunnel is closed due to severe flooding after heavy rain during the night. So make the most of the sunny interval while it lasts."

The radio broke into T'Pau's *China in Your Hand* while Stephanie wondered what she was going to say to Mike.

***

Stephanie didn't like hospitals much. The sterile odour turned her stomach. She found herself wondering how Karen could work in this place. Mike was being kept in for observations after his appendix burst on the operating table. *Typical*, she thought, for Mike to go one better than everyone else. No simple appendectomy—he had to dally with peritonitis.

Radfield had wanted to talk to him, but Stephanie offered to be the messenger and he could talk later.

"What's the prognosis?" she'd asked.

Radfield hooked off his rimless glasses and proceeded to polish them with his handkerchief again. He was a policeman, not a doctor, he'd said. All he could tell her and that she could pass on to Mike, was that somewhere on the N16 between Termas São Pedro Do Sul and Olivera De Frades in the Dão region of Portugal, Karen and her bike had parted company with the road and each other.

"Are the Portuguese police investigating?"

"No apparent suspicious circumstances, why?"

Stephanie shrugged. She needed to ask. Besides, Radfield's involvement hinted at something that maybe the Portuguese police hadn't considered. She was still numbed by the shock, so expected a tough time when she went to see Mike and wasn't disappointed.

At first he said nothing. Then he said less. Blue eyes stared unseeingly from below the unruly mop of dark hair—somewhere in Portugal with Karen.

After his discharge from hospital he moped around his flat, unable to go back to work so soon after his surgery. They flew Karen back from Portugal a few days later. Stephanie contacted the RAC and they arranged everything. Dave Fry spent as much time as he could with Mike, but with starting his new job, he was busy much of the time. So Stephanie took some time off work to help where she could.

"It's not possible," Mike said.

"It's always possible," Stephanie replied.

"No. You know how Karen rides. Nothing else about and she overcooks a bend or something."

"We don't know that for certain. We don't have the police report. It could have been heat exhaustion or anything."

Meanwhile Karen lay silently in her hospital bed. The hissing of the life support an accompaniment to their silent vigil by her side as each of them took turns. When her personal belongings arrived they took the trouble to go through them. Not that there was anything much; her bag with passport, purse, a few Escudos, keyring with house and bike keys and the two pannier bags with her clothing. Stephanie sorted it, put the clothes through the wash and left the handbag and its contents in her chest of drawers.

"Do you want the bike shipped back?" her contact at the RAC asked.

"Better," she replied.

The police report arrived two weeks after Karen's return and Radfield asked them in to go through it, confirming Stephanie's suspicion that there was more to this than the Portuguese police believed. They read it through but it told her little more than they already knew. When they found her, Karen was halfway down a ravine between the river Vouga and the N16. Skid marks in the dust indicated a loss of control. There were no other vehicles around and no witnesses. The only person who could shed any light lay in a hospital, comatose.

Radfield placed it on the desk. Mike exchanged eye contact with him. "You're not convinced, are you?"

"No. When is the bike being shipped back?"

"According to Steph, the RAC have things in motion. Should be a week, they reckon."

***

"Radfield's tight lipped," Mike said.

"So it seems, except when he wants a favour." Stephanie reflected that Radfield, having become aware of her IT expertise had on occasion during those weeks taken to asking for some off the record help when it suited him. "What are the Portuguese police saying about the accident?"

Mike stood and reached for the coffee pot, poured himself a coffee and sat. "According to Radfield and their report, they regard it as an accident—case closed. Except..."

"Mm?"

"What does "mm," mean when it's out?"

"Except what? Radfield thinks differently, yes?"

"Yes. Any update from the RAC about the bike?"

"Not yet. It's in the hands of the recovery people. Could be anywhere, why?

"When it gets back, Radfield wants it. He plans to get forensics to look at it."

"Seriously?" she asked. "He's definitely convinced there's some kind of criminal conspiracy? That it wasn't an accident?"

Mike leaned back in his chair, studying her. "Haven't you asked yourself why an apparently good rider suddenly loses it on a deserted road?"

"We don't know that it was deserted, just that there were no witnesses coming forward and the report states that the skid marks show no indication of another vehicle being involved."

He smiled. "Yeah, that's why Radfield would like to take a look at the bike. Something doesn't fit. Why, for example haven't the local police taken much interest?"

"Because it's a straightforward accident?"

He shrugged. "Quite possible. But Radfield may be right and someone should check it out."

***

"Could Miss Ross' injuries be caused by anything other than a road accident?" Radfield asked.

The surgeon returned his gaze before switching it to Stephanie "Your sister's injuries are consistent with falling down a sheer drop such as the one where she was found."

"But could they have been caused by anything else?"

"Such as?"

"Such as," Radfield said, "A sustained beating."

"Well, the head wounds could be consistent..."

"She was supposed to be wearing a helmet," Mike interrupted. "What about neck injury?"

"Now that you mention it, there were contusions to the base of the skull, but not the neck. Several broken bones in her arms and two cracked ribs."

"Brain movement?"

"No. No, odd that, her head injuries are caused by something striking the skull rather than twisting of the brain."

***

Karen's mother travelled from Edinburgh. Dave offered to take her and Stephanie and to the hospital. Stephanie wondered how she would react to squeezing into a Transit that was so old the headlights needed bifocals. Always immaculate and expecting everything to be just so, Stephanie expected a protest at the sight of the rusting heap that Dave and Mike used to transport their sidecar outfit to its doomed race meetings. The smell of oil mingled with the rust. Peeling paint and old maps, sweet wrappers and cans littered the interior. Mrs Ross said not a word, nor even raised an impeccably plucked eyebrow. She just climbed in and took a seat. During the brief journey they said little. There was little to say. Dave concentrated on his driving and said nothing.

The traffic ground to a stodge before oozing its way forward once more. Two or three cars would squeeze through the brief light cycle, clogging the junction for the next batch. Gridlock was but a short span away. Stephanie was glad that she chose to use a motorcycle for commuting, as this stop-start nightmare was normally something that happened to others.

Mike was waiting for them at the hospital and Mrs Ross briefly hugged him before they went in.

Chapter 4

Beziers - Bristol, August, 2018

Daily Herald

Friday, 25th May 2018

Murder Victim Identified

Police are investigating the murder of Frank Cotter, who was discovered in his home during the early hours of the morning.

No motive has been suggested yet and according to Detective Inspector Radfield, Cotter may have had links with the criminal underworld. Police are looking for any witnesses w⌐

Cotter, 62, was linked to the disappearance of the Koh-I-Noor, thirty years ago. The police are also urgently seeking the whereabouts of a known associate, Philip Maguire, 65. The public are urged to inform their local police if they see him, but under no circumstances to approach him.

Chief Inspector Radfield said today "Mr Maguire is a person of interest in ⌐ ing inquiry

North Korea Ready to Talk

Kim Jong Un has indicated that he is ready to talk to the USA following President Trump's cancellation of his planned visit to discuss nuclear disarmament.

The White House has suggested that talks may resume next month. However, the cancella⌐ tic⌐ uncertainty.

The flight was delayed. Mike informed Pascale when they met for lunch.

"Crew problems, apparently," he informed her. Not that this eased her distaste for flying. It wasn't the flying that irked her, rather she found the whole security theatre involved tedious and humiliating to the point where she would avoid flying if it was at all possible. Now she fumed silently at both Mike and Radfield for placing her in this position. Despite the delay, they had to arrive at the airport as if there was no delay, so she had more time to fume inwardly in the impersonal atmosphere of the airport.

"I have better things to be doing," she snapped.

"Maybe, but see it through, eh?"

"Pah!"

Eventually they were called to the gate where the aircraft had just arrived from the inbound flight. By now they were already three-quarters of an hour late. Pascale watched as the plane was fuelled, not expecting to be called forward until this was complete. As she watched, the baggage was loaded, the attendant finished refuelling and wandered up to the ground crew and got his signature, before uncoupling his equipment and driving the tanker away.

Still no sign of being called forward. Pascale's inner hackles rose. Something wasn't right. She glanced across at Mike who was frowning as he watched the little theatrical performance as well.

"Not looking good," he said.

Then an announcement. A technical fault with the aircraft. More information in fifteen minutes. They found a couple of seats. Mike opened his book and started to read, unfazed by the further delay.

"If it drags on too long, they will cancel the flight," he said.

Pascale raged inwardly and muttered to herself. *I have better things to be doing.* She repeated to herself. *This is the last place I want to be.* The enforced delay triggered her anxiety. She felt trapped as if she was no longer in control of her destiny. She felt her pulse quicken and her palms were sweaty. The desire to scream her frustration stifled by the realisation that she would probably be arrested. Adrenaline coursed through her system pounding in her temple and shortening her breath as every nerve screamed to get out of that place—*now!*

"You had a choice," Geneviève said. "You could have refused."

Pascale turned to look at her. Geneviève sat easily on the seat next to hers. *And why is it that you never age?* Pascale wondered.

"What are you doing here?"

"I have always been here."

"Hm. In my head, no doubt."

"It's as good a place as any."

"So why here? Why now?"

"Now is the time. Fábián Rousseau is released, no?"

"So I understand. What of it?"

"So why does Radfield want you to go to England? Why now?"

Pascale mused on this as she had been musing for the past twenty-four hours since Mike Jenner had showed up. *Yes, why now?*

"They were insistent," she explained, almost as if to convince herself into justifying her compliance.

"Yes, maybe, but you could still have said no. But you wouldn't, would you? You know deep down there is unfinished business here. Thirty years is a long time, but now, perhaps there will be a resolution."

"You have a ghost to lay to rest." Death's voice echoed in her mind.

Just as she was about to respond, there was an announcement that the plane was ready for boarding. She glanced at her watch—an hour and a half late. She turned back to Geneviève as she reached for her bag and stood. The seat was empty. She slung the strap of her bag over her shoulder.

"Who were you talking to?" Mike asked.

"No one."

"I could swear…"

"You were dozing. A dream perhaps?"

"Ah, perhaps."

They walked out onto the tarmac that was basting in the summer heat, the harsh light hurting their eyes.

As they took their places in the cool of the air-conditioned cabin of the aircraft, the pilot welcomed them aboard and informed them that the delay was due to a computer fault affecting the reverse thrusters. This was now locked out, so they could proceed with the flight.

"Well, at least we know what it was," Mike said.

"As if that makes a difference," Pascale replied grumpily. She fastened her seatbelt and half listened to the safety brief, her mind with Geneviève. *Yes, maybe now. Resolution.*

***

Detective Chief Inspector Radfield was one of those men who never seemed to age. Perhaps, Pascale reflected, because he was always middle-aged. Even thirty years ago when he was in his mid-twenties, he looked fifty. Now, she reflected, his age fitted his skin. A few extra pounds around his girth and maybe the hairline was a little higher than she recalled, but otherwise he looked exactly the same.

I could swear that's the same raincoat.

Radfield stood as they entered his office. "Madame Hervé, a pleasure. After all these years. I see that rumours of your demise are somewhat unfounded."

She reached out and took the proffered hand. "Yes, Chief Inspector, I am a survivor."

"I do hope so," he sighed as he sat. "Do you recall Frank Cotter?"

"Of course." She glanced across at Mike and realised that he was party to what was about to be disclosed. *Well, if nothing else, it demonstrates that he can be relied upon to keep a confidence,* she thought.

"Well, Frank Cotter was murdered back in May."

"I see. And what does this have to do with me?"

"Ahem," he shifted awkwardly. "We are unable to locate his erstwhile business partner. Seems to have gone missing. Then there's your old partner, Madame Duval…"

"You are suggesting that there is a link?"

"I am. Fábián Rousseau."

"Why?"

"The Koh-I-Noor."

Pascale was puzzled. She glanced across at Mike, but he showed no emotion. "But that was all done thirty years ago."

Radfield shook his head. He had a habit of polishing his glasses as he spoke as it gave him the opportunity to avoid eye contact. "The Koh-I-Noor was never recovered."

"What? But we recovered it. Geneviève changed the real gems for fakes and returned the genuine ones."

"That and the other diamonds were all fakes."

"As was the one that was used to replace the stolen one while we were busy chasing our tails over the real one," Mike said.

Radfield smiled. "Indeed. A little confusion to muddy the waters. Put the bad guys off their game."

Pascale thought about the implication for a moment. "So there were two fakes?"

"Correct."

"And for the past thirty years, the one we believed was the real thing has been in the crown jewels?"

"Yes."

"And the real one?"

"Well, now, isn't that the question? A question, it seems that *Monsieur* Rousseau is asking. Certainly he seems to have asked Mr Cotter. The thing I didn't mention is that Frank Cotter was tortured before he died."

Pascale took a moment to consider what Radfield had divulged. "Cotter had a partner. Phil…"

Radfield nodded. "Yes, Phil Maguire."

"What of him?"

"Served time for the Hatton Garden job along with Cotter—although like you Cotter was believed to be dead. We caught up with him a few years later. He was released about twenty years ago."

"And since then?"

Radfield shook his head. "Since his release, Phil Maguire had vanished. No one knew where he was or what had become of him. Could be dead, for all we know."

"That," said Pascale, "is probably what he wants you to think."

As the afternoon was growing old, Radfield decided to call their meeting to a close. "We've arranged accommodation for you." Mike led Pascale out of the police station and they took a taxi to the hotel.

"What does Radfield want?" she asked.

Mike shook his head. "Not sure. He is worried about your safety—mine too and Steph's. In fact everyone who was involved with that ride thirty years ago is at risk."

"I was perfectly happy as I was, in ignorance of all this."

"It would have caught up with you sooner or later."

The taxi stopped outside the hotel. "Wait," Mike instructed the driver as he alighted. He walked with Pascale up to the entrance. "I'll see you later," he said, "If you like. Dinner? Seven?"

42

She nodded. "Yes, why not."

"It'll be nice to catch up."

Pascale reached across and kissed him lightly on each cheek before turning back to the hotel and walking inside.

"See you at seven," she said over her shoulder.

She would not be keeping that appointment.

***

Bristol, August, 1987

"I want to go to Portugal," Mike said.

"Why?" Stephanie asked.

"I want to find out what happened."

"We know what happened, it was an accident."

"I don't believe it was."

"Mike," she said. "You're upset..."

"I'm not stupid. Karen was a good rider, she wouldn't lose it on an empty road and you know it."

"We don't know it was empty, just that there were no witnesses. Anyway, how do we know it wasn't heat exhaustion?"

"Well, I want to go and find out for myself."

"I'm not sure that's..."

"I can go on the next trip that Maguire Motorcycle Tours are running."

"You can't," she replied. "You're in no state. You're still recovering from surgery, you'd never cope with that kind of trip."

"I want to," he repeated belligerently.

"Mike..."

"Something happened out there, don't you care?"

"That's not fair and you know it."

"Sorry, I didn't mean..."

"I know, you're upset, we all are. Look, I'll take you home you need the rest. Come back tomorrow..."

"I thought I'd bring the tape machine, play her some music."

"Good idea," she said, hoping that it showed he was coming up a little from his depression. Grasping his arm, she led him like a child away from the inert form on the bed.

***

Something woke Stephanie. Stirring, she pushed her husband Roddy's sleeping form away and squinted at the clock. Its luminous figures blinked 04:30 at her. Fuddled by sleep she listened. Downstairs the telephone chirruped. "Damn," she murmured, throwing the duvet aside and pulling on her robe. "One of these days I'll get an extension up here."

"And complain when it rings," Roddy muttered sleepily.

"Must you always be such a smartarse?"

"It's the company I keep," he murmured as he drifted back to sleep.

The chill of early morning filled the house, despite the lazy warmth filling it later in the day. Barefoot she padded downstairs and answered the phone. "Yes?"

"Miss Ross?"

"Sergeant Radfield?"

"Miss Ross, you'd better get down to the hospital..."

The urgency in his voice electrified her, banishing the sleep from her brain. "What's up?"

"Someone's tried to kill your sister. I have already called Mr Jenner and Mr Fry."

Waking Roddy, she dressed quickly and they drove through the empty streets to the Royal Infirmary in his battered Cavalier. Mike, Dave and Radfield were waiting for them—along with another familiar face.

"What are you doing here?" she asked Ted Stanshawe. Roddy nodded and smiled at his erstwhile colleague. "Ted."

Ted's face lit up into a smile of recognition and turned back to Stephanie. "I heard your sister was in here and figured...well, I heard about the attempt on her life...and thought..."

"That there was carrion for the picking?"

"You can be so cruel."

"Experience is didactic."

"Ouch."

"So?" she pressed home her advantage.

"So, I heard a whisper and I want to know what's going on. There's a story here."

"Is there?" she responded with a desert wind whipping through her voice.

"Clear off," Radfield interrupted. "When we've got something for you, we'll call a press conference."

Ted remained steadfast. "I could be of some assistance. We could help each other."

"I doubt it." Turning her back on him, Stephanie asked Radfield "What happened?"

"Someone gained entry to the ward and switched off the machine," Radfield replied.

She glanced across at Mike who moved his head in a barely perceptible shake.

"Who?" she asked.

"We intend to find out," Radfield replied.

"Well did anybody see…?"

"No," Radfield sighed heavily. "At least we haven't found anyone yet, but we will keep trying. Hospitals are full of people moving about, even during the night. A stranger could walk in here relatively easily."

"And did," Mike said bitterly.

"And Karen?"

"The night sister found her," he replied.

"And?"

"Well, she's okay. That is, okay in that there's no change in her condition for the worse."

"Why?" Stephanie asked.

"Perhaps Mike's conspiracy theory has some weight," Radfield suggested heavily.

"Ah, conspiracies," Ted interrupted. "I'm good at those."

"You still here?" Radfield asked flatly.

Ted returned the sour humour with a broad grin exposing the gaps in his teeth. "You don't know what you're missing."

"And perhaps I should go to Portugal," Mike said.

"No," Radfield replied. "You are in no state."

"But... I am. I'm okay now. Steph can keep an eye on Karen."

"I think Stephanie should go."

"Oh, you do, do you?" she said tartly.

"I don't think..." Roddy started.

"Neither do I," Stephanie finished. "Sergeant, I'm not an investigator."

"You don't need to be. Just go and have a holiday."

She looked from Mike to Radfield. "What's going on here?"

Radfield took his glasses off and polished them, thereby avoiding her eye.

"Mike?"

"We'll talk about it in the morning," he replied. "But I think I should go."

"Okay," Stephanie said acidly, "we'll talk about it in the morning. I don't think anyone should be going anywhere."

"Hear, here," Roddy said. But no one was listening.

"What about me?" Ted asked with his best phoney puppy dog look.

"What about you?" Stephanie asked, teasing him with her best obtuse blank stare.

***

The RAC phoned the following day. Radfield took Stephanie's call and gave her an address, "the forensics lab," he explained. She called the RAC back and repeated the address to a puzzled RAC operator. "That's the police…"

"Yes," she said, stopping the conversation there.

So when the remains of Karen's Suzuki GSX550 finally arrived home, the sorry mess found its way to the police labs.

Dave Fry arrived at the offices of Alpha Technologies bearing his usual supply of customer disks just as Stephanie was preparing a jug of coffee. "I suppose you'll be stopping, then?" she asked, flicking a lock of red hair away from her eyes.

"I wouldn't say no to a coffee. I've not slept much since I got home last night—or was it this morning?"

She nodded. Mutual understanding needed no words.

After Dave went, Stephanie called Radfield and asked him about the forensic investigation of the Suzuki. "You're sure that they'll find something?"

"No," he replied. "But unless they look, we won't know, will we? Besides, after last night I think we may be in luck."

"Well what about this nonsense about me going to Portugal?"

"Mr Jenner won't rest until someone does and as he's in no fit state, you will be the best person to go." He paused for a moment. "Much as it goes against my grain to involve civilians, I think there might be some scope here to have eyes on the ground. Something's not right here and I could do with some assistance. Budgets and all that…" he trailed off awkwardly.

"And do what, exactly?"

"Have a holiday," he said. "It's extremely unlikely you'll discover anything," he said a little more brightly. More brightly than he felt and Stephanie detected as much but didn't push it.

"Oh?"

She could almost sense him shrugging on the other end of the line. "As you said yourself, you're not a professional investigator…"

"Thanks," she said, dripping nitric, "for the huge vote of confidence. So what's the point of me going?"

Radfield smiled broadly to himself and sipped his coffee. "I've got some files to get on with. What about you?"

***

Radfield telephoned Stephanie a couple of days after the Suzuki arrived home. "Get over to the police HQ. The others, too."

A lab technician met them and took them to a garage that served as a vehicular mortuary. Featureless and grey, the remains of once prized possessions littered the floor in sad little heaps—the hopes and dreams of their proud owners a faded memory. The technician led them across the floor, seamlessly avoiding the twisted broken and rusted assault course to where a couple of his colleagues were poring over the Suzuki's remains.

With care, he reached out a gloved hand and held up an exhaust downpipe for their examination. "What do you make of that?" he asked.

"Exhaust downpipe," Mike replied.

"Mm, and what do you notice about it?" He traced a finger along the pipe.

"Nothing, looks pretty ordinary to me." Stephanie ventured.

"That," he said, eyes flashing over the top of his glasses, "is what is strange. There are a couple of interesting things to note. Firstly, a hot exhaust coming into contact with the ground and other parts of the machine should have debris burned into the surface. This one has a little oxidation..."

"Rust," Mike interrupted.

"Mm, rust," he replied. "But otherwise, where is the burned plastic from the fairing? Look," He picked up a piece of fairing lower and placed it against the downpipe. "This is where the fairing contacted the exhaust and broke—you can see the line of the break and the indentation of the pipe."

"But no burn," Mike said.

"Exactly, no burn. Now, look at this." The technician led them to another piece of wreckage. "The instrument console. Look at the ignition switch."

"It's switched off," Radfield said.

"So, anyone could have done that after the crash," Dave pointed out.

"Quite possible, but where is the key?" The technician asked.

Mike turned to Stephanie who shrugged. Then she remembered. Karen's personal belongings were returned when she flew back. In her bag were a bunch of keys, the Suzuki ignition key among them. She hadn't given it much thought at the time.

"It was in her bag... So, what, exactly we are saying here, is..."

The technician sighed. "What we are saying, is that when this machine went down the precipice, the engine was not switched on."

"So," Stephanie said, "Mike is right, this was no accident."

"Undoubtedly."

"Portugal, then," he said.

"Portugal," Stephanie replied.

"I'm going," Mike said. "No arguments."

In that moment, she realised that arguing with him was futile. Nothing was going to dissuade him.

***

"Did you speak to Mike today?" she asked Dave when he arrived later that evening. He raised an eyebrow that asked silently about her missing husband.

"Roddy's out somewhere," she confirmed.

He followed her through to the kitchen and waited while she finished the washing up.

"Er, yeah. Strangely enough he was reasonably positive, almost perky."

"Good," she said. "Maybe this is what he needs to bring him back to the world of the living. Perhaps I was wrong."

Dave opened his mouth to speak, but a look from her green eyes made him think better of it and he remained silent.

Stephanie placed the dish she'd been wiping on the drainer and turned to face him. "I'm worried. There's something going on here and Radfield isn't telling us everything."

Chapter 5

Somewhere by the sea, Late August, 2018.

Pascale hated the rain.

It spattered against the window like a celestial tap-dancer, swept in from the cold grey sea. Sometimes, in her more lucid moments, she wondered which sea. If she knew, she would have some idea of her whereabouts.

Her world was the small room with its bed, table, chair and cupboard bathroom. In the middle of a cold stone floor, a tired rug sufficed as the only covering. The table was a simple affair left over from the nineteen sixties—all plastic and Formica and no taste.

She hated the rain. Cold grey water splashing down on the cold grey sea from a cold grey sky. Another ship nosed past the jut of land at the end of the bay. She wondered where it sailed from and where it would sail to when it left this place. Straining, she looked west along the headland. The ships disappeared behind it and mostly they reappeared from there. She presumed that the promontory concealed a port. Which port?

She supposed that it was still August. Or maybe early September. Time drifted and she lost track. When was it that she could last remember? It was mid-August when she walked into the hallway of her hotel. Mike had returned home and they were planning to meet later that day to discuss events over dinner. It was August. She knew in her own mind that wasn't so long ago. Was that days or weeks though?

They delivered food and coffee three times a day. She never saw their faces and only heard their voices muffled by the door between their rooms. The taller one usually brought in her tray. The other stood, leaning indolently against the doorframe, watching through the eye slits in his balaclava in case she made a run for it. At least that's what she presumed. If she attempted to strike up a conversation, they ignored her.

She knew the taller one's name: Chris. They let it slip one night. They played cards into the early hours and sometimes she would wake. The moon, high in the shimmering sky, flooded the room with its silver light. The muffled voices from the other room carried on the still air.

"Well?"

"I'm thinking."

"C'mon, Chris, it's only matches..."

Pascale heard the sound of a chair scraped against the floor. "Godammit! She could be listening..."

"Sorry, it slipped out."

"Well, be more careful in future, right?"

"Right, right, sorry."

The voices dropped to a murmur and she drifted into a dreamy sleep. She didn't much care what their names were. She kept quiet about her newfound knowledge. One day it might be useful.

How long she'd been there she couldn't say. Sometimes it seemed like years, other times it seemed like days. She drifted from wakefulness, when she wondered about her predicament, to sleep, when oblivion washed over her like a blanket and back to reality and the room. Sometimes in those dreams she watched helplessly as Geneviève set out in her Peugeot, slamming the door shut, looking over her shoulder and driving off to catch Fábián Rousseau. Always the same, yet she was never there. Had she been, it might have worked out differently.

The room. A self-contained world, sealed from the outside. A holiday home, she decided, lacking the personality of a regular occupant. The mismatched furniture and cutlery, the weary carpet barely covering the cold slate flagstones.

Sometimes she gave up the attempt to work out where she was and turned her attention to when. When had she last known where she was?

The hotel, that's right. Mike walked away as they reached the hotel.

"See you at seven?" Mike asked as they stopped at the front door.

"That will be nice. Yes, seven. I will see you then."

And then what? She went up to the room and everything appeared normal. As she stepped inside, she felt something in the room was wrong. A presence, a subconscious feeling only but enough to make her turn to see what, but it was too late. Her world went black.

And here she was at rain-by-the-sea. *England! Such a grey little island,* she thought to herself.

She started to count the days but somehow they all blended into each other. Eventually she realized that her permanent stupor was due to some drug in the food or drink. She decided not to eat or drink. She could exist on the water from the tap in the bathroom. Her plan depended on her incarceration being relatively short. She waited until Chris backed out of the doorway and his companion closed it behind him. Then she took the plate into the bathroom and emptied its contents along with the coffee into the toilet bowl.

By the end of the day she was feeling more awake and able to assess her surroundings as well as the gnawing in her stomach. She was aware of engines in the distance. High pitched engines. Racing engines?

August? Racing?

It was night when they dumped her in the room—she remembered being driven through the dark. Before that...before that, what? An aircraft. That was it, an aircraft. She thought about this. Dimly she could recall the drumming of its engine and the bumpy turbulence. A light aircraft, probably a single engine, or a turbo prop. Did this mean that she had crossed the sea and this was a Channel port? She struggled with half formed memories as

50

the effect of whatever drugs they had given her wore off. She recalled clearly the two men in the hotel lobby. Used as she was to observing her surroundings, her recent retirement had made her slow.

I should have realised.

Closing her eyes, she followed her footsteps through the hotel, up the stairs—she never took the lift—to the hallway. She opened the door and stepped into the room. He must have been waiting behind the door as she entered.

Chris! Yes, Chris! And someone else, whose face was familiar. I know who you are!

Chris and his companion, but a third man. Chris pushed something in her face during the struggle and she lost consciousness. She must have woken several times during the next few hours. Parts of the journey came back to her as she allowed her mind to wander, touching the memories lightly, stimulating them into life. Placing herself back there in that moment.

A car journey. She was in the back of a car. Chris was driving, she could see his head above her. She was lying across the back seat, the other man was alongside her, one arm restraining. Chris was speaking, his voice distant. Something about the man, Ronald. Ronald who? She was aware that she was moving, the rag was pushed over her face once more and everything drifted away.

Pascale closed her eyes and forced the memories to come back to life.

Flying. Aero engines are distinctive with their loud buzz, cutting through the atmosphere, pulling the craft through its fabric. A turboprop, definitely a turboprop. She was slumped in a seat alongside Chris. Half in half out of wakefulness she was aware that the light was going. Outside the last few rays of the spring sun were dripping across the seat and warming her face. She turned her head to look out of the window. Chris sensed the movement and pushed the ether-soaked rag into her face once more. The sweet smell turned her stomach as she drifted away again. But now she can remember what she saw. She saw the sea. The low sun, slinking below its curved horizon, was hovering for the last few moments of the day above the calm waters of the sea. Which sea? Also, they were heading north. Then it wasn't a channel port.

Pascale stood and walked to the window. Her mind now clear, she looked across the bay. The sun hovered just above the promontory casting the bay in a warm glow, the water lapping the shore reflected the dying glory of the day. As the sun slid behind the finger of land it left behind the pink and purple haze of impending night. West, so this was the Irish Sea.

And the land behind me?

Unless she was in Ireland, then this was the Atlantic.

The airport was one of those open provincial places, no huge terminal and covered walkways. She felt the sea breeze touch her face as they bundled her into a vehicle and they drove through the night. Twisty roads and the ghostly glow of the trees in the headlamps. Then a town. A seaside town. She remembered lights and the sound of people in the streets and those high pitched engines. Motorcycle engines. Then here, in this room, they left her, calling three times a day to feed her and keep her comatose.

Now she was awake and could think about escape. Now she was awake and she knew where she was.

"Well, that took time," Geneviève said.

Pascale looked back from the window. Geneviève sat nonchalantly at the table, swinging a leg easily as she watched Pascale struggle with her memory before returning to the open book in her hands.

"What are you reading?"

Geneviève held the worn tome up so that Pascale could read the title. "A Pin to See the Peepshow?"

"A murder story," she said. "Based upon a real case in England. Fascinating. She was executed, you know."

Pascale sighed. Fascinating it may be, but a novel was an irrelevance as far as she was concerned. "What are you doing here?"

"The same as you. To see what Phil Maguire wants."

"I know what he wants," Pascale said.

"The Koh-I-Noor."

"Yes, so why suggest that you don't?" *God! But she can be irritating sometimes.*

Geneviève turned a page, feigning reading. "He thinks you know where it is?"

"Presumably. Hence this charade of kidnap."

Geneviève nodded. "And?"

"And, I have no idea where it is. So I will have to escape before he comes here. They tortured and killed Frank Cotter."

Geneviève nodded. "But you do know where it is."

Pascale stared back at her. She shook her head. "If I knew where it was, I would have told Radfield and I would not be a captive on the Isle of Man."

Geneviève smiled. "So you worked it out. You always were the better detective."

"August. Motorcycle Engines. The Manx Grand Prix." She shrugged, once her head had cleared it all made sense. Chris had given away more than he had realised. "But I do not know where the Koh-I-Noor is."

"You have known for years. You just haven't worked it out yet."

She barely heard the door open and she was about to retort.

"Oh, I think you do."

She turned at the sound of his voice. Phil Maguire had barely changed over the past thirty years. Unlike his erstwhile compatriot, Frank Cotter, Phil had looked after himself. Still lean and muscular. Some grey now showed around his temples, but for a man in his mid-sixties, he had weathered well. Or, perhaps, unlike Frank Cotter, he was still alive, Pascale reflected.

52

"I don't know where it is." Pascale turned back to the table, but Geneviève had gone.

"Oh, I think you do." Maguire sat on one of the chairs and gestured Pascale to join him.

Silently, she complied.

"We're on the same side, you and me," he said.

"We are?"

"Well, you worked for me didn't you?"

Pascale smiled. "Is that what you think? Even now?"

***

Montpellier, January 1987

The shadowy figure stepped out from behind the half-closed door. Pascale sensed rather than saw the movement. Instantly, she swivelled on her heel and stepped back, bringing the Beretta up to eye level, both arms outstretched and hands wrapped around the butt. She froze for the barest of moments before squeezing the trigger and watching the figure disappear into the darkness of the doorway.

Almost immediately a slight sound from across the street electrified her senses. Dropping to a squat, she swung her torso round as she aimed the Beretta, both eyes open, sighting along the barrel. A kid, pushing a bicycle—nothing to worry about. She lowered the pistol and moved her gaze along the street, beyond the child and into the shadows of the Post Office doorway. Slowly, warily, she stood.

"Okay, Pascale, you can come out now."

Alain Marchant's voice echoed through the intercom in the roof above the plywood street. Stepping between the *Boucherie* and the Post Office, she mounted the open plan metal steps to his office.

"Well done, Pascale, fancy a coffee?"

"You mean I didn't kill anyone I shouldn't have?" She smiled as Alain poured coffee from the machine bubbling away in the corner of his office. The place was so familiar, like a well-loved but tired old pullover. The smell of coffee permeated the room filling it with a life that was no longer there. Alain caught her eye and recognised the memory. His predecessor had died in the line of duty and it weighed heavily in that room.

He shook his head. "No. Reckon we can let you out on the streets still."

"Thanks." She smiled as he handed her the steaming mug. She sipped the hot liquid, saying nothing as she watched Alain writing out his report. Finished, he looked up. He studied her across the tiny office with its paraphernalia littered across the desk and spilling onto the floor. Clear grey eyes swept over her face, taking in the olive skin, dark eyes, small nose and full lips below dark hair pulled back into a long plait.

"I've a job for you."

Cupping her hands around the warm mug, she raised an eyebrow. He made a play at leafing through some papers on the desk while she waited. This was a game they played regularly. He would build up the suspense and she would wait as if on a knife-edge while he delivered details about the next job. Unfortunately it was usually exceedingly dull.

"We want to get close to Fábián Rousseau."

"Oh…"

He shook his head. "But it is not so simple. He is notoriously secretive. So we get close to his associates. We have discovered a diamond smuggling operation he is using. A subcontract if you like."

"And I am to go undercover?"

"Almost. We want you to go back to your old job for this one."

She inclined her head. "Why?"

"Because we want them to know that you are a police officer. You remember Geneviève Duval? You were at the academy together?"

"Yes."

"You report to her first thing tomorrow morning."

"And then?"

"And then, you will be contacted."

He stood. The interview was over.

***

Douglas, Late August 2018

"We thought you were dead," Phil said.

"Most people did. My handler decided that it would be useful for me to remain officially dead." She sighed. "I was never on your side, Maguire, I was undercover with the GSIGN. And I cannot help you. I do not know where the Koh-I-Noor is. I did not know until Radfield told me when I arrived in England that it was still missing. So torture me if you must, like you did with Cotter, but I'll tell you no more than he did, because I know as much as he did."

Maguire smiled for a brief moment. "It wasn't me who tortured Frank."

"Ah. Then Rousseau?"

He nodded. "Yes, Rousseau and like it or not, we are on the same side here, because he believes that one of us who were involved has the key to its whereabouts and he will not rest until he has uncovered it."

He stood. "You have a choice *Madame* Hervé, work with me or face Rousseau alone."

She said nothing for a moment. He walked to the door and opened it.

"And if I refuse to cooperate with you, what will you do?"

He turned and shrugged. "I will do nothing. Rousseau will do whatever he thinks is necessary to obtain the information that he wants."

"As I said, I don't have it."

"Tell him, not me."

"Ha!"

He smiled, but there was no mirth or warmth. "*Madame*, you understand betrayal. It's what you did for a living. But I have no choice—I will have to trust you this time as I trusted you before. This time, though, we have a common foe. It's up to you." He stepped into the hallway outside and turned before closing the door. "I'll be in touch."

The door closed and she was alone.

***

They didn't come.

She waited, having made her plans, for them to bring her breakfast. Then she was going to make her break. As the day wore on, she waited. Once or twice she went to the door and pressed her ear to it and listened. Nothing. Outside the sea lapped the shore and the gulls keened overhead. The sounds of normality in a macabre, abnormal situation.

She was alone. It took a while to realise that Phil, Chris and companion had gone. Why? She thought about this for a moment. Why would they just leave? Why had they kidnapped her in the first place? Just to talk? To ask about an alliance? She dreaded the worst.

Eventually she tried the door. It opened. The kitchen was deserted. Empty cans overflowed from the pedal bin and the sink was full of unwashed crockery. Stale cigarette smoke hung in the atmosphere and she could detect a hint of curry—the remains in the pedal bin confirmed her assumption. Warily she walked through the house, pausing and listening like a feral cat before opening each door. Not that she needed to worry. The rest of the house was as empty as the kitchen. Puzzled, she wandered about looking in cupboards but found nothing. Almost nothing.

Something nagged in her mind as she wandered back to the kitchen. Something she had seen. Something so normal to her that she had missed it. On the kitchen table she found a handgun. A Beretta nine millimetre automatic pistol. *Her* Beretta nine millimetre automatic pistol.

My God! The bastard has been in my home!

Picking it up, she slipped it into the waistband of her jeans and walked out of the house.

Behind her the sea sparkled in the late August sunshine. The air was cool, fresh and westerly. Ahead, the lane climbed a rise through some trees towards the sound of traffic. *The main road*, she concluded. As she reached the top of the rise she came upon railway lines running along a cutting in the rock and following the line of the coast. They were narrow gauge as she expected, there being no regular gauge railway on the island. Watching for trains, she stepped across the lines and clambered across the embankment to the road.

Despite the cool wind, she was warm by the time she reached the top of the rise. For a moment there was a lull in the traffic—a brief silence dangling heavy in the air as she waited. Then she heard the approach of a motorcycle. The high pitched howl of a snarling four cylinder engine as the rider changed down on the approach to a bend then the throaty growl as he powered on for the straight. Then more blips before changing down. He came into sight. A lone rider on a Kawasaki Z900RS. She watched as he straightened his mount and headed along the road towards her, the exhaust note becoming a throaty whine as he opened the throttle and the big four sprang forwards. She stepped into the road and waved vigorously.

The rider braked hard, the front wheel biting into the tarmac to an accompaniment of screeching rubber and the sour tang of burning. He killed the engine as his mount stopped, leaving the sound of ticking in the exhaust's wake. Flipping his visor open, he glowered angrily at her.

"You silly cow!" He snapped. "You could've got yourself killed."

"Yes," she said, unruffled, waiting for him to flick the sidestand down and dismount. "I know."

"Well, what..." He stopped mid-sentence, thrown by her lack of reaction. And then...

"My God!"

"Freddie? Freddie McLean? Really?"

"Pascale! Good Lord! What are you doing here?"

"I need some help."

"You've a funny way of asking."

"Sorry, it was necessary." She looked at the man facing her and the years fell away. Ghosts from the past seemed to her to be becoming something of a habit. He was about her own age and now that he had removed his helmet, she could see a rounded face topped with cropped dark brown hair speckled with grey at the temples.

"Pascale," he said. "As I live and breathe. I thought..."

"That I was dead. Yes, I know. Well, I am not. And you? Why are you here?"

"I'm covering the Manx. It's what I do, remember? Write articles?"

"Yes, I remember, write articles," she said flatly. "When you weren't doing something entirely different. It's been so long. Thirty years now."

"Okay, so, Pascale. So what are you trying to commit suicide for?"

"It's a long story—I've been kidnapped."

His eyebrows shot up to his closely cropped hairline. "And you've escaped?"

"Not exactly. I just walked out."

"Just like that?"

She shrugged. "Just like that. Come with me, I want to show you something."

Walking back across the railway lines, she descended the short rise to the cottage. Freddie followed at a discreet distance. He wandered around the cottage behind her, with a bemused expression on his face. She had to admit, that apart from the curry wrappers in the pedal bin, there was little evidence of recent occupation and certainly nothing to raise suspicion.

"My gun was lying here," she said, placing a hand on the table.

"Why?"

"I wondered that. Maguire wanted me to help him and the man we are up against is a dangerous man. That, I guess."

"Perhaps they want you to have it—it may be incriminating."

That thought had occurred to Pascale when she first found it. If it had been used in anger, it was likely that the only fingerprints on it would be hers. She slipped the magazine out. "One round is missing."

"When did you last use it?" Freddie asked.

"Couple of weeks ago during a practice session."

"And?"

"I reloaded it." She clipped the magazine back. "I have a feeling that Maguire may have bought himself some insurance. I need to get off the island."

"The ferry could be a problem—everyone else will be trying to get back at the same time."

"What about the airport?"

"Ronaldsway?"

She stared at him. "Ronald."

"I'm sorry?"

"They kept going on about someone called Ronald during the flight. They were on about Ronaldsway."

"Figures." He shrugged and walked out of the cottage and back up the hill to the road with Pascale following several paces behind.

"I really need to get off the island," she repeated.

"How?"

"I don't know, fly I guess."

"Have you any money?" He paused, causing her to almost walk into him.

"No."

"Mm," he turned again towards the road.

"Can you help?" she asked.

"Maybe," he replied enigmatically. "Tell you what, I'll nip back to the hotel and pick up a helmet and meet you back here."

"And?"

"And, I'll take you back to Douglas—we can think about what to do next then."

Freddie rode off and returned about half an hour later with a helmet on his arm. He handed it to Pascale along with a pair of gloves. Pulling on her jacket, she mounted the Kawasaki behind him.

Back at the hotel, Freddie shifted the sleeping arrangements allowing her to use his room while he bunked down with his travelling companion. While she was settling in, he picked up his phone and dialled.

"Hi, yeah, it's me. No, no, I'm okay. Yes, I know I'm supposed to be on holiday… But you'll never guess who just landed in my lap…Yes, yes, that's right. I've found her. What do you want to do?"

He listened for a moment or two, casting an eye at the closed door of the bedroom.

"And Phil Maguire?"

He nodded as he listened. "Okay, I'll make the arrangements," he finished, terminating the call. She would find out about Phil Maguire soon enough. In the meantime, she needed to get off the island.

Chapter 6

Portsmouth, September 1987

Phil Maguire was waiting in the terminal building. He was a tall, lean man with rugged features enhanced, rather than marred, by a broken nose. A legacy, Mike later discovered, from his boxing days several years previously. His short, fair hair had an attractive unruly look about it, but any boyishness ceased at his steely, grey eyes. Strangely, though his mouth twitched frequently into gentle humour, those eyes rarely smiled. He stood and ran a hand through his hair before glancing at his watch.

"You must be…"

"Mike, Mike Jenner."

Next to him on the bench, Frank Cotter snored in loud, comatose bliss until Phil nudged him with the toe of his boot. Frank jerked awake, then relaxed as he realised where he was.

A short, powerful man, Frank contrasted with his companion both in intelligence and looks. Phil, immaculately dressed, was wearing a short sleeved pilot shirt and grey leather trousers with a matching top lying on the bench. Frank's garb was more casual: a stained tee shirt and faded jeans, beneath a well-worn lancer jacket, were more his style. His chin was covered with a two-day growth of stubble and his bloodshot eyes bore evidence to too much of the good life.

Frank sat up and reached for the box of jelly babies lying next to him on the bench, selected one and popped it into his mouth before rising awkwardly and reaching out a hand.

"Frank Cotter," he said. "Pleased to make your acquaintance."

"I thought you were dead to the world," Phil said easily.

Frank allowed himself a sly grin. "That's what you think. I was aware of everything that was goin' on."

Phil ignored the comment and turned to stare out of the window to the queue that was starting to build for the Le Havre crossing. A few more bikes were gathering. "Better go out and see if any of them are ours," he said.

"Ah," Frank replied rising awkwardly. "So which one are you?"

"Silver TR1," Mike said.

Frank nodded and set off for the door. "I'll be on my way then."

He was almost through the door when he remembered something. Returning to the bench he retrieved his box of jelly babies before winking at Phil and stepping out into the night. Fifteen minutes later he returned with several other leather-clad riders clutching helmets and looking slightly adrift. "Found 'em outside," he explained. "They're supposed to be with us."

Phil Maguire was seasick. The ferry turned outside the harbour and rolled with the swell on the surface of the choppy water, turning his normally healthy tan a sick shade of grey. His forehead shone with a patina of cold sweat. Frank was unperturbed and Phil clearly hated him for it. While Phil gathered the party together in the forward bar to brief them about the following day, Frank was busily devouring a hamburger. Groaning wanly, Phil clutched at his protesting abdomen.

"Shit. Do you have to?"

Frank feigned surprised innocence. "Mm? Oh, sorry. I was hungry. Want some?"

Phil gulped down the desire to retch and turned away from the food. Desperately trying to ignore the hamburger, he turned to the gathered party.

"I've billeted you in groups of two or three except for the couples—you'll have rooms to yourselves. Mike, I've put you with a bike journo who will be joining us at Le Havre, name of Freddie McLean. That okay?"

"Fine," he said. "What about you, are you sure you're alright?"

"I always get sea-sick," he grumbled. Turning to Frank, who was chewing happily he said "Can't you go somewhere else and eat that?"

"Sorry for breathing," Frank mumbled through a mouthful of bun, feigning hurt.

"You will be if you don't put a sock in it and take that thing away," Phil replied malevolently.

Tendrils of cool grey mist heralded the start of a new day. As the sun lifted its head slowly in the eastern sky, dull red against the pale translucent shadows of the town, the docks of Le Havre took form and the cranes appeared like huge dragons slumbering until the call to wake. Within the hour the mist would clear leaving the promise a fine day belying the early morning chill.

They had experienced bad weather in the channel overnight. Although Mike's only awareness was drifting into half sleep occasionally and feeling the swell as the ship rolled from one wave crest to another. During those moments of semi-consciousness he wondered about the bike—had the crew secured it properly? Would he return to the car deck to find it on its side, the fairing smashed? These were nothing more than the vague fanciful notions of a half-asleep mind.

Overnight ferry crossings can be a mixed blessing. In theory, after a night's sleep, the traveller is refreshed and ready to face a day's driving through France. The practice, however, can be rather different.

When they were woken by the Tannoy at about five a.m. Mike had hardly slept and was still ready for another couple of hours' shut-eye. He was feeling drained and unkempt. His hair was a tousled mass of dark brown bird's nest, bags sagged below his eyes and he dared them to remain as he glared at his pale reflection in the mirror and ran a razor over his chin. *God, I look awful.* Ghosts had healthy tans by comparison. His mouth felt like glass paper and he could have murdered a coffee or two.

Breakfast, unfortunately, was another problem. The galley opened for business an hour before docking. Consequently everyone rushed at once to be fed. Mike felt that he couldn't be bothered.

"I think I'll wait," he muttered to himself as he looked at the queue. He preferred to wait until they were in France and could stop in a café at the roadside anyway. He was unconcerned about what Phil and Frank may have planned—he was stopping for breakfast in France and would brook no argument. As it was, the arrangements were so fluid, they could do as they pleased and no one cared very much.

The ship now suffered from the all-pervading odour of stale vomit— Phil was not alone in suffering sea-sickness—quashing any appetite that he may have had so the prospect of a postponed breakfast was all the more appealing. In France he could eat in a more leisurely atmosphere once the fresh air had revived his desire to eat.

Consequently, he was tired, hungry, and suffering from caffeine withdrawal symptoms when they rolled their bikes off the ship and into the lifting mist of Le Havre. Shivering from the damp atmosphere Mike wondered if he would ever see it in sunshine, as so far every morning that he had experienced here looked the same, grey and gloomy.

Phil and Frank disembarked before the rest and they made their way through the diesel fumes engulfing the car deck to the cool of a late September morning and along to where the others were parked by the Terminal building just after exiting customs. Not that customs were slightly interested—they waved the riders straight through before Mike had time to retrieve his passport from his jacket pockets.

Geneviève Duval and Pascale Hervé were waiting with Phil and the others. With them was a slim man on a BMW K75S. Mike took in the short-cropped hair, upright stance and assured manner. He wondered if he was ex-military. "This is Freddie McLean," Phil introduced him. "You two are billeted together."

"Freddie is an acquaintance of ours, so we may as well ride together," Geneviève said, introducing herself to Mike.

Mike paused to look at Freddie's BMW K75S, a neat three-cylinder machine that was half touring bike and half sportster. Its owner stood next to him. "You must be Mike," he said holding out his hand "You know a friend of mine, I believe."

"I do?"

"Ted Stanshawe?"

Mike turned slowly to look at the man standing beside him. About the same age as himself with dark close-cropped hair above a saturnine face, he had the decency to look embarrassed.

"And Ted didn't just happen to telephone you and ask you to talk to me, did he?"

"Erm…"

"I see."

"Well, he said there was something going on, and, well, er…"

"He asked if you could do a little investigating for him, ask a few discreet questions, things like that?"

"Yeah, somethin' like that."

"You do surprise me. So you're a journalist too?"

He wriggled awkwardly and gestured at his bike. "It's not mine," he mumbled, glancing at Mike shiftily. "I've got it on test. That's what I'm here for primarily."

"Oh?"

"Yeah, I'm based over here—I write for *La Moto*."

"And?" What, Mike wondered, had Ted got on him? Apart, that was, from his own ability to persuade Lucifer to sing baritone in a heavenly choir.

"Well, as I said Ted got in contact…"

Mike stared into the man's eyes. "You haven't told him anything?"

Freddie shook his head. "Good God! No. Not yet anyway…."

"Well, don't."

Freddie raised his hands. "Okay, okay. Not yet. But when it's all done, there's a story here."

"I thought you were a bike journalist?"

"Yeah, I know, but this story could be big."

Mike conceded that he might be right. However, for the moment they needed to exercise discretion.

Geneviève was slim and petite, Mike thought that she stood at no more than five feet three or four inches. Her apparently blonde hair—the dark parting gave the game away—was cut in a bob; high at the neck and following the jaw line, with a fringe along her forehead, surrounding a heart shaped face with wide blue eyes. Like her companion, she was dressed in leathers. A red and white two piece matching her Ducati Paso.

Pascale Hervé was taller than her companion. Dark hair flowed in an unruly curtain about her olive face. Brown sloe eyes crinkled with wry amusement as she held out a hand. Unlike Geneviève she wore more traditional clothing, a lancer style jacket and lace up jeans. Image is all. When you ride a Harley, you've got to look cool. He smiled to himself—Harley riders all thought that.

Phil called the group to order and they gathered around his Maguire Motorcycle Tours logoed Honda. "Right," he said, "I expect you'll have already formed small groups. Can we have no more than about four to a group? Otherwise it gets too disorderly. Keep to the speed limits—the police can be tough on offenders and want money up front. Oh, yes, lunch and coffee stops are up to you to find on the road. Dinner will be in the hotel at Parthenay at eight thirty. Any questions?"

There were none.

"Okay," he pulled a map out of his fairing pocket and unfolded it. "We're taking the Route Industrielle from here," he pointed to the roundabout at the entrance of the ferry terminal. "From there we pick up the motorway—cross the Pont de Tancarville, then turn off the motorway at Quillebeuf. Then we head south to Pont Audemer and on to Gaçe..."

They listened in silence as Phil traced the route with a slender finger on the map. Maguire Motorcycle Tours had already issued them with a route plan, but Phil spent ten minutes or so ensuring that everyone knew where they were going. "Frank and I will be around throughout the ride. To start with we will set out behind you. If you get into trouble, just wait and we'll catch you up. Anything else?"

People stood around and self-consciously shook their heads as they do when asked if there is anything else and they would like to ask a dozen questions but haven't the nerve to risk looking silly.

"Well," Phil said. "Off we go and enjoy the ride."

Blinking with tiredness, they negotiated the early morning traffic. Geneviève led and Freddie tucked the BMW in behind her with Pascale hovering in his offside mirror. Mike took up the rear on the big Yamaha. It always took him a little time to adjust to riding on the Continent, not so much the driving on the right, as the differentness of it all. Particularly the signposting—he could say plenty about French signposts. On one occasion, he had followed the wrong road out of Le Havre in error, because the wretched signs convinced him that this was the desired route out of town. Did he find myself on the motorway? No, an unwitting victim of the cunning signposters of France, he finished up on the far side of the docks in a no through road. The irony being, that if he wanted to, he couldn't find his way there a second time. *How they do it, beats me*, he mused as he flicked up through the gears as they made progress out onto the dual carriageway.

They followed Geneviève who led the small convoy out to the motorway. They turned right out of the docks and joined the Route Industrielle, following the signs towards the *AutoRoute* and the Pont de Tancarville. There was still a dense mist on the Seine and as they built up speed on the *AutoRoute*, the cool dampness in the atmosphere worked its way through Mike's leathers. By the time they reached the bridge he was shaking from the high chill factor. He glanced enviously at Freddie who had chosen textile clothing more suited for colder climes.

While Phil was briefing them Mike had asked Geneviève and Pascale if they had had breakfast.

"No," Pascale replied. "We left Paris in the early hours. Too early for breakfast."

"I was wondering," he said, "whether we should stop along the way..."

"Good idea," Geneviève replied. "Pont Audemer is no distance."

As the bridge came into sight the view was breath-taking. At least it would have been if Mike's breath had not been taken by the cold already. The sun was starting to break through the low mist still shrouding the Seine. The suspension bridge rose majestically out of the fog and shafts of sunlight shone through it, causing the pillars and latticework to cast translucent shadows in the swirling vapour.

They crossed the bridge and rode through patchy fog. This, combined with carriageway repairs, made riding conditions treacherous, reducing their pace to a crawl.

Once on the southern bank of the Seine, the fog dispersed, leaving in its wake a watery sunshine. They turned onto the D roads and by eight o'clock they had reached Pont Audemer when France was beginning to stir, so they stopped with some relief in the small square outside a bank.

"I'll get some cash," Mike said, crossing to the cash machine. Freddie, Geneviève and Pascale waited while he withdrew the notes and they crossed the bridge leading to the town centre. On the corner overlooking the river they found a café serving breakfast.

While not breakfasting on the ship may at first seem to be a disadvantage, once on the road, that first stop in France for the purpose was something Mike always anticipated with pleasure. It could have been the way they made their coffee, or the croissants, the fresh baguette or the sound of French voices—or perhaps all of them.

That first breakfast was for him a homecoming and his first taste of France after an absence. They sat over their coffees, soaking it all in, the smells, sounds and sights. Mike also had to gear himself to thinking in French and he relished the opportunity to roll his tongue around the language again. The two women murmured exchanges in their native tongue and Mike listened, adapting his mind to the vowel sounds and responding where appropriate in French.

"So you're based over here?" he asked Freddie.

"For the moment. I'm doing some work with *La Moto* so based in Paris. I've got the K on test."

At nine o'clock, they were on the road again and headed south along the N138 through the tree-lined countryside to Bernay.

The traffic was starting to increase in density and one thing became apparent that Mike had noticed on previous trips to France, the relatively small number of non-French cars on the roads. Renaults, Citroens and Peugeots dominated the highways. Also, those wonderful vans that had the appearance of being manufactured from corrugated iron. *Now, only the French could make something as ugly as that and successfully market it*, he mused. There were relatively few to be seen by now, and he smiled when he saw one rattling along the road on some early morning errand, belching fumes and misfiring as it made dangerously rapid progress along the now rather busy road. Just the sort of thing, he thought, for Dave and himself to use for their racing transport.

***

La Hutte was little more than a crossroads in the desolate plain that is northern France; a café bar, a couple of shops and a petrol station served the few houses of the village.

Mike needed fuel, so they stopped and filled their bikes' tanks with petrol before they turned off the N road and took the D roads through the small towns along the banks of the Sarthe; Fresnay, Sille La Guillame and Sablé to bypass Le Mans to the southwest. There was logic in Phil's method. The 'D' roads tend to be long, straight and relatively unpopulated. They also skirt the larger towns. French signposting in the conurbations invariably lead the unwary traveller to *centre ville* where one will find—eventually—more signposts for the required route out of town, frequently after passing them.

The more seasoned traveller will avoid town centres and use the quiet back roads. Phil's route worked on the principle that the 'D' roads would enable them to make reasonable headway as Parthenay involved a total trip of nearly three hundred miles.

The landscape of northern France tends to be flat and bleak; fields of crops stretch off towards the horizon in every direction, broken only by the long, straight roads carving through the monotonous vista. Rows of giant electricity pylons tramp their way across the fields and into the distance, stamping man's authority on the natural world.

Occasionally the flatness is relieved by the small towns and villages rising up from the land and following the line of the road, often, like La Hutte, little more than a few houses and shops with the inevitable café bar and periodically a petrol station.

The promise of fine weather had failed to materialise and a low, heavy cloudbank hung ominously over the horizon.

They stopped at Sille La Guillame for lunch. Parking the bikes in the steeply cambered square they walked across to La Orchadie where they worked their way through huge pizzas.

At about one o'clock they were again on the road and having skirted to the west of Le Mans at Sablé-sur-Sarthe turned east to La Flèche.

They crossed the Loire at Samur_and reached Parthenay at about half past six. By this time Mike could feel his concentration starting to lapse, so the planned stop there for the night at a two star hotel just off the centre of the town was timely.

They parked their bikes in the patron's garage where he was most insistent that they secure them, watching as they unloaded their overnight bags and locking the doors afterwards. Later arrivals had no choice but to park in the rough car park at the back of the hotel. He retained the key; *Les Motos* would be safe, he assured them.

The hotel was in a side road with a walled off car park adjacent, with the garage in the far left corner, adjoining the main building. Next to the garage was a doorway leading to a courtyard surrounded by the body of the building, with the rooms opening out onto a secluded lawn.

Having shouldered their overnight bags, they followed the patron through the door along the pathway and into the bar. Their rooms were on the first floor. Once on the landing it was obvious that at one time the building consisted of two premises and had since been converted. The stairway led into the middle of a square landing with a supporting wall surrounding the stairwell, giving the area an odd maze like feel. They followed the patron around the structure to the room, where he left them to settle in.

As they had until eight thirty before the evening meal was served, Mike lay down on the bed and allowed his muscles to relax after the ride. He had always found that the first day on the continent was spent adjusting to a different road system and recovering from the jet lag effect of the ferry crossing. Pascale and Geneviève were tired after their long ride, but didn't feel inclined to lie down.

"I could do with a drink," Pascale said.

"Why not?" Geneviève replied. She turned to Freddie who nodded and followed them to the bar.

At eight, Mike sauntered into the bar for dinner. Apart from a few locals talking and laughing with the patron, the place was almost empty. A television was burbling away unnoticed in its alcove on the wall. There was no sign of Freddie nor the two French girls.

Phil was sitting at a table, sipping a beer and waiting. Occasionally he checked his watch. Eventually his patience was rewarded when Frank shuffled through the open door and sat opposite him. Frank reached for the bottle and glass waiting on the table and poured half of the beer into the glass, drinking deeply and emitting a sigh of satisfaction before pouring out the remainder.

"Well?" Phil asked impatiently.

Frank shrugged indifferently and took another gulp of beer. "He's talkin' to the RAC."

"Problems?" Mike asked, taking a stool next to Frank.

Phil scowled at his companion who smiled and winked at Mike. "Nothing we can't sort out. One of the lads got a swing arm bearing gone. We've arranged for the RAC to get another to him and then he'll catch us up."

"Shouldn't take too long," Mike replied. "There will be a dealer somewhere near here."

The menu was duly placed in front of him and he was left to make his choice. He decided on *omelette garnie*; omelette, lettuce and chips.

As he was making his choice, the others arrived. "Where did you get to?" he asked.

"Market day," Pascale said. "There were still some stalls trading."

"And?"

Pascale shrugged. "Nothing of any interest." She picked up the menu, perused it and passed it along.

Once they had finished their meal, they relaxed with a coffee and watched Pascale settle to a game of cards with Phil, Frank and one or two of the others. Geneviève sat next to Mike and idly contemplated her companion. "I hope they know what they are doing," she observed to no one in particular.

"Good, is she?" Mike asked.

"Mm," she smiled.

Mike's mobile rang.

"Mike Jenner."

"Mike, it's Ted, Ted Stanshawe. We met at the hospital, remember?"

"Uh huh, what do you want?"

"What makes you think I want anything?"

"Stephanie warned me about you."

"Ah. Well...where are you at the moment?"

"Parthenay."

"Well, I knew you were up to something."

"Did you now?"

"Do I get an exclusive?"

"Goodbye Ted." He disconnected and placed the telephone on the table, waiting for it to ring. He wasn't disappointed.

"Look, Mike, mate, I just want to know what's afoot."

"Twelve inches." He disconnected again.

He tried again. "Don't hang up. I know something's going on."

"I'm on holiday."

"Yeah, right."

"Why shouldn't I be?"

"Come on, I'm not stupid."

"Really?"

"Come on, you and I know that something's up. Your friend is injured on one of these Maguire Motorcycle Tours trips and now here you are going on one yourself."

He had a point. "You're sharp, I'll give you that."

"So what gives?"

He glanced at Geneviève who appeared to be engrossed in the card game on the next table. "Now is not a good time," he said.

"Ah," Ted replied, catching on. "Look, I've been doing a bit of digging. Seems that Phil Maguire sold out the bike touring company last year. Made a few bob in the process. Still works as a courier for them."

"Really?" Despite himself, Mike allowed his piqued interest to inflect in his voice and Ted latched onto it.

"I'll keep digging, eh? And get back to you, okay?"

"Do I have a choice?"

Ted Stanshawe once worked alongside Roddy Schaeffer on a provincial tabloid. According to him, he was a news hound. As Mike listened, he pictured the boyish looks and the gap-toothed smile below a mop of light brown hair. A picture that said "trust me", a picture that got people talking, because he was such a nice young man. According to just about everyone else, everyone, that is, who had seen their names screamed across the headlines, he was a bloody nuisance. Having said that, and despite warning Mike about him, Stephanie liked Ted and despite his irritating enthusiasm, and constant snuffling (I'm allergic to the twentieth century, he once said. Give it thirteen years and you'll be cured, she replied) he had on occasions proved useful.

Mike recalled Stephanie filling him in about her encounters with Ted. It was Ted who uncovered a trail of dirt leading straight to a work colleague that exposed embezzlement. It was also Ted who nearly got her arrested for obstructing the police. When Ted's story made the nationals he was offered the opportunity to work with one of the Fleet Street titles and took it. Since then she hadn't heard from him until the night in the hospital. His arrival on the scene was, although she would hardly tell him, just a little welcome. If nothing else, she knew she could trust him because he was honest. He had a knack of digging up little-known facts that people would have preferred remained buried. She wondered what he had heard but presumed that sooner or later she would find out. If he could discover anything in his digging, he would share it. The price, unfortunately would be fifteen minutes of unwelcome fame. It was with this in mind that she told Mike to make use of him if he got in contact, but be careful.

Almost as soon as he disconnected the phone bleeped again.

"Mike,"

"Hello Dave."

"How are you?"

They went through the platitudes that people do when they want to say something completely different, yet don't quite know how. "What about Karen? How is she?"

"Oh, she's much the same," Dave said. "And you?"

"Watching a poker game at the moment. How's Steph?"

Mike heard a stifled chuckle. "She's her usual self."

"Colour me surprised."

"So everything's fine there, then?"

"Early days, Dave. Early days. Stay in touch."

He looked with idle curiosity for a second or two at Pascale and the two couriers as they played their game. It was a game he had never played and little understood. Geneviève ordered a coffee and asked if he wanted one. He did. "Is she likely to win?" he asked, nodding towards Pascale as she looked over her cards at the other players, her eyes dark impenetrable pools. She caught him watching and slowly winked, divulging a rare show of mischief before turning back to the game

Geneviève smiled. "More than they realise. Today she will probably lose, tomorrow as well, maybe. Eventually the stakes will rise sufficiently and then she will win."

"That's hustling."

Geneviève smiled knowingly. "I believe it is."

***

Mike woke. For a moment he lay awake, listening to the silence.

That was it, silence. No, he had heard something. He could hear the steady breathing of Freddie in the other bed. Turning slowly onto his side he peered in the dim light cast by the neon streetlights outside to the bed on the other side of the room.

Pulling on his tee shirt, jeans and trainers, he crossed the room and crouched by Freddie's sleeping form. Gently he shook his shoulder. As Freddie's eyes opened Mike held a finger to his lips and motioned to the open door.

"What?" Freddie said softly.

"Dunno. Think I heard something."

Freddie grumbled to himself, then sat up. "Okay, let's go see." He hastily dressed and together they tiptoed out of the room onto the deserted landing. Mike paused, stretching his senses, listening for the soft footfall that wasn't there, his skin tingling with nervous anticipation.

They stopped outside Pascale and Geneviève's room and listened. Mike put his ear to the door but couldn't hear any breathing. He gently opened the door while Freddie maintained a watch along the corridor and looked inside. The beds were empty, the sheets pulled back as if left in a rush. What, he wondered, was the urgency that made them leave as if in a hurry?

"Well?" Freddie asked.

"The other two are missing."

"Where?"

"Well if I knew that, they wouldn't be missing."

"Okay, okay, let's go look."

One step at a time, they descended the creaking stairs—each one a heart stopping moment when time stood still and they waited for something dreadful to happen.

Once in the bar, they stopped and listened. Nothing. They crept through to the door behind the bar. Somewhere a tomcat yowled to a queen, sending shock waves through their nervous systems. The keys for the door to the courtyard hung on a hook by the bar. Breathing slowly, Mike lifted the bunch off its hook, freezing when they jangled like a klaxon in a silent priory. His heart wasn't far behind in the decibel stakes. And going by the glare Freddie shot him, neither was his.

When he pushed the key into the lock, the door swung away from him. He hissed a curse under his breath and carefully replaced the bunch of keys on the hook before pushing through the door and out into the moonlit courtyard.

"What is it?" Freddie whispered.

"The door's already unlocked."

Once in the square behind the bar they paused and looked around—all the rooms were dark. They walked through the passageway, treading noiselessly in soft trainers, to the car park where the bikes gleamed dully in the weak moonlight.

Mike looked up—clouds were scudding across the half moon. He shivered involuntarily.

A padlock secured the garage. Or had been, it was hanging open on its hasp. Inside they could hear whispered voices. Mike eased the garage door open, pausing guiltily when it creaked. He stood motionless, his mouth dry and his heart thumping noisily—the blood pounding in his ears. When no one rushed out to see what the noise was, he pulled gently at the door again—hardly daring to breathe. Creaking, it swung open. Once more they waited, listening intently, every nerve straining. Still no discovery.

Taking a deep breath they stepped into the garage and Freddie pulled the door behind them, wincing at the noise it made. Mike wiped his palms, damp with perspiration, against his jeans and promptly swore to himself.

As their eyes adjusted to the gloom, they could see Geneviève crouched by the left-hand side of Mike's TR1, the left-hand side cover in her hands. She retrieved a torch from her bag and its beam cast a soft yellow light around the interior of the garage and they ducked back into the shadows by the door. Mike found himself wondering vaguely where Pascale was. He glanced back at Freddie who was looking about the garage with a puzzled expression on his face. So, presumed Mike, he was wondering the same.

Fascinated, they watched as Geneviève retrieved a small black plastic packet from inside the cavity in the frame behind the side panel. She opened it and peered inside. There, in the glow of the torch, was the unmistakable glister of a diamond. A rather large diamond.

Pascale stepped out of the shadows. Neither Mike nor Freddie heard her. Before either could react, Mike was face down on the concrete floor, winded and staring at the dull gleam of an automatic pistol waving inches from his nose while his right hand was on nodding terms with his left shoulder blade. As he stared down the maw, he could see Freddie likewise looking down the barrel of a pistol held by Geneviève. He wondered if this was what Karen felt. Only, he couldn't ask her, he reflected bitterly. Pascale was about his size and weight, yet when squatting on top of him with a knee in his back she may as well have been a sumo wrestler. Her dark eyes returned his stare as she leaned across his inert body and glowered along the barrel of the gun. "What are you doing here?" she hissed.

"Shouldn't I be asking that question?" he asked, nodding with some difficulty towards Geneviève.

Geneviève turned, lowering her own pistol.

"Put the gun down, Pascale," she said. Pascale glanced away towards Geneviève then back to Mike. He remained still until she reluctantly lowered the pistol, clicked the safety back on and slipped it into a pocket. Letting go of his arm she slid away from him with the stealth and agility of a large cat.

Mike rubbed his arm as he got back to his feet and stepped back to stand alongside Freddie.

"You okay?" Freddie mouthed.

Mike nodded, rubbing his shoulder. "I think it's about time we stopped being mushrooms," he said. "Don't you?"

Geneviève raised her eyebrows as she turned to face him. "Mushrooms?"

"Yes, kept in the dark and fed . . ."

Geneviève interrupted him with a wave of her hand. "Ah, yes, I understand." She reached into her bag and handed him an identity card. He took it and whistled appreciatively. "Lieutenant Geneviève Sophie Duval, Sûrèté Nationale. Well, well, I am impressed. And?" He turned to Pascale who scowled in the half-light.

"Brigadier Pascale Hervé," she said with a truculent tone in her voice, leaving Mike under no illusions about how she viewed the interruption.

He nodded and turned his attention to Geneviève. "Well, I am listening, Lieutenant." he said, handing back the identity card.

"As am I," Freddie said with an edge in his voice that Mike hadn't heard before.

"Last Sunday there was a diamond robbery in London," Pascale said.

Mike watched her as she leaned back against one of the bikes, hands in her pockets with a coiled tension belied by her apparent relaxed posture. *Ready to pounce at any moment,* he thought.

"Mm, I remember, I heard about it on the radio."

Geneviève handed the pack to Mike "Look inside."

He opened the pack and looked at the glittering stones. "What about the other one? The big one you had a few moments ago."

Geneviève reached down and picked up a second packet and took out the stone. "This was stolen last June."

Mike's eyes widened as he recalled. "Same time as the TT," he said to Freddie, "Remember?"

"That's the Koh-I-Noor?"

"Yes," Pascale said. "There have been several diamond robberies during the past few months. CID was given a tip off and decided to see where the stones went before moving in. The Koh-I-Noor is being smuggled through the same route."

"And that's where you two fit in?"

"Yes."

"And us?"

Geneviève hesitated. "Detective Radfield was against the idea..."

"Go on," Mike said.

"We hoped that the thieves would use your motorcycle."

"Why?"

Geneviève shifted awkwardly. Pascale took up the story. "Because the British Police traced the gang to Bristol. That is where the British office of Maguire Motorcycle Tours is based. It is probable that they were placed on your bike before or shortly after you left for Portsmouth."

"I hadn't thought about that," Mike said. "So I was bait," he finished.

Pascale shrugged. She didn't seem too concerned, Mike noted.

"Radfield and I have some discussing to do," he said eventually. The acid in his voice suggesting that it might be uncomfortable for Radfield.

***

Mike listened to the chirruping of the ringing tone in his ear as Freddie stood next to him, listening in. Eventually it was answered.

"Do you know what time it is?"

He glanced across at the bedside clock. 01:13 a quarter past midnight in Britain.

"Yes," he said.

"Mr Jenner..."

"Tell me about Geneviève and Pascale," he snapped.

"Ah."

"Ah, just about fits," he replied.

Mike could hear the sigh, before Radfield replied. "I asked Geneviève to look out for you."

"Didn't occur to you to warn me what was going on?"

"We thought you would be more natural if you didn't know."

"I see."

"I'm sorry."

"So, what, exactly, is going on?"

"What did Lieutenant Duval tell you?"

Mike repeated Geneviève's story about the stolen diamonds and the finding of the Koh-I-Noor on his TR1.

"Okay, well, the Sûrèté and CID have been working on this for a while. We didn't realise that there was a link with Maguire Motorcycle Tours until I started asking questions about Miss Ross. It was their idea to send Duval and Hervé along to follow the diamonds once they were in France. We decided, that is, I thought, well, given that you were determined to go, we agreed that you would be the ideal person to use..."

"Use being the operative word."

"Sorry."

"Just tell me next time you have bright idea, okay—then perhaps I won't end up looking down the barrel of a gun."

Chapter 7

Pascale walked across the tarmac to the ferry. Freddie McLean had been as good as his word and arranged a crossing. As it turned out, although the racing was still ongoing, there were crossings available for a foot passenger despite her fears.

She had wondered about Freddie. It was all too convenient.

"Not exactly a coincidence," he admitted. "I was alerted as soon as you went missing. We all were."

"All?"

"Under covers—you'd know about that."

She did. "So you contacted Radfield?"

He nodded. "A private arrangement, so no one is going to ask any awkward questions. He sorted the crossing for you." He glanced down at her waistband where the Beretta resided. "You've not seen any newspapers then?"

She shook her head, puzzled. "Why?"

"It doesn't matter. Radfield will fill you in."

She would have to deal with that later, she decided. Radfield wouldn't be too happy with her walking about armed, yet Maguire had taken it from its secure location in her house. *What about Guillaume?* She wondered.

She had phoned him and, as it turned out, he was fine and none the wiser for any break-in. She relaxed a little after that and waited until Radfield and Freddie could arrange a crossing back to the mainland. In the meantime, Phil Maguire made no attempt to contact her.

The salty sea wind caught her hair and blew it across her face as she walked. She reached up to push it away from her face, but in vain as the wind caught it once more. Eventually, she gave up the struggle until she was up the steps and seated in the club lounge of the catamaran. There were few other passengers and none were taking any notice of her.

I am honoured.

"Make the most of it," Geneviève said, sitting alongside her.

"I wondered when you would show up."

"You are worried about the gun."

Pascale sighed and looked out across the bay. Above, the sun shone in a clear blue sky. A perfect, untroubled world far above the intrigue and death below.

"There is a round missing," Pascale said

"Why do you think that is?"

"I'm not sure. But it will be for no good."

She felt that she was caught in a maelstrom that had its beginnings thirty-one years ago. A simple enough case…

"But you even betrayed me."

Pascale turned to look at Geneviève. "No. I did not betray you."

"I was supposed to be your partner."

"You always were." She turned again to look out at the heavens. Geneviève was partly correct. It wasn't betrayal, she told herself. More that she was not entirely open about her mission. She couldn't be. After all she was under cover. Genevieve understood that well enough.

"You should have told me."

"I couldn't," Pascale replied. "You know I couldn't."

She was met at Liverpool. Uniformed police stepped forward and surrounded her as she disembarked. A sergeant introduced himself. "Pascale Hervé?" he asked.

"Yes."

"Pascale Hervé, I am arresting you on suspicion of murder. You do not have to say anything. But, it may harm your defence if you do not mention when questioned something which you later rely on in court. Anything you do say may be given in evidence."

***

Pascale woke and stretched. The hard mattress in the cell was sufficient but these days her body ached more readily than it once did. Her mood was one of bemusement rather than anxiety. Now she was sure why her gun had been left at the cottage and why there was a round missing. But equally, whatever evidence the police thought they had, she was confident that she would get herself out of this mess.

The spyhole flap slid back and she exchanged eye contact with the eye that peered through it. The flap slid back with a clunk and she heard footsteps departing along the corridor. Eventually, they returned and she was given some breakfast. *The English* she mused *and their obsession with cooked breakfasts.* She eschewed the fried food and satisfied herself with the toast and butter, sipping the tea with mild distaste preferring a cup of strong percolated coffee. Not that she was concerned about the omission of coffee as she was equally dismissive of the English attempts to make good coffee. They didn't, she concluded.

Eventually they came for her and led her to an interview room. A plain room with cream coloured walls, a table and recording machine with a mirror along one wall. A two-way mirror, she correctly presumed. Still, she remained unconcerned. She looked again and frowned. The reflection in the mirror was one she had seen before. A shadowy figure wrapped in a black cape. She was sure she could see the glow of his eyes as he looked out from the mirror into the interview room. She pouted at him and looked away. Whatever it was that he wanted, she wasn't sure that she was interested.

"I'm hurt."

"I'm sure that you will survive."

Two police officers, a man and a woman walked in and sat opposite her. "I am Detective Sergeant Brown and this is Detective Constable Travers," the man gestured to his colleague.

Pascale nodded and remained silent.

"Who were you talking to just then?" Travers asked.

"No one."

Travers frowned but didn't follow it up.

Brown slid a photograph across the table so that Pascale could see it. "Do you know this man?"

Pascale picked the image up and studied it, although she did so for show, having recognised the man in the picture as it was sliding across the desk. She pushed it back. "Yes, why?"

Brown sighed with irritation. "Who is he, then?"

She smiled. "Then perhaps you should have asked that question Detective Sergeant?"

"So just answer the question."

"Of course. He is Philip Maguire."

"Thank you. And when did you last see Mr Maguire?"

Pascale frowned. She wasn't too sure. "A few days ago, I think."

"When exactly."

"I cannot be sure. I was imprisoned for some while, so cannot say."

"Imprisoned?"

Pascale arched an eyebrow. Clearly they were not up to speed. "Have you spoken to Freddie McLean? Or DCI Radfield?"

They looked at each other. Travers pushed a plastic bag containing a pistol across the table. "Yours?"

Pascale sighed. This wasn't going as she expected. "Yes, but you know that."

"And a round from this weapon killed Phil Maguire," Brown said flatly.

"Mmm, I did wonder why it had been left there." She decided to play for time. "Is my husband alright?"

"What?"

"This gun was locked away in my apartment in Montpellier. Someone must have gained access to it. I want to know if Guillaume is alright." They weren't to know that she was well aware that he was fine, but it put them on the back foot and she was happy to play the game.

Travers looked at Brown then back at Pascale. "So far as we are aware. We have heard nothing from the French police. We are concerned about what happened on the Isle of Man while you were there. The Manx police want you to go back to answer charges."

She sighed. *Oh, well, that didn't work.*

So she recounted her experience since Mike Jenner's arrival at her place of work and the days she spent captive on the Isle of Man. All she could hope was that they would believe enough of her story to ask the right questions of the right people—Radfield being a good start, she thought dryly. Meanwhile, if they were planning on charging her, perhaps now was a good time for legal representation?

Chapter 8

Pascale's head felt heavy when she woke at half past seven the following morning. She was alone. Geneviève had already risen and gone downstairs to breakfast. After taking a couple of ibuprofen, she dusted some eyeshadow over her eyelids and applied a little lip-gloss before tackling her hair. Irritably she tugged at the comb as she tried to tidy the tangles in her long, dark tresses, hurting herself, yet wanting to hurt Radfield, Mike and Freddie—whoever was responsible for the plan falling apart.

Damned amateurs interfering. Bloody hell!

Part of her wanted to abandon the whole enterprise and to return home, yet another part of her recalled why she was here in the first place. Eventually, having vented her aggravation on her hair and looking halfway acceptable, she descended the stairs to the bar for breakfast.

Geneviève Duval and Mike Jenner were already seated at a table, sipping coffee. Mike looked up as she entered and there was a cloud that crossed his eyes as their gazes met and he saw the suppressed annoyance in hers. It was subtle and brief and no one noticed. She was reluctant to be involving civilians and Geneviève frustrated her by going along with it. But Geneviève was the boss, so she remained silent and grumbled to herself inwardly while she attacked her croissant.

She sat alongside Geneviève with her back to the door. The bright morning sunlight shone through the open door behind the two women, creating a halo effect around their heads although halos were the last things those two deserved, Mike decided. Geneviève was casually dressed, in denim jeans and a team France Rugby shirt. Pascale wore a tee shirt and her leather jeans. Geneviève looked up from her coffee and smiled as Freddie walked to their table and pulled up a chair next to Mike who nodded and sipped his coffee in silence.

"Bonjour."

Freddie nodded and sat. *"Bonjour."*

He helped himself to a coffee and broke off a piece of bread.

"Still sore?" Pascale grinned mischievously, her smile hiding her irritation.

"Not particularly," Mike responded moodily. He was but he wasn't going to give her the pleasure of an admission.

"How far do we expect to travel today?" Geneviève broke the unwieldy silence.

"According to Phil's itinerary," Freddie said, "The Spanish border. We cross at Hendaye—then from San Sebastian pick up the E3 straight through to the Portuguese border at Vilar Formoso."

"A long ride."

"Mm. I don't know about you guys," Mike replied, "but I'll be pretty tired by the time I get there. Today's trip is about three hundred miles. I shall sleep soundly tonight. What about you?"

Geneviève shrugged. "We shall see."

Mike chewed thoughtfully on his croissant and drank his coffee, allowing his thoughts to wander. He was unaware that Geneviève was speaking to him.

"Mike..."

"Mm? Oh, sorry. I was miles away."

"I asked if you know the area we are going to."

"Oh, it's in the Dão wine region, I think, not far from Viseu. It's a spa town, I believe."

Geneviève nodded and took another sip at her coffee. He was aware of a look in her eyes—almost as if she didn't trust him. He felt uneasy. After the previous night, despite Radfield's assurances, the trip was taking on sinister undertones. *I know, I know*, he thought to himself, *we were looking for something that might give us a clue to what happened to Karen, but this was so sudden and I certainly didn't expect to be used as a mule. Presumably,* he reflected, *that was what Karen had been unwittingly doing.*

He glanced at his watch. "Five to eight. I think it's time I moved, Phil will be chasing us."

"Me too," Geneviève stood and drained her cup. Pascale followed suit.

"Let's hit the road, then," he said.

"Yes."

Mike squinted as he walked to the dark garage from the bright sunlight with one of the pannier inner bags slung over his shoulder. The proprietor had left the doors open ready for their departure and Geneviève and Pascale were there before him, their bikes glinting in the warm early sunshine. Phil and Frank stood by Phil's Honda, with a yellow Michelin map unfolded on the seat.

"Okay, gather round, I'll run through today's route, then we can get under way..."

They listened as he traced a finger on the printed line as he did the previous day.

Something caught Pascale's eye. Something that shouldn't have been there. Moving away from the group as they listened to Phil's lecture, she walked back to the garage and into the cool interior. Although it was dark inside there was enough light to see what she was looking for. She crouched down by the place where Geneviève's bike rested the previous night and traced a finger on the floor. Satisfied, she walked back into the sunshine and over to Geneviève's Ducati and again, crouched down, peering closely at the front wheel. Phil had just about finished his route plan and was looking questioningly at her, as were the others. Geneviève crouched down next to her.

"What's up?" she asked.

For a reply Pascale wiped a finger across the brake caliper and held it up for her to see. "The rest is on the garage floor," she said. "You didn't notice spongy brakes when you wheeled the bike out this morning?"

Geneviève shook her head. "No, I didn't touch the brake."

"What's going on?" Phil wanted to know.

"Leaky bleed nipple," Pascale replied. "Nothing much to worry about."

"So why did you go into the garage?"

"I wanted to check how much had leaked. Looks like it wasn't tightened properly when it was last serviced."

"Okay," he sighed, believing her. "Look, I'll nip into town and get some fluid, then we can get this sorted and on our way."

"Thank you," Geneviève said.

Phil wandered off with Frank in tow while Geneviève, Pascale and Mike stood by the bikes, joined a few moments later by Freddie.

"Problem?"

"Leaky brakes apparently," Mike replied.

"Do you think Phil believes it was an accident?" Geneviève asked.

Pascale shrugged. "I think so, but who knows? If he thinks otherwise, he will want to call the police."

"Maybe," Geneviève replied. "Maybe…"

"Which is all very well, but if it wasn't an accident, who undid your bleed nipple?"

"Who indeed?" Geneviève mused. "Who indeed?"

"Whatever," Mike said. "Someone knows what you are so we will need to be vigilant."

"Yes."

"What about Pascale's bike?"

They checked the Harley over, then moved onto Mike's Yamaha but both machines were free of any evidence of tampering. "Looks like yours was the only one," Pascale observed.

"We will check each day," Geneviève instructed.

They waited a few moments before Phil and Frank returned with a half-litre bottle of brake fluid and Geneviève topped up the reservoir and bled the brakes.

"Everything okay?" Frank asked as he leaned over, watching Geneviève work. "How come you didn't notice the brakes going soft yesterday?"

"The nipple was only just off tight," Geneviève lied. "So the seepage was slow."

Frank nodded as if satisfied and ambled across to his Honda and walked around it apparently checking it.

"Are you sure it was unintentional?" Phil asked, crouching down beside Geneviève.

"What do you think?" she replied flatly.

"It's possible someone's been fiddling with the bikes."

"Why?"

"Why not? People do."

Geneviève turned her head to meet his gaze. "There is no evidence of tampering elsewhere."

Phil straightened his legs and stood. "No. Maybe you're right."

When Geneviève had finished, Mike rolled the TR1 out of the garage, and pressed the starter. The big twin groaned a couple of times and burst into life. Once the engine had settled into a steady tickover, he selected first gear. "Okay?" he asked.

"Okay," Geneviève responded with a wave. Pascale nodded.

"Let's rock and roll, then."

The early morning sunlight was already beginning to warm the day as they negotiated the one-way system through Parthenay and picked up the D743 towards Niort. In her mirrors Pascale could see the dark shapes of the other three bikes. They maintained a steady pace for a while. The road was straight and for the moment, unpopulated. Before long they caught up with a convoy of three trucks. Pascale reduced speed and remained a reasonable distance behind them—peering along their offside periodically and moving across the road to glance down the nearside as she awaited an opportunity to overtake.

Their speed had dropped to 20mph and they were beginning to tire of the stench of diesel fumes when Pascale saw a clear stretch of road ahead. She changed down two gears and accelerated hard. Geneviève followed and Mike clung to her taillight. Glancing in his mirror he watched Freddie and Phil's Honda shadow them seamlessly onto the wrong side of the road. Their speed picked up rapidly as the bikes hurtled forward—Pascale watched as the needle climbed rapidly around the speedometer dial.

The trucks blurred on their right-hand side. The road ahead appeared to narrow dramatically as the increased speed altered her perspective. There was room for two, maybe three bikes, but she wondered about Phil clinging to the rear of the group like a barnacle to a breakwater.

A Citroën BX rounded the corner ahead of them just as Pascale drew level with the leading lorry and slipped smoothly in front of it. Geneviève followed and Mike ducked in behind her, closely followed by Freddie. They were approaching continuous white lines on the entrance to the bend. Phil opened his throttle some more, squeezing extra acceleration out of the big Honda—pulling over to the right just in time to avoid the car, but he was on the wrong side of the white line when he passed the leading truck. Pascale wondered if he saw the Gendarme waiting at the side of the road. They always hunted in pairs and she speculated on his partner's whereabouts as the Citroën passed with flashing headlamps and angry parps of the horn.

Mike released the breath that he had been subconsciously holding and sucked in several lungsful of fresh air, glancing in the mirror to see Freddie tucked in behind him and Phil behind him. They eased back to a legal speed and cruised sedately towards Champdeniers behind Geneviève and Pascale.

It didn't take them long. A thin wail of a siren accompanied by flashing blue lights in the mirrors was enough to tell them to pull into the side of the road. They obeyed like children awaiting chastisement for discovered misdeeds as the convoy of trucks rolled past.

The two policemen dismounted from their BMWs, flicked the sidestands down and sauntered across to where Phil waited astride his Honda. Phil lifted his visor and rested the machine on its stand at their approach, but the first policeman signalled him to remove his helmet. Irritably, he obeyed. Frank, who had not engaged in the overtaking manoeuvre, likewise, clambered off his bike and stood indolently leaning against it as he watched the ensuing spectacle with barely disguised amusement. Pascale dismounted and started to walk back to the group but Geneviève placed a restraining hand on her arm. "Wait," she said. So they waited and watched.

The second policeman wandered around the Honda, glancing at the tyres and lights while his colleague dealt with a sorely embarrassed Phil.

"Your papers, *Monsieur.*"

Phil wordlessly reached into his fairing pocket and pulled out his documents. He handed them to the policeman.

"*Merci.*" The policeman casually leafed through the documents. "And who do we think we are, *Monsieur*? Joey Dunlop, *n'est-ce pas?*"

Frank sniggered at the joke but was silenced by a glare from Phil. The policeman meanwhile made an elaborate show of examining the documents. "We are in a hurry, *Monsieur*…er..Maguire?"

"Not particularly," Phil replied tautly.

"You are aware that you must not cross the continuous lines, *Monsieur*?"

"Yes."

The policeman ignored Phil's discomfort. "Those laws that we have in France apply equally to foreigners, *Monsieur*. When you drive in France, you obey her regulations. *Comprenez vous?*"

"Yes, yes," Phil snapped with growing impatience. "I wanted to get past the truck before the opportunity ran out…"

"You are going nowhere at the moment, *Monsieur*," he said with a hint of smugness as he watched another convoy of trucks trundle past, closely followed by a group of the motorcycle party. One of them slowed and looked in their direction, but Phil waved irritably at him to carry on.

Acknowledging with a wave, he cracked open the throttle and the BMW twin surged on. "There they go, *Monsieur*, your hurry was in vain, I think."

"Yes," Phil replied bitterly.

The second policeman, having completed his cursory examination of the bike, re-joined his colleague and remained silent, watching while his colleague withdrew a notebook from his pocket with a flourish and proceeded to write a ticket—referring to Phil's driving licence for the relevant details.

"That will be nine hundred Francs, *Monsieur*," he said with a broad smile.

"Nine hundred Francs?" Phil was horrified. "You're joking!"

"I do not joke, *Monsieur*," the man's tone was cool, disapproving. "I have very little humour."

"Could've fooled me." Frank said with a grin.

"What was that?" the policeman asked sharply.

Phil silenced Frank with a glare. "Nothing. Nothing at all."

The second policeman, who, up to this point had said nothing, leaned across to his colleague and spoke softly, almost inaudibly, to him in French. The first man smiled.

"Ah, yes, my colleague reminds me that you may appeal, of course."

"And?" Phil asked, sceptical.

"If you are lucky. Very lucky, the conviction may be overturned." He sighed. "That is extremely unlikely, of course. However, you would have to attend a court hearing some months from now."

"I see."

"It is possible that the court may decide that the offence requires a fine—that is the chance you take."

"But this nine hundred Francs . . . "

The policeman treated Phil to a Gallic shrug. "Ah, *Monsieur*, that is merely a deposit against your court appearance. If you choose not to attend, well, that is, how do you say it? Ah, yes, that is quits." Beaming expansively, he tore the ticket out of his pad and handed it to Phil.

"Damn!" Phil pulled his wallet furiously out of his pocket and counted out the notes before handing them over.

"*Merci.*" The policeman counted the money as Phil handed it to him before slipping it into his tunic pocket and buttoning it down. He then scribbled a receipt and handed it to Phil. "*Bon journeé.*" The two policemen stepped back and complemented their ear-to-ear grins with brisk salutes before turning and walking back to their bikes.

Phil jammed his helmet back onto his head, his face puce with fury. "Bastards!"

Frank opened his mouth to reply but Phil silenced him with a glare that sliced though granite. "Don't," he snarled. "Don't even think about it!"

Frank clearly thought better of commenting and satisfied himself with a chuckle as he reached into his jacket and pulled out a box of jelly babies. Popping one into his mouth, he winked in Pascale's direction before pulling his helmet on and remounting his Honda. Pascale smiled in return and remounted her own bike, gesturing to the others to follow suit.

The entertainment over, they restarted their bikes and negotiated the side roads away from the town—heading east on the tiny unclassified roads to Saint Maixent.

Here, the road led through a pine forest—a convoluted route through tree-shrouded countryside. Dappled light penetrated the boughs, creating a stroboscopic effect as the bikes twisted and turned through the dense, lonely forest. They barely met another vehicle throughout the morning until they reached Chef Boutonne.

The morning sun was now high in the sky. Like many small towns in France, Chef Boutonne was built around a small square at the end of a tree-lined avenue, with prosperous houses set back from the road.

Pascale pulled onto the car park in the middle of the square. The others followed, placed their machines on their propstands and dismounted. Geneviève stopped and turned when she realised that Pascale wasn't following. Pascale placed her helmet on the bike's seat and reached into a pocket of her black leather jacket, withdrawing a comb. Using one of the bike's rear view mirrors, she studied her olive complexion and checked her make up as she combed her hair. Satisfied, she sauntered in silence to where the others waited.

"Finished?" Geneviève asked, amused.

"I have my image to keep," Pascale replied, falling into step as she walked across to the café alongside Geneviève. As they sat at one of the outside tables, the patronne appeared from inside the dark interior of the building to take their order.

On another table, the group of riders who passed them in Campdeniers were halfway through their coffees. One of them lifted a hand in salute and Mike returned it with a smile.

Mike ordered a Rio, a fruit drink from the juice of blood oranges while Geneviève and Pascale satisfied themselves with mineral water and Freddie selected a cola. As she disappeared into the café, they watched Phil and Frank park their bikes alongside theirs and walk across to join them.

Phil sat heavily at one of the tables and Frank slumped down beside him. Wearily, Phil ordered two coffees and made a decision.

"I'd better call in—let 'em know what's happened."

Frank studied a jelly baby before biting its head off and calmly popping the rest of the body into his mouth after it. He chewed his prey unconcernedly.

"Yup."

"Fat lotta good you are." Phil sighed irritably. "They won't be pleased."

"No."

"Yeah, I'd better phone," Phil said, drumming his fingers on the table.

Frank carefully selected a red jelly baby from the box.

"Okay."

Phil smiled despite himself. "Oh, two syllables."

"Sod off," Frank replied amicably. "Just remember, it wasn't me that forgot your advice about the law 'n all."

"Yeah, yeah, yeah." Phil grumbled as he stood. Jingling the change in his pocket, he negotiated the tables on the pavement and walked into the café's dark interior. He returned a few moments later having placed his order for coffees and used the phone booth at the back of the café to make his call, stepping out into the sunlit street. He walked back to the table and resumed his seat. Frank looked across indifferently as he sat and sipped at his coffee.

"So?" he asked

"So, don't be a bloody fool and do it again. Also, don't contest it. I've to accept the nine hundred francs and put it down to experience."

"Suits me."

"It wasn't your nine hundred francs."

"There is that."

"Gissa jelly baby."

Having rested, they strolled back to the bikes. Mike paused to look at Freddie's BMW K75S, a neat three-cylinder machine that was half touring bike and half sportster. It was an attractive machine and deserved to sell well, he thought.

"Like it?" he asked Freddie.

"Aye, nimble and light enough." He glanced across at Pascale who was buckling her helmet and frowning at him to do the same.

He nodded in response and gestured to Mike. They mounted their bikes and got themselves underway.

Lunchtime found them in Cognac.

Pascale was toying with her salad *entrées* when Geneviève interrupted her reverie.

"This is a strange route Phil has chosen."

"Yes," she sighed. "I suppose so. If he chose it, that is. Although, if you think about it, it's more or less a straight line south."

Stephanie and Karen had come this way a few years previously, Mike recalled. They had spent days poring over yellow Michelin maps planning routes and stopovers. Indeed, he wondered if they got as much pleasure from that as they did from the ride itself, although the photographs they brought back suggested that they had a terrific ride through glorious countryside, lovers as they were, of rural France—a passion that he shared. Geneviève smiled and placed her fork on the plate before resting her chin in her palms meeting his gaze.

"So what is it that troubles you?"

"Apart from last night, you mean?"

"I detect an underlying pain," she said.

"How perceptive," he replied flatly.

"What is it that brings you here?"

"My friend, Karen. Something happened and she had an accident. A staged accident. Inspector Radfield hopes that I'll find something out."

"And you did."

"Mm, not exactly what I expected, though."

"The unexpected is never expected, so you should always expect it, no?"

He smiled. "You just lost me there." He twisted round in his chair to obtain a slightly better view of the main street outside and its ancient bridge.

"Karen loved this place. She said it was full of old world charm. I suppose it is, really."

"She came this way on her trip—how do you know?"

"Sorry, I don't. I mean, I expect they probably came this way. They're taking us to the same destination. That said, she and her sister, Stephanie came this way regularly."

The conversation paused as the first course was served. Geneviève poured herself a glass of mineral water from the carafe provided, before passing it to Pascale then to Mike.

"Steph has a photograph of her on the bridge outside." He recalled the picture fixed to the fridge door with a combination of blu-tac and a fridge magnet. Karen was leaning against the balustrade, her back to the town centre. In the background, her bright red Honda four hundred four leaned on its propstand. Karen was sticking out her tongue at the camera. A breeze caught her hair, blowing it across her face.

"What, exactly, happened?" Geneviève asked.

"Apparently she rode off a precipice next to the Rio Vouga. The forensic people discovered that the engine was dead when the impact happened, so no one really knows what happened."

"I'm sorry."

"You think she discovered something?" Pascale asked. Although she had given every indication that she had not heard, Mike became aware that she had been following the conversation intently.

He shrugged. "Don't know."

"Mm, I think she did—it fits." She looked across at Geneviève. "There is your bike this morning, no?"

"You are jumping to conclusions," Geneviève snapped. "We have no way of knowing what, if anything, she discovered. Await the evidence, eh?"

"Pah," Pascale snorted, then smiled a wink in Mike's direction. "The boss is always right, mm?"

"I am," Geneviève replied easily.

As the day drifted into afternoon the sloping vineyards and *chateaux* were bathed in the soft, warm glow of the golden sun. Their lengthening shadows danced on the tarmac to their left as they headed south. They crossed the Dordogne at Libourne and carried on south to Langon where we crossed the Garonne. By now, it was about five o'clock. They stopped for a while at a café, taking refuge under a pavement umbrella.

The route took them to the outskirts of Mont De Marsan and its massive ring road. As the afternoon grew old, Mike felt a niggling pain start to irritate his right temple. He ignored it for as long as he could but, by the time they reached the ring road around Mont De Marsan, he was beginning to tire and the embryo of a migraine was starting to make itself felt. On the outskirts of the town he pulled the Yamaha into the side of the road and dismounted. Geneviève and Pascal watched with concern as he fished through his bag and took two tablets.

"You okay?" Freddie asked.

"Mm, I'll live," he smiled with more optimism than he felt. *Why is it*, he wondered, *that I play down my migraines—I always lose out to them eventually.* All he was doing was delaying the inevitable.

They travelled west towards the sinking sun, joining the E3, following the coast and on towards the border with Spain. As they skirted to the east of Bayonne and Biarritz, the sun dipped below the horizon, leaving a pink sky in its wake, deepening to purple and indigo.

The dual carriageway was congested with traffic as they negotiated the resorts and it was nearly nine o'clock when they finally reached Saint Jean de Luz.

They stopped outside the hotel. Mike was barely able to hold his machine upright. Geneviève and Pascale dismounted. Pascale stood next to him and placed a hand on his shoulder and Freddie took the other while Geneviève disappeared without comment into the hotel. Mike remained on his bike, his head pounding with pain, resting it on the handlebars. He was oblivious to the traffic. A train arrived unnoticed at the station on the opposite side of the road. Tannoys announced its arrival and forward destination and it moved off again with squealing wheels pushing against the metal rails, slicing his brain in two.

"Are you all right?" Pascale asked softly

"Migraine," he replied weakly.

Before long Geneviève returned. "We can park *Les Motos* behind the hotel."

"Yes," Mike said, turning the ignition key and pressing the starter. "I can manage that."

Wincing, he engaged first gear and moved into the traffic. At the end of the street, he turned right into the side road leading to the back of the hotel. As he leaned the bike onto its side stand, he felt strong, firm arms wrap around him and lift him gently away from the Yamaha. "It's okay," Freddie said. "Just relax and lean against me. We'll get you up to the room."

"Thanks," Mike mumbled, stifling the waves of nausea.

"Think nothing of it," he replied, supporting him to the reception of the hotel where Geneviève and Pascale were waiting.

Geneviève tried the lift, but it wasn't working, so they trudged up the stairs to the third floor. They trudged, Mike swooned against Freddie, half conscious, fighting waves of nausea. The tablets had failed to work. When a migraine takes hold, the stomach goes into stasis, refusing to absorb anything, let alone medication. All that was left was to sleep it off.

The room when they arrived was welcome. Nothing more than a standard three-star room with three beds and an en-suite bathroom, it was a refuge nonetheless. The door swung open and Freddie turned on the light, dropped his bag and gently deposited Mike on the bed. Mike gave in then. Almost immediately he leapt off the bed and dived across the room to the bathroom where he allowed his stomach the luxury of disgorging its contents, waiting until the spasms finished. When he staggered back, Freddie was placing his bag on one of the beds. Mike collapsed onto the other bed, reached into his bag, extracted his migraine tablets and swallowed two.

"It's always worth a try—maybe they'll work, maybe not." He leaned back and closed his eyes. Geneviève placed a hand on his forehead, icy cold against the fever on his brow.

"How are you now?" she asked softly.

"Mm, I just need to sleep."

Geneviève stood and turned to Freddie and Pascale, motioning them to leave with her. "Okay, we'll go down to the bar and leave you in peace."

"Ta."

They slipped silently out of the room and Geneviève switched out the light behind her. In the half-light cast by the street lamps outside, Mike drifted into a listless dream-ridden sleep. Even in sleep, he was aware of the pain. Pain that felt as if someone has taken an axe to the skull. A sharp, searing, pulsating pain that felt as if it would go on forever.

As it was, it lasted a little over eight hours.

Chapter 9

The cell door opened and the custody sergeant beckoned Pascale out. She stood and followed. At the desk, Radfield was waiting.

"Have they treated you well?" he asked.

"Yes," she replied tersely. "I want to go home now. Unless you are going to bring charges?"

Radfield shook his head. "No charges, Pascale." He led the way out to his car. "Come on."

They drove in silence for a while. Pascale watched as the countryside flashed by and as they went through the interminable 50mph roadworks of the M6, not flashing by so much as crawling. "They think I know where it is," she said.

Radfield raised an eyebrow while watching the traffic in the stop-start queue. "And do you?"

Pascale shook her head. Something, though, made sure that Fábián Rousseau thought she did. *What is it? What do I know?*

"You have history with Rousseau," Radfield was saying, startling her out of her reverie.

"Yes. Geneviève tried to pin him down on more than one occasion. Each time, he slipped from our grasp. Eventually, he got us warned off."

She drifted off into silence. Her thoughts twenty years in the past.

***

Marseille, July, 1997

Anton watched Pascale Hervé as she killed the Harley's engine and leaned it on the sidestand. The exhaust echoed into silence, leaving in its wake the distant sound of ships in the harbour and the keening of sea birds overhead.

Marseille. The spicy warm smell of the Mediterranean hung on the late evening breeze. He breathed it in as he sat on the step and basked in the last of the sun's warmth. Gulls squabbled over scraps left by tourists.

The Harley Davidson Springer Softail was in good company. Apart from the exotic cars, there were several other motorcycles parked in front of the exclusive downtown club. Pascale gave them a sidelong glance as she checked her hair and make-up in the handlebar mirror, half a dozen Japanese café racers, a Triumph Trident, a brace of Ducatis and the MV Augusta.

Anton stood as she mounted the steps and brushed past him without a glance. Grinding the butt of his cigarette under his heel, he followed the waft of Chanel through the door of the club, where it was promptly engulfed by the wall of smoke. A few of the clientele looked up disinterestedly at the tall, dark-haired woman, dressed in a black leather jacket, denim jeans and western boots, as she strode through the fug.

A tuxedoed flunkey walked across the room on an intercepting course, placing himself in her path.

"*Madame*," he said firmly. "I am sorry, but..."

Anton grinned as Pascale speared him with a withering stare, causing him to flinch briefly.

"I am expected. Étienne Paccard..."

"Ah, *Madame*," the man melted into obsequiousness. "But of course. This way, please."

Pascale followed, staring with distaste at the man's back. Smiling inwardly, Anton stepped into line behind her, as she made her way to the cashier's cubicle.

***

The atmosphere in the back room was, if anything, thicker than outside. A blue haze hung serenely over the table and the three men seated around it. A single lamp suspended from the ceiling hung so low over the playing surface that it cast the players' faces into shadow.

Anton slipped past Pascale as the door was opened and took his seat, an imperceptible glance passing between them.

"*Messieurs*," the flunkey started. "*Madame...*"

"Pascale," she interrupted brusquely.

The man seated opposite the door stood, his cold grey eyes appraising as he proffered his hand. "Étienne Paccard. We spoke on the telephone. Pascale, er..."

"Just Pascale," she replied, ignoring the outstretched hand.

Paccard looked again and she saw then the first inkling of recognition.
He remembers.

"Pascale Hervé... As I live and breathe."

***

Montpellier Several weeks earlier.

Geneviève stood from her desk as Daniel Viala walked across the office. She nodded to Pascale who likewise stood. They followed Viala to the door of his office. Geneviève knocked on the open door as he sat at his desk. He looked up.

"Yes?"

"Can we talk?"

"Of course." Daniel gestured them into the room. "What is it?"

Geneviève slid the photograph she was holding onto his desk. "Recognise him?"

Daniel picked it up and scrutinised it. "Fábián Rousseau, what of it?"

Geneviève smiled. "That picture was taken a few days ago."

Daniel Viala frowned. "That's not possible. Rousseau has been dead for… ten years."

"It would seem not. Meet Fábián Rousseau aka Étienne Paccard, now living in Marseille. He runs a club there."

***

Marseille, July, 1997

Paccard inclined his head, smiled and returned to his seat.

"Well, it's been a long time. I thought you were dead."

"Likewise. I guess we both survived, eh?"

"Well, after all this time, you are looking well. Take a seat, *Madame*."

François and Bernard muttered surly "*bonsoirs*" as Pascale took the remaining chair, opposite Paccard.

"The rules," Paccard started.

"No upper limits." Pascale reached into her bag and withdrew a stack of chips and placed them on the table.

"No limits," Paccard smiled from behind eyes hidden deep in shadow. "Cut to deal. Ace high?"

There were no objections, so they cut the pack. Anton drew a king and dealt.

Pascale lost steadily during the first few hands, folding early and keeping her stakes modest, leaning back in her chair as she watched the rest of them play.

Anton was losing heavily, too. True to form. He was aware of Pascale's scrutiny, an unlit cigarette dangling from the corner of her mouth. Paccard had offered her a light early in the proceedings but was curtly rebuffed. "I'm trying to give up."

The stakes rose steadily. Bernard excused himself and left, causing Paccard to grin. "Can't stand the heat, eh?"

The others laughed politely as he dealt another hand.

Pascale continued to lose.

"Perhaps it is time to change decks," she said.

"Of course," Paccard started to rise. "I will ask Louis…"

"No need." Pascale reached into her bag and placed a cellophane wrapped deck on the green baize. Paccard looked as if he were about to protest but she stifled it with a disarming smile. "If no one objects?" François and Anton shook their heads. Paccard scowled before shrugging irritably. *"Bof."*

Pascale dealt.

Still she lost and Paccard appeared to regain his composure.

François bowed out.

Anton looked at Pascale's dwindling pile of chips. As if reading his mind, Paccard smiled. "You have had enough too, Pascale?"

She returned his wintry twitch with a flicker of her eyelids. "I will decide that. Deal please."

"As you wish."

Pascale picked up her hand and studied the cards before placing them face down on the table. Paccard raised an eyebrow. She nodded, pushing two of the cards away. "Deal two."

Paccard turned over an ace of spades and a five of hearts. Pascale lifted the corners of her hidden cards and let them drop.

Anton drew deeply on his cigarette. "One." A jack.

"Dealer takes three," murmured Paccard, drawing a nine and queen of diamonds and an eight of spades. "Pascale?"

She scanned the fifty thousand francs remaining by her elbow, broke off ten and slid them to the centre of the table. Anton followed suit, matching her bet.

Paccard moved ten across, then placed a further twenty from his stack. "Raise you."

Pascale placed thirty thousand onto the pile. Again, Anton followed her lead.

"And," Paccard smiled with his mouth, his eyes revealing nothing. "I'll raise you fifty."

They looked at the remaining ten thousand next to Pascale's cards. That was it, Anton decided. It was all over. Pascale's jaw muscles rippled briefly. Paccard, eyes hidden, watched wordlessly for a moment before breaking the tension.

"You haven't enough," he mused, watching her, fingers steepled, smiling humourlessly. His teeth flashed white in the dull light. "I do not accept personal cheques."

"Observant," Pascale replied, reaching into her bag. "But inaccurate. I raise you one hundred."

"Fold," Anton muttered, unheeded by the other two. The tables were turned now. Paccard breathed deeply as he assessed the fifty by his side and reached into his pocket.

"No personal cheques," she said.

"But…"

"There is little time left," she murmured, glancing at her watch. "*Vite,* eh?"

"I cannot match that. If you will accept…"

Pascale shook her head, the barest flicker of movement as Anton watched keenly. "No. The MV."

He stared at her for a moment before replying. "So, that's what it's all about."

She smiled. "Well?"

Paccard shrugged, reached into his pocket and withdrew a key. He held it aloft briefly before tossing it onto the kitty. "Will that do?"

Pascale silently calculated the value of his stake. "That raises me slightly, I believe."

"It does."

She reached into her jacket and removed an ignition key, dangling it above the table. Paccard cocked his head in unspoken question.

"Harley Davidson Springer Softail. Now I am raising you, eh?"

"Perhaps now will you accept my cheque? My credit is good."

"No," She too had a line in wintry twitches.

"This is not reasonable," Paccard protested, his voice rising to a whine. Pascale stared at him, emotionless, immobile. Her dark eyes cold. Black ice.

"Then," he breathed in defeat. "I have no choice. I fold."

Pascale grinned and swept the pot into her bag. "Thank you, it has been a pleasure."

"What did you have?" Paccard asked softly.

She turned the remaining cards over: a two, a three and a four of mixed suits. "Five high."

Paccard's nostrils flared briefly in anger as he revealed his own cards. "Three queens."

Pascale shrugged. "Too bad, eh?"

She smiled and tossed the MV's ignition key across the table. Anton reached out a hand to catch it. "Thank-you."

"Don't lose it again." Turning to Paccard. "You are acquainted with my younger brother, Anton, I believe."

Paccard stared at them, eyes flicking from one to the other, seeing the same dark eyes and olive skin anew. He hurled Anton a glance that he cared not to interpret, before laughing softly.

"I should have known. You look so alike. She is luckier though."

***

Anton followed her into the night. The breeze from the Mediterranean was balmy still, from the heat of the day.

"Were they marked?" he asked.

"Probably," she shrugged.

Standing on the steps, he watched as she mounted the Harley. "You know," he said. "I've known you all my life, yet tonight I realised that I hardly know you at all."

She sat, saying nothing, arms resting on the handlebars, waiting for him to finish.

"You hustled like a professional in there. Yet I never even knew you could play poker."

Flicking back the sidestand with her left foot, Pascale smiled. "Well," she said. "You never asked."

***

Geneviève waited for the sound of the Harley. She wound down the window of the Peugeot as the bike pulled alongside. Pascale rested her machine on its sidestand and walked over to the car and leaned into the window.

"Switch it on."

Geneviève switched on the receiver lying on the dash. Over the crackle of static they could hear voices. Étienne Paccard was complaining about his losses. Another voice curtly admonished him.

"We have more important matters to deal with, Étienne."

Geneviève looked up at Pascale. "Who is that?"

"Bernard Aguillon. One of the others at the table."

They carried on listening. Bernard was talking again. "Fábián, what about Hervé, she knows who you are. You told us she was dead."

"Don't worry, Bernard, she is sound. One of ours. Now that I know she is alive, we can make use of her again."

Pascale exchanged glances with Geneviève.

"Where did you put it?" Geneviève asked.

"Under the poker table. It is well enough concealed and they have no reason to suspect."

"And Anton? I do not like to drag him into this."

Pascale smiled. "Anton is fine. He knows only what he needs to know. Besides, he has his moto back, which is what he wanted."

***

Somewhere on the M5, August 2018

"So did it work?" Radfield asked.

Pascale sighed heavily. "For a short while. We were able to follow some conversations, but they discovered the listening device, which also put an end to any possibility of me infiltrating the gang."

***

Montpellier August 1997

"Come in!" Commandant Viala ordered.

The two women entered his office.

"Shut the door."

Pascale stepped back to the door and pulled it closed behind them. They stood facing him across the desk.

Pascale looked down and noticed that Geneviève had, likewise, seen the listening device lying there, exposing their guilt.

"What did you think you were doing?"

"I…" Geneviève started.

Viala held up a hand. "I do not want to hear it. He sat back in his chair and sighed heavily. "From now on, Rousseau, Paccard or whatever he is calling himself these days, is off limits."

"But…"

"No buts. Leave well alone. I do not want the department to face an internal investigation if he complains again."

"That bullion robbery…We know he is responsible…"

"I do not care. Do you understand?"

The two women exchanged glances.

"*Do you understand?*"

They nodded.

"Then I expect to hear no more of this. Get out."

***

Somewhere on the M5, August 2018

She looked across at Radfield as the memories came flooding back and she shrugged. "Geneviève and I were expressly forbidden to involve ourselves with Rousseau."

"But you did anyway?"

"Geneviève did. I wish…"

Radfield turned to look across at her and caught the haunted expression on her face. "What happened?"

"Guillaume and I had been having some difficulty. We nearly separated. I was distracted. If I had not been, I might have been able to stop her."

***

Pascale woke with a start. The digital readout from the clock on the bedside cabinet cast a green luminous glow across the room. Its display read 01:15. Something had woken her. A noise downstairs. Reaching into the drawer in the cabinet, she pulled out her pistol, removing it from its holster. Slipping out of bed, she shivered as her feet touched the cold floor. Pulling her fleece gown tightly around her she slid her feet into a pair of heel-less slippers and held the pistol tight as she flip-flopped her way to the door. Opening it, she listened for any noises. Nothing. Maybe she had dreamed it. Maybe not. Until she had checked, she wouldn't be sure.

Creeping down stairs, she winced as the stair creaked under her weight. She stopped, ears cocked. A murmur, a low groan, coming from the front room. An intruder after all, she thought. She flicked the safety catch off and stole panther-like to the door of her lounge. Again, the low moan. Holding the pistol in her right hand, she reached across to the light switch with her left and as the light came on, she snapped;

"Don't move... *Geneviève!"*

Geneviève Duval looked up from the sofa where she was sitting. A wan smile crossed her face. Beneath the blonde bob, her skin was pale with a patina of cold sweat on her brow. "Pascale," she said softly.

"What are you doing here? How did you get in? I could have killed you!"

Geneviève waved a hand dismissively. "We are police officers, how do you think I got in, eh?" She coughed softly and leaned back, closing her eyes.

"You're hurt," Pascale started.

"Yes..."

Pascale now looked more closely at her friend. A dark stain spread across her abdomen beneath the hand clutching the sodden clothing. The blood was inky, almost black, indicating a major organ. The liver, Pascale realised. Geneviève needed immediate hospital treatment and she said so. "You've been shot. You need the hospital, now."

"No!"

"I must call..."

"No," Geneviève interrupted. "There is nothing anyone can do. I am dying. I will not die in hospital."

"But."

"No buts, it is too late for me. I need to you to listen and to help me. Do this one last thing for me, eh?" Her eyes were pleading as she stared back at the horrified Pascale.

"Who...?"

"Fábián Rousseau."

Pascale slowly sat next to Geneviève as she took this in. "But we were expressly ordered to stay away from Rousseau."

"I know. But how were we to get the evidence we needed, mm?"

Pascale sighed. "So you ignored the orders?"

Geneviève coughed and smiled before wincing with a spasm of pain. Looking down at the dark ooze between her fingers, she said "Yes. I know where the bullion is hidden. There's a farm north of Martigues." She shivered. "I'm cold, not long now."

Pascale said "I'll get a blanket," before leaving the room and returning a moment later and wrapping the blanket around Geneviève. She sat again beside her friend.

"They've built a false wall and used the bullion as bricks. If you remove the paint, you will find it. Neat, eh?"

Pascale smiled. "It's been done before, but yes, neat."

"There's something else… He uses an assassin. A professional."

"Who?"

Geneviève drifted into a listless half slumber and then snapped back to the present. "The murder weapon," Geneviève said, "it's in Rousseau's car. A silver Mercedes, in the glove compartment. You must be quick; he thinks he has time as I won't have told anyone."

"Murder weapon?"

Geneviève smiled wanly and looked again at the dark stain still spreading across her abdomen. "Mine."

"Attempted murder."

"Not by morning. Stay with me. Please."

So they sat, Pascale reluctantly going along with Geneviève's request not to call the ambulance. "I still think about that English boy sometimes," Geneviève said, grasshoppering.

"English boy?"

"The one we met in Portugal."

"Ah, Mike Jenner," Pascale smiled as the memories from a decade previously flooded back into her mind. Closing her eyes momentarily, she saw again the skinny young man with dark, tousled, shoulder-length hair framing a heart shaped face with pale blue eyes and a crooked smile. It amused her that his leather jacket appeared two sizes too large when draped about his slight frame. Yet, for all his lack of stature, he handled his large Yamaha vee-twin with the deft competence of a seasoned veteran. Mike Jenner, she thought; a pretty, feminine boy, which was just how Geneviève liked them.

"He'll be pushing forty now," Geneviève said.

"As are we," Pascale reminded her.

"But I'll not grow older," Geneviève smiled.

Pascale didn't answer, her thoughts were still on that trip a decade ago and Mike Jenner. She preferred the hairy biker type, the more hirsute the better. Indeed, she had sometimes wished that Guillaume hadn't shaved. On the occasions that he let his beard grow for a few days, the feel of the rough bristle against her skin had the capacity to send a shiver down her spine. But that was in the past. Time to move on.

"I always thought you were sweet on him," Pascale said, retrieving her shoulder bag from the coffee table. She slid her hand into the bag, past the event horizon and rummaged for the tobacco pouch and lighter lurking amongst the kludge in the depths. Rolling a smoke, she said, "I always wondered why you didn't do anything about it."

"Who says I didn't?" Geneviève replied.

Pascale stopped mid light. The flame hovering before the unlit tobacco as Pascale arched her eyebrows in a look that said *"do tell and leave nothing out, I don't want to have to use my imagination"* without the questioner uttering a sound.

"I went to England the following year. We had a wonderful two weeks together."

"So why didn't you...?"

Geneviève waved a hand listlessly. "Life. My career here, his over there, things just got in the way." She paused. "There is one more thing I want you to do."

Pascale absent-mindedly plucked a stray strand of tobacco from her tongue. "What?" she asked.

"You will know when the time comes."

They drifted into a companionable silence and, eventually, Pascale dozed, her friend's head resting on her shoulder, the sound of her breathing soft and shallow, faint shivers coming from her dying body.

It was cold when Pascale woke to the sound of her mobile phone chirruping in her shoulder bag. She was alone on the sofa with the blanket half on, half off. Puzzled she looked about, but there was no sign of Geneviève. "I must have been dreaming," she muttered to herself, pulling the blanket around her as she fumbled in her bag and pulled out the insistent phone.

"Âllo?"

"Brigadier Hervé," she recognised Commandant Daniel Viala's voice. "Sorry to call you today, but..." There was a pause as he chose his words. "We've found a body..."

"One of ours?" Pascale asked flatly.

"How...?"

"It doesn't matter," she replied. "Where?" She listened to the directions and promised to be with him in half an hour.

***

As she walked through the cordon to where Daniel was waiting, she recognised Geneviève's blue Peugeot. The driver's door was open and Geneviève's lifeless body lay skewed in the driver's seat, two bullet holes in her abdomen. There were two matching punctures in the car's windscreen.

"I'm sorry," Daniel said as he motioned Pascale to the crime scene.

"You can move her now," the pathologist said as they walked up to where he was examining the body.

"Can you give an indication of time of death?" Pascale asked.

The man shrugged…

"I know," she replied, "not before the post mortem, but an educated guess?"

"After midnight," he pursed his lips, "and no later than three a.m."

"So, one fifteen would be about right."

Daniel narrowed his eyes. "You know something?"

"Rather more than I should," Pascale said flatly. "She was going after Rousseau."

"But, you two were given express orders…"

"And she disobeyed them and this is the consequence," Pascale said, interrupting. "If it helps, I know where he has the bullion hidden from the bank job, and if you look in the glove compartment of his Mercedes, you'll find the murder weapon—he won't have had time yet to get rid of it and he's arrogant, he isn't expecting us to come after him anyway—we had express orders, remember? And, he is banking on Geneviève not telling anyone."

"How could she?" Daniel reached for his phone. "You had better be right about this or there will be serious trouble… I'm talking uniform and traffic duties." He tailed off and snapped instructions into the handset and Pascale watched her friend's body being manhandled onto a stretcher. She reached out and gently closed the staring violet eyes.

"I'm sorry," Daniel said, breaking her reverie. "I know you two were close…"

"We started out at the academy together." Pascale crouched down and looked into the interior of the car. Something caught her eye—an envelope with a UK stamp. She lifted it out and turned it over.

Daniel reached for his phone as it rang. He listened for a moment or two before snapping it shut and turning back to Pascale. "I don't know how you knew, and I'm not sure I want to, but we have recovered a pistol from Fábián Rousseau's car. We will see what forensics has to say about a match."

"It will," she said, slipping the envelope into her pocket.

"Perhaps, when we have time, you will offer some sort of explanation?"

"If I can," she sighed. "If I can, I'm not entirely sure I understand myself."

You know who he is.

Pascale turned but saw only Viala. Daniel frowned. "You'd better go home," he said. "You're not making any sense. Get some rest. We'll talk later." He looked down at the body in the open body bag. "I wish I could say merry Christmas, but in the circumstances…"

"I know." Pascale nodded and turned to Geneviève as the bag was zipped shut. She slipped her hand into her pocket and felt the envelope. Inside were two cards. One was from England. The other was a picture postcard that she recalled from visits to Geneviève's flat. It used to be pinned to a corkboard. Opening the first card, she read the message: *"Gen, nice to hear from you after all these years. Since my divorce, I'm now a free agent, so I'd love to get in touch again. Call me, love, Mike"*

Pascale sighed. A call she would have to make. But not now. There was another she had to make first. She flipped open her phone and dialled.

"Pascale," Guillaume said. "I didn't expect to hear from you."

"No…I…"

Pride is not an easy thing to swallow and Pascale nurtured hers like a prize orchid, but she swallowed it anyway.

"Guillaume, I'm sorry, it was my fault…I was just calling to say…"

"That's okay, I know. So you'll be round later? Lunch?"

"I'd like that." She ended the call and looked again at the card, tears pricking her eyes. Not at Mike's doomed message of hope, but the one on the second, an image of somewhere they had visited long ago. Marred only by a pinhole in the middle where it had been affixed to that board all those years and, written in Geneviève's bold, round hand a brief message *"Call Guillaume. Today."*

***

Somewhere on the M5, 2018

"I wondered what happened to her," Radfield said. "Sad."

"Yes. And stupid. Such a stupid waste." There was a bitterness after all these years. She kept the card. It was now pinned to a board in her kitchen—a reminder of loss and regret, of hope and reconciliation. And a place half remembered. Viseu.

"So Karen is Mike's second wife, then," Radfield continued blithely, not noticing her reverie.

"He would have married Geneviève, I'm sure of it," she replied. "But when he found out that she had been killed, he started dating Stephanie's sister, yes. They seem well suited."

"So it was her death that Rousseau was doing time for."

Pascale nodded. "It took a while to get to trial. He was convicted in 2003" Geneviève never revealed the identity of Rousseau's assassin and the assassin had vanished before Rousseau's arrest. It was odd, she thought to herself, for Rousseau to have been so careless, but the more she considered it the more she realised that it was not carelessness on Rousseau's part, but cunning on the assassin's. This man had covered his tracks and left his employer to take the fall if things went wrong, slipping away like a shadow. No one knowing who he was. He used a weapon that could be traced back to Rousseau and used Rousseau's car.

"He's back," she said.

"Who?"

You know who he is. Geneviève said in her head.

And then another voice. A voice she had almost forgotten, a voice she had consigned to an over active imagination. *"You have ghosts to lay to rest. And an injustice to resolve."*

Pascale stiffened. "Oh, my God! It all makes sense."

"What?" Radfield asked.

"I need to go back to France. And I will need my gun back."

Radfield was about to decline, but she stopped him before he could speak.

"There's something I need to check. And you know full well that my gun was used to set me up. I need it back please."

"What is it that is so urgent?"

So she told him.

"Rousseau's assassin. Rousseau... All along we have been chasing a ghost, a ghost who never existed."

"You've lost me."

"The Wizard of Oz."

Radfield turned to look at her. "What?"

"Rousseau. All along, we have sought Rousseau. We were looking in the wrong place and for the wrong man—it is the assassin we must find. That is who will have killed Maguire and Cotter. There is a neatness, and in Cotter's case a sadism, that fits his methods. We have assumed that Rousseau is using him again." She smiled. "The Wizard of Oz. I need to go back to France and meet the Wizard of Oz."

"So who is he?"

She shook her head. Despite Geneviève's voice in her head, she had no idea and said so. "We never found out, because we were never looking."

"You have ghosts to lay to rest. And an injustice to resolve."

***

The shower was running in the *en suite* when Pascale woke. Sleepily, she reached for her watch on the bedside cabinet. Six a.m. she threw back the duvet and started to dress.

The shower stopped and Geneviève entered the room wrapped in a towel. "Morning, Pascale, do you think Mike will be better this morning?"

"As soon as you are ready, we will find out."

Once dressed, they made their way to Mike and Freddie's room and knocked on the door.

"Come in," Mike said.

Pascale pushed the door opened walked in followed by Geneviève.

Mike was sitting on the bed and looked more like his usual self and Freddie was standing alongside him, half-dressed and still wet from the shower.

Pascale looked him over with an inquiring eye. "You are feeling better?"

"Morning, yes, I think so. I overdid it yesterday."

"Do you suffer these attacks often?" Freddie asked, towelling his hair.

"Not as much as I used to. They're usually triggered by tiredness. I broke my own rules—went too long between meals and my blood sugar dropped too low. Ended up paying the price though. Should've known better."

Freddie finished dressing in shirt, jacket and leather jeans. "I had no idea it could be so disabling. It was an education."

Mike grinned. "So's watching you squeeze into those jeans. I would've thought a size up would be more fitting."

Freddie opened his mouth to retort, but Pascale stopped him mid-flow. "No lingering headache at all?"

"Aye, it's gone completely now. I feel a bit washed out, but that's the postdrome. I'll be fine once I've eaten."

"So good for the ride, then?"

"Yes. Fine. Er, changing the subject, I don't remember getting undressed."

Geneviève laughed. "You didn't. Pascale and I did the honours."

"And Freddie?"

"No, he just left you there after carrying you up."

"I see. Well, Time I got up and…" Mike glanced down beside the bed. They had brought his luggage up to the room. "And," he said, "I need to call home."

When the others had gone into the bar for their breakfast, Mike made his way to the phone cubicle. He dialled Stephanie's work number and she answered after a couple of rings.

"Hi Steph. How are things?"

"Ted Stanshawe has been nosing around, ferreting for information. I gave him a flea in his ear—I hope you did likewise when he telephoned you. He asked if Freddie has been in contact with you.

"Tell Ted, Yes, Freddie spoke to me. Tell him from me, he's a shit."

She laughed. "In the meantime, I'm doing some company searches to find out who, exactly, owns Maguire Motorcycle Tours now that Maguire is no longer the owner. It appears to be a front with no obvious substance. Let me know the name of the other courier—I want to do some checks. They're probably okay, but you never know. Karen is fine, well, as fine as we can hope for."

"What about Radfield? Or are you going off *piste*?"

"If I have anything to tell him, I'll tell him."

"Off *piste*, then."

"If you want to put it that way. Anyway, how is the trip going? I tried to call you last night but you weren't answering."

"I had a migraine," he replied.

"Ah. What triggered it?"

"Doing too much and not enough rest, I think."

"As if you didn't know that was one of your triggers."

"Mm. How are you?"

"Oh, I'm fine. Look, I've got to go…"

"Yes, sure. I'll call again tomorrow."

Phil Maguire had ordered breakfast for half past six. So he made his way into the bar before time moved on too far and joined the others.

"Maguire said that as Portugal is a long way, we should travel as much as possible, in the cool of the day," Geneviève said

"Smart thinking," he replied, sipping the strong dark coffee. "He's not just a pretty face, eh?"

Shortly after seven, the small armada of bikes ventured out into the cool salt laden morning, past the harbour and the fishing boats coming in from their night at sea and followed the E3 off the roundabout to Hendaye and the border with Spain.

The *Bureau de change* was open on the French side, so Geneviève slid off the Ducati and walked towards it. Calling over her shoulder she said "I'll join you on the other side. I may be a few minutes."

"I might as well get some cash out as well," Freddie said.

Mike engaged first gear and trundled forward, following Pascale's Harley, through the French customs, where the booths were empty. They rode on towards the Spanish side. Oddly, at this hour in the morning, very oddly, they were manned.

The Spanish customs officer waved them to a stop.

"English?"

"Yes," Mike replied. Nodding towards Pascale, he said, "French."

Pascale smiled at the man, but with no warmth—there was something reptilian about that smile, Mike thought to himself

Pointing to a clear space away from the through route, the man said, "You will park over there, please."

Puzzled rather than concerned, Pascale and Mike obeyed. They rode to where his colleague was waiting. The officer walked unhurriedly over to the riders. Pascale watched the man carefully, taking in his demeanour. He was a tall, lean man with a thin moustache and dark eyes—partially hidden by the peak of his cap. His colleague was a smaller, portly individual with greying hair and nicotine-stained teeth who smiled expansively as Mike hauled the Yamaha onto its centre stand and removed his helmet. Pascale remained seated. She glanced across at Mike who returned her glance. While Pascale appeared unmoved, Mike had the frightened look of the guilty man etched upon his face. *Amateur,* she thought idly to herself, her own visage betraying nothing of her inner thoughts. *These two could prove to be a problem, yet.* She turned her head and looked back across to the French side where Geneviève was still withdrawing cash. She frowned as she could see no sign of either her or Freddie.

The first man by this time was drawing alongside Mike. "Passport, please," he said.

Wordlessly, Mike fished in his pocket and pulled out his passport. Still showing no emotion, Pascale did likewise. They handed them to the official, who leafed disinterestedly through them.

His colleague, Nicotine Teeth, turned to Pascale. "You are travelling to Spain on business or pleasure, *Señora*?"

"Pleasure," she said sullenly. "What is this about?"

Leafing through the passports, still, the first man, Moustache, ignored her question and asked "And where are you going?"

"Portugal, the Dão region," Mike told him. He unlocked his top box and pulled out an itinerary that Phil had given them. Nicotine Teeth waved it away, disinterested. Mike replaced the papers and locked the top box.

Moustache closed the passports and pointedly retained them. "You will open the valises please."

He sighed heavily and unlocked the panniers, allowing Nicotine Teeth to fish around in them.

Moustache motioned to Pascale and she slid effortlessly from the saddle of the Harley in a snake-like move before turning to the back of the bike. She opened the leather panniers slung over the tiny pillion pad. Meanwhile, Nicotine Teeth returned his attention to Mike's bags, but finding nothing of interest, replaced them and turned his attention to the other pannier and the camera bag. Having found nothing suspicious, he pointed to the pocket in the fairing. "How does this open, please?"

Growing irritable, Mike replied "With the key."

"Please."

Shaking his head, Mike unlocked the fairing pocket, removed a small pocket book of maps. "See?" he said. Nicotine Teeth took the maps, flicked through them and handed them back to Mike.

Glancing across at Pascale, Mike hissed, "What happened to the open borders policy?"

Pascale treated him to a suitably malevolent glower followed by a grin. "Pah."

Nicotine Teeth ignored the exchange as he placed his hand into the fairing pocket and fished around. Satisfied that no contraband was concealed inside, he stood back, curiosity written on his face. "You can listen to the radio as you drive, *Señor*?"

Mike's mood was shifting from irritation to boredom. Pointing to the headset in his helmet, he said "I have an intercom."

"Ah, I see."

Moustache decided that he had seen enough of Pascale's bike and turned his attention to Mike's Yamaha along with his colleague. Tapping the dual seat, he said "What is under here, *Señor*?"

"Nothing much," Mike replied sourly. "Battery, tools, stuff like that."

Pascale watched the charade, wondering if they were going to uncover the contraband. Again, she looked back across to the French side. Still Geneviève had not come across, nor could she see Freddie. She felt edgy. If these two were working to rule, then they were sure making heavy weather of it, she thought sourly to herself. She returned her gaze to Nicotine Teeth as he interrogated Mike. Meanwhile, Moustache was still working his way around the Yamaha, looking under the bike, poking about in the fairing. Despite her calm exterior, Pascale was beginning to worry.

Moustache said nothing, but stood with an expectant expression on his face. Sighing heavily to himself Mike opened the seat as instructed and allowed the man to peer under it—at the small toolkit, spare bulbs, fuse box, the top of the battery and the air intake.

Meanwhile, Nicotine Teeth stood watching his colleague and looking across at Mike with a slight smile on his face. Pascale could feel a trickle of sweat running down between her shoulder blades, yet felt oddly chilled. She watched as the man returned his attention to the fairing, running his hand over the silver painted plastic, grimy now, with road dust, before moving across to the side panel under the seat. Pascale thought she would stop breathing. If she felt her chest going tight, she wondered what Mike was thinking. She flicked a glance at him and saw a frightened man, so guessed that the two customs officials could see it. They would now dig in until they found the source of his anxiety. *Shall I say something? Perhaps they will find nothing and I can stay silent.*

"What is behind here?" Nicotine Teeth was asking, his hand pausing on the side panel. Mike tried not to exchange a furtive glance with Pascale, but the flicker was there and he saw it. She fished in her pocket and took out her cigarettes. Fiddling around with the rigmarole of extracting one and lighting it, she watched.

"It's just the side panel. Covers the air box," he said, controlling his breathing as best he could. Pascale said nothing and stared at the ground. She glanced back again to the French side. No sign of Geneviève. *Should I do something now? No. Wait and see.*

Nicotine teeth stepped forward and bent over it to take a closer look, communicating with his colleague in machine gun Spanish. Turning to Mike, he said. "Remove this, please."

Pascale was pretty good at recognising a lost cause when she saw one and this had all the symptoms of terminal illness. Mike looked up at her with a plea for help etched upon his face. Pascale, presumably, he thought, did not intend to step in to help and he could not understand why. She stood there giving all the appearance of indolence as she sucked on a *Gaulois*. So, drawing one last breath of free air, he unclipped the side panel from its studs.

Moustache rocked back and forth on his heels. "Let me see, *Señor.*"

Sighing, Mike handed the small plastic cowl over. Pascale avoided his gaze. She took another puff at the cigarette. *Where is Genevieve? Should I intervene? Perhaps not. Wait and see...* She dropped the stub and ground it out with the toe of her boot as events unfolded as if in slow motion.

Nicotine Teeth leaned forward with interest, but Moustache motioned him away with a wave of his hand. He proceeded to peer with interest into the hole inside the frame before poking his fingers inside and wriggling them around. Mike watched this exercise with heart busily tap dancing against his teeth. Frantically, he looked across at Pascale, but she was busy studying the tarmac as she ground the dog end into it. He stared across to the bank on the French side, willing Geneviève to come to their aid. Nothing happened. Continental banks were notoriously slow even when they only had one client to deal with. Mike died a thousand deaths in two seconds flat.

Moustache continued to poke around in the cavity for what seemed like hours but in reality must only have been a second or two when his expression changed. Moving his fingers a little more awkwardly, he eventually withdrew them, clutching a small black plastic packet. Holding this up for a moment, he fixed Mike with an interrogative stare.

"What is this, *Señor? Señora?*" his expression deadly as he shifted his gaze from Mike to Pascale who exchanged glances, but said nothing, then returned it with even greater malevolence to Mike. Shaking his head numbly as Moustache opened the packet for him to see the diamonds was about the only response he could muster.

"You will come with us, *Señora, Señor,*" he said quietly.

Between them, they marched Mike and Pascale to the office building. Briefly Pascale cast a glance over her shoulder to the bank, but Geneviève was nowhere to be seen. She maintained an unruffled expression as she walked.

Shall I say something now? Where is Geneviève? Wait until I am inside. See who is in charge.

Mike glanced across at her, his eyes wild with anxiety and puzzlement. He hoped she had something up her sleeve, because she appeared to be unaffected.

The officials separated them and took each to a different room. Mike found himself in a small and featureless cubicle with a table and two chairs. A flickering fluorescent tube cast the only light on the peeling, cracked plaster on the walls and the cold stone floor. The door was flung open and he was pushed into the room. They shut and locked the door behind him. Left to contemplate his fate, he vented his spleen by kicking one of the chairs.

"Shit!"

His anger temporarily abated, he sank to the floor and rested his head in his arms. *I only have myself to blame*, he told himself. He didn't entirely believe it though. *What are Geneviève and Pascale up to?* And why, he wondered, did Pascale go so meekly when they were arrested? He was still sitting on the floor with his head in his arms when he heard footsteps outside and lifted his head listlessly. The door opened and a plain clothed official entered, followed by Moustache, who closed the door and stood in front of it, at ease, hands behind his back.

The new arrival was a stocky man in his mid-forties, with a bulging stomach, dark thinning hair and a thick black moustache gracing his upper lip. In his hand he had Mike's passport. He gestured to the chair Mike had earlier kicked across the room, before drawing the other one to the table.

"Please sit, *Señor.*"

Wordlessly, Mike complied. The official sat in the opposite chair and proceeded to leaf through the passport.

"*Señor* Jenner," he said disinterestedly.

"Yes."

Studying the passport, he said "Tell me about the diamonds."

"Nothing to tell," Mike replied sullenly, sounding much like Pascale, he thought silently to himself.

"Do not test my humour, *Señor,*" he said flatly. "I have none."

Mike tried a new tack and said defiantly "Shouldn't we be talking about a solicitor, or the British Consul?"

Unfortunately the man remained unruffled. "When you have answered my questions, *Señor.*"

"No, I want . . ."

"What you want," he said firmly, "*Señor*, is of little importance to me. The British Consul is unaware of your presence here, so it will not concern him unduly if he does not hear from you. Now, tell me about those diamonds."

"Oh no. The British Consul."

The man laid the passport on the desk and proceeded to study his fingernails. "I could, of course, keep you here indefinitely, pending my enquiries. The Spanish legal system is slow, *Señor,* very slow. So, I am a patient man. I have plenty of time. You will be wise to reconsider your position. After all, you are about to be charged with a very serious criminal offence. The British Consul can wait until after we have had our little talk."

Mike stared at him in stony silence.

"Tell me about the diamonds, please."

"I don't know anything about them."

The official shrugged expressively. "Please, *Señor*... your accomplice, she has much to say…"

"Pascale? What has she been saying?"

"Oh, enough to convict you. Unless, of course, she's lying. Then if you assist us," he shrugged again. "Well, we can speak to the judge, see about a reduced sentence…"

"Unless, of course, you're lying," Mike said. "Pascale wouldn't… I don't know anything about the diamonds," he finished lamely.

The official sat there, staring blankly at Mike, not twitching a muscle in his fleshy face. The sweat of the day started to gather on his brow and Mike imagined him mopping it as the day wore on and he approached the time for siesta. Little beads, mingling with the faint odour of stale garlic. Mike smiled despite himself and the man frowned.

"What is so funny, *Señor*, that you can smile?"

Mike sighed. "I've been set up, dammit! And, you have nothing, or you wouldn't be pressing me."

Two black pebbles stared back at him. "Indeed, *Señor*," he said coldly. "If they are to be believed, all smugglers are set up. Do not take me for the fool."

"Perhaps," Mike said, getting into his stride. *If you're gonna go down, go down big time.* "They are to be believed. After all, an unknowing dupe is less likely to be discovered—and the perpetrators get away Scot-free if it all goes wrong. I was under the impression that it was standard practice."

The official studied him across the table, drumming his fingers on the passport. He hadn't expected this. But, then, neither had Mike. *Where are those two bloody French cops when you need them?* His mouth just spat it out before his brain had the opportunity to censor it—*no change there, then.*

"You are very well informed, *Señor*," he said, his face etched with scepticism.

"Not especially," Mike sighed. "I just keep up to date with the news. I suspect that for every dupe that's caught, there are plenty who slip through the net without even being aware of the role they've played."

110

"*Señor*, who is behind your operation?"

"I haven't the faintest idea. Perhaps you should ask Pascale Hervé."

"*Señor*, Spanish prisons are not very pleasant places to be. You would be wise to refresh your memory. And I will be speaking to Madame Hervé in due course."

"I don't know."

"*Señor*, I repeat," he said, his irritation growing. "Do not take me for the fool. You cannot expect me to believe that."

Mike got angry. It happened sometimes. When it did, those in the immediate vicinity usually took notice. "Godammit! You can believe or disbelieve what you bloody well like, I don't…"

He was interrupted by a commotion in the corridor outside. Amongst the raised voices, he recognised Geneviève's. The door exploded inwards, pushing Moustache forwards, nearly knocking him off his feet. Before he had time to recover, Geneviève burst into the room. Remonstrating volubly, Nicotine Teeth attempted to follow her but was cut off midstream by the door slamming in his face. His pained yelp as it closed raised a wicked expression on Geneviève's face—maniacal almost. She was on the point of meltdown—her blazing eyes, pale skin and trembling body emanated violent and voluble wrath as she stormed like a disruptive volcano, into the interview room. She waved a sheet of paper in one hand as she advanced on the official, who stood in an attempt to intercept her.

"*Señora*…" he started officiously.

"Sit!" Geneviève commanded.

Startled by the ferocity of Geneviève's reply, he slumped back into his seat. Mike's command of Spanish was limited, but as he discovered that morning, Geneviève's was excellent and richly colourful. Most of what was said bypassed him and he managed to decipher only one word in every dozen or so.

With angry shakes of her hand, Geneviève thrust the sheet of paper under the man's nose before slapping it forcefully on the desk.

"This," she said malevolently. "This is for papering the walls, no?"

The official attempted to get a word in. "*Señora*…"

"You imbecile! Have you any idea of the damage you may have caused?"

The official opened his mouth to speak but Geneviève had no desire to break her flow.

Moustache remained standing in one corner of the room, quietly enjoying his superior's humiliation.

Reaching into her bag, Geneviève said "A delicate operation may have been ruined by this incompetence." From the bag she pulled out her identity card and waved it before the official. "Months of planning wasted, because you do not read your correspondence."

"*Señora*…"

"Oh, shut up," she said contemptuously. She turned to Mike. "Michael, come on, we go! Now!"

Geneviève gave the man a contemptuous stare—more effective than the world's combined nuclear arsenal—before swearing fluently at him in Spanish and turning to Mike.

"Come on, move it! Let's go," she ordered as she turned on her heel and wrenched the door open before departing in a tornado of wrath. The official stared after her in a helpless heap. Mike stood and started to follow her. He paused briefly, grinning as he retrieved his passport.

"Another time, perhaps."

Freddie was waiting outside. "I arrived just as they were taking you in," he explained.

"It was just as well," Geneviève said. "I had no idea where you were until Freddie told me."

"We wondered where you got to." Mike said.

"Had to go into the bank. The cash machine wasn't working. What matters," Geneviève continued, turning to Mike, "is are you prepared to carry on to Portugal? I cannot force you, of course, and you are free to turn back."

Wordlessly Mike clipped the side panel back onto the studs on the bike's frame, carefully pushing until it snapped into place. He then walked around the Yamaha, checking that the panniers and top box were securely fastened. Freddie, Pascale and Geneviève watched in silence as he made his checks.

"We've come this far, I would like to complete what we have set out to do, that is, if you would," Geneviève said eventually as he made no attempt to answer her question.

"Do you have any suspects?" he asked at last.

"Possibly."

"And are you going to tell me who?"

"No."

"Why?"

"Because you will be less suspicious if you don't know."

"I see."

"So, we may be able to find out where they intend to take the diamonds."

"And find out who's behind this," Freddie grinned with anticipation. "Ted would love this."

Wordlessly Mike donned his sunglasses and stared at him. "I'm sure he would." Turning to Geneviève, he asked, "What was that piece of paper you were waving about in there?"

Rolling her eyes heavenwards, Geneviève replied "Only a fax from my office to all the likely customs posts that we were expected to use. Advising them that you were under my surveillance, with the co-operation of the relevant authorities. It was at the bottom of the 'in' tray. I despair."

There was an underlying irritation in Pascale's voice. "You didn't tell me,"

"I don't tell you everything, Brigadier."

Pascale appeared unmoved by the rebuke. "So we tipped them off. The two guards took advantage of the situation and made a fool of their senior officer by the looks of it. Or they weren't aware because they weren't told."

Mike laughed, easing the tension al little, "There's no answer to incompetence." Then a thought that had been nagging at the back of his mind surfaced. "So why didn't you say something? Seriously? All that claptrap about exposing us…"

She shrugged. "I considered it, but didn't because I do not carry police identification."

"What?"

"Pascale usually works under cover," Geneviève explained. "Police identification would be dangerous…"

"Fatal, even," Pascale finished. "So I decided to wait it out."

Geneviève shifted her gaze to the French side of the border and raised a hand as Phil and Frank came through. "Everything okay?" Frank asked as he pulled alongside us.

"Fine," Pascale replied. "Geneviève needed some cash."

Frank lifted a hand in salute and powered away behind his colleague.

"Time we were on our way," Freddie said. "We've got some miles to cover."

***

San Sebastian was a sprawling conurbation, hugging the coast of the Bay of Biscay. While it boasted a smart up tone shopping centre, this was but a small part of the town. Much of it was derelict inner city, with black, grimy buildings, sooty from the polluted air of the riverside industry. Dowdy, ugly tenement blocks dominated the skyline and the turgid river was thick with pollution. As they rode west into the industrial wasteland responsible for the dying river, the road surface deteriorated. In the grubby outskirts of the city, Pascale pulled into a petrol station and the others followed. They dismounted and Pascale filled the Harley's tiny tank. Reaching for her purse, she walked across the forecourt and into the office. She presented her credit card for payment. The attendant fed the card through the swipe machine.

Nothing happened. Furrowing his brow, he muttered to himself and tried again.

Nothing happened.

He tried again.

The machine remained uncooperative. Balling his hand into a fist, he struck the machine.

Still nothing. The attendant tried swearing at the machine to no avail, so he rained several more blows on the unfortunate machine before kicking the table for aiding and abetting the visa machine in its refusal to issue a ticket. As this also failed to produce a result, he returned his violent attention to the Visa machine itself, whacking it heavily on the side.

Pascale stood, arms folded, watching the performance with a smile on her face until they were interrupted by a teenage girl who materialised from the interior office, clutching a till roll. Wordlessly, she opened the front of the Visa machine, withdrew the empty till roll, replaced it with the fresh one and shut the machine. She pressed a button and the machine chattered in response, producing a ticket. She tore off the ticket and handed it to Pascale whereupon she signed it. The girl smiled before withdrawing to her inner sanctum having uttered not a word.

Shaking her head, Pascale returned to the others waiting on the forecourt. "What's so funny?" Freddie asked.

"It would take too long," she replied. "Ask me tonight."

"I'll keep you to that," he said.

The road climbed, snaking its way into the mountains. Past hydroelectric plants, harnessing the kinetic energy of the tumbling white waters of the river as it rushed in headlong flight to the dubious welcome of San Sebastian below.

They rode briskly. The sharp bends and steep inclines were a challenge for Pascale's riding skills on a machine designed for the long, straight American highway. She was aware of the heavy steering as she hauled the bike into the tight bends, relishing the fight. She tucked well into the right for the lefthanders and drifted across to the centre of the road for the righthanders before easing the radius by straight-lining as much as was possible. She followed braking and gear changing with leaning, accelerating and changing up. Almost immediately she had to plan her line for the next bend. Their riding settled into a steady, relaxed rhythm as the little convoy made its way south towards the Spanish plain.

As they climbed further into the mountains the cool air they encountered increased the chill factor and Mike was shivering uncontrollably from mild hypothermia by the time they came across a bar where they could stop for a while and warm up. Pascale pulled into the car park in front of the Basque style building with its steep eaves and half timbers and dismounted. It struck Mike that she was unaffected by the temperature. Nothing ever seemed to disturb that woman, he thought sourly.

They sought warmth in the bar where they sat for a while sipping coffees as they warmed up.

Once refreshed, they pressed on and, as the morning progressed, the sun thankfully grew warmer and before long, they descended onto the plain.

Dusty and arid, the overall colour of the land was a sandy brown, with the solitary road sweeping like a ruled line through the undulating panorama. The heat was now intense, causing the horizon to distort in the haze and the road surface to apparently liquefy in the shimmering air.

Every so often one of the brown hillocks was crowned with a hoarding advertising sherry, tyres or cars. Occasionally, the huge silhouette of a bull could be observed, rising out of the barren landscape, looming menacingly against the azure sky—dominating the desolate skyline.

These hoardings increased the sense of isolation as the motorcycles tramped their way across the vast and underpopulated plain. So, too, did the evidence of previous travellers—the remains of picnics, polythene bags, cartons and drinks cans littered the ditches.

The wind moaned across the plain like the monotonous dirge from a bar room radio. Cool at first, but warmed by the white hot sun, it became a blast furnace that dry roasted the plain and its inhabitants.

The wind's abrasive nagging, tugging at the bikes and riders frayed their nerves. On the outskirts of Vitoria Gasteiz Pascale pulled the Harley into the side of the road outside a bar. The riders were now suffering from the intense heat. Their clothing was clammy with sweat and clinging to their skins.

Geneviève dismounted and rested her Ducati on its sidestand.

"Dunno about you, but I'm gonna change out of these leathers," Mike said.

"Good idea," she replied, fanning her face. "Hard to believe that we were freezing a couple of hours ago."

The four of them disappeared into the interior of the café.

Inside it was dark and cool and they waited by the bar to be served while, one at a time, they went to the grubby toilet cubicle to change from leathers to denim. Pascale glanced across the dimly lit room to a booth cast in even darker shadow and saw a figure sitting with a cognac and cigarette. They briefly made eye contact before Pascale looked away again, waiting her turn. Mike had now changed and took the drinks from the bar.

A few moments later, he stepped out into the searing heat and glare of the high Spanish sun, clad now in denims and clutching four glasses of cola. Sipping at one of the drinks, he placed the others on one of the tables scattered along the pavement and cast a curious eye about him. Placing his own drink on the table with the others, he wandered across to a bank nearby and browsed the exchange rates. The Pound had risen sharply against the Peseta once more. He harrumphed to himself—although good news for the traveller, the continuing strength of sterling was a problem for exporters and in the long term damaging for the UK economy, he mused to himself. He turned to walk back to the bar as Freddie and Geneviève, denim clad, like himself, emerged from the semi-dark of the café's interior.

Inside, having waited for the others to get changed, Pascale took her turn. Having slipped out of her leather jacket and jeans and replaced them with lightweight denim and canvas. She also changed her tall boots for a pair of lighter ankle boots, as had the others. She closed the toilet cubicle door and made her way across the café to the booth, taking a seat opposite Alain.

"You are late," he said, stubbing the cigarette out in an ashtray. He pulled a face. "Horrible Spanish things. Disgusting."

"We were delayed. It was cold in the mountains, so we stopped for a while to warm up," Pascale replied.

"Well, what have you to report?"

"The English guys know about the diamonds."

"I see. And?"

"And, nothing. Geneviève seems to be in control of matters. They are working with us for the moment. Have you found out anything?"

Alain lit another cigarette. "They appear to be what they seem—McLean is a journalist working on a motorcycle magazine and Jenner is a courier. The UK police are aware of them. We have been in contact with a detective Sergeant Radfield. Although…" He trailed off.

"Although what, Alain?"

He shook his head. "I get this feeling that Radfield isn't telling me everything."

"I see. And what about Cotter and Maguire?"

"Ah, now, they are more interesting. Both have a background in petty crime, but nothing recently. Juvenile convictions mostly, although the UK police have suspicions about recent robberies, but have no direct evidence to link them to it. Has either of them spoken to you?"

"No. And Rousseau?"

"Nothing. Silence. No one is talking. What about you? Has he been in contact?"

"I have heard nothing either," she shook her head.

"Well, it is probably time you rejoined the others. They will be wondering where you are. Where are you staying when you arrive in Portugal?"

"Termas São Pedro Do Sul," she replied as she stood.

Alain nodded. "I will make contact there."

Denims would not provide the same level of protection as leather in the event of a spill. Nevertheless, the high temperatures encountered in Spain meant that heat exhaustion could have been a serious problem had they continued to ride in leathers. Wearing denims therefore made a fall less likely. So, in theory, the need for the protection provided by leather was diminished. Already, they felt more comfortable for having made the change and secured their leathers on the bikes.

As they rose to leave, Pascale emerged from the cool dark of the bar, picked up her cola and drank deeply.

"Where have you been?" Mike asked.

"Inside, talking to the locals," she said, finishing the glass and placing it on the table.

Geneviève shook her head. "Pascale avoids the sunlight…"

"Sure you don't hang upside down at night?" he asked archly.

Pascale responded by sticking her tongue out as she straddled the Harley. Freddie opened his mouth then shut it again, having thought better of it. *Wise*, Mike thought to himself.

"Come on, it's time we were on the road," she said.

"Slave driver," Freddie muttered.

"You have something to say?" she asked archly.

"No, no," he grinned, gulping at the last of the fizzy liquid. "Not me—I know better."

"I should think so too."

***

Burgos was another drab, slum-ridden town in the parched plain. The sun was approaching its zenith as the traffic ground inexplicably to a halt in the outskirts of the town.

Phil had a plan that they should stop for lunch in Burgos. Pascale wondered vaguely as they crept slowly through the traffic whether the sun was affecting his judgement.

As the vehicles stopped, enterprising teenagers rushed into the melee, armed with buckets and filthy rags. They wiped the dead insects from the windscreens of their captive market, with as much expedition as possible, seeking payment, before the mechanical throng ground forward again.

For a handful of pesetas, these cheeky urchins smeared the insect entrails and dust across the windscreens, leaving them more obscured than before.

The riders trickled their bikes through the queue, keeping them moving, managing to avoid the teenagers' dubious services.

After negotiating the back streets of Burgos, they stopped at a restaurant and asked for lunch.

Phil and Frank joined them shortly before they finished chewing their way through gargantuan tortilla sandwiches—dry bread divided by tired omelette. Phil rested his Honda on its sidestand and angrily set about wiping furiously at the smeared remains of countless dead insects now congealed and baked into a hardened mass on the windscreen. Pascale walked out to join them.

"Problems?"

"Soddin' kids!" He snapped angrily.

"We managed to avoid them."

"Lucky old you."

Frank dismounted and ambled over to Phil where he watched idly for a moment before speaking. "Use some mineral water."

Phil sighed, staring at the mess that was now considerably worse than when he started. "Yeah, Guess I'll have to, dammit."

Frank returned to his bike reached into his top box and fished out a bottle of mineral water, then shuffled back to where Pascale stood watching the entertainment, before handing the bottle to Phil who took it and rubbed vigorously at the mess.

"Bloody nuisance."

"I dunno," Frank replied conversationally. "I thought they were onto a good thing."

"You would," Phil snorted. As he looked up, he caught Pascale's eye. There was a brief unspoken exchange. He gave the barest of nods before returning to the matter in hand.

Pascale's group set out just as Phil and Frank sat down to their meal. "We'll probably catch you up later," Frank said, eyeing his tortilla sandwich with well-deserved suspicion.

***

Somewhere in the middle of that desolate expanse between Burgos and Valladolid, the rear tyre on Geneviève's Ducati punctured. They stopped at the side of the road and dismounted. Geneviève swore softly and kicked the flat tyre.

"Now what?"

"We repair it," Pascale said easily.

Geneviève raised an eyebrow.

"I've a repair kit on the Harley."

Geneviève heaved the machine onto its centre stand and removed her helmet and jacket, while Freddie, Pascale and Mike followed suit. Geneviève crouched down and spun the rear wheel, pushing wisps of hair away from her face as she did so. Pascale opted for a bandanna to keep her hair off her face and relatively tidy under her helmet.

"Well," Geneviève remarked, pulling a nail from the rear tyre and holding it up for inspection, "There's the culprit."

Pascale unclipped her tool roll strapped to the sissybar. Inside were a small packet with glue, several rubber patches, tyre levers and three gas cylinders for reflating the tyre. Crouching down she worked the wheel spindle loose and together they wriggled the wheel out from the bike.

By this time, the grease and dust were mingling with the sweat as it ran down their face and arms. Eventually, they had removed the tyre from the rim and pulled out the inner tube. It was a simple matter to glue a patch over the damage and replace the tube before working the tyre back onto the rim.

"Water?" Mike asked, walking over and proffering a bottle of mineral water.

"Thanks." Pascale took a long pull at the mineral water and held the bottle out to Geneviève, who took the bottle and drank deeply from it.

Pascale returned to the wheel, wriggling it back onto the spindle and refitting the chain while Freddie and Geneviève shared the bottle between them and was about to start tightening the spindle nut when Freddie's demeanour caught her attention.

"What's up?" she asked.

"Oh, we have company, it seems," he observed as Phil and Frank pulled up and dropped their machines onto the sidestands walking over to the party.

"You need any help with that?" Frank enquired.

Pascale shook her head. "Thanks, but I've done plenty of these in my time, I can manage."

He shrugged and took the bottle of water Freddie proffered and drank.

"There's a place in Valladolid could do you a proper job if you need a new tyre," Phil said. "I'll get my documents, I've got a list of dealers and stuff."

He returned a moment later with details of a motorcycle dealer in Valladolid who would carry out a vulcanised repair on the tube or replace the tyre, whichever would be necessary. "Need any more help?" he finished.

"No," Geneviève said. "Thank you, we will manage."

"Okay. Well, we'll probably hang around on the outskirts of Salamanca and make sure you come by."

They watched as Phil and Frank donned their helmets and rode out onto the carriageway before disappearing behind a dun-coloured hillock.

"Well, that's it." Pascale said, clipping the toolroll back into place.

"Ready to rock and roll?" Mike asked.

"Yes."

***

They were greasy and dusty, so stopped at a bar in Valladolid, where they used the meagre facilities to wash and subsequently slaked their thirst with cola and lemonade.

While they were there, they decided that it was time for another meal stop as they were ravenous. Burgos seemed a long time away. But, like many bars in Spain, the restaurant was closed so they made do with *tapas*. Geneviève decided to carry on with Pascale's repair, at least until they were settled in at Termas São Do Sul, rather than delay the journey further. The repair seemed to be holding up well enough, she thought to herself.

The heat of the afternoon sun baked them as they rode to Salamanca; the hot, dry air coming off the plain was like opening an oven door.

They sweltered and suffered saddle soreness—the perspiration from their thighs and buttocks, being unable to escape, formed a breeding ground for bacteria—causing irritation and itching.

They pulled in at a supermarket in the suburbs of Salamanca where they stocked up with cheese, bread, fruit and mineral water.

A little further along the road, they found a picnic site, hidden from the highway by a row of trees. Having eaten, Mike laid out his jacket and slept for half an hour—the late afternoon sun warm on his face, he could hear the dry grasses and the leaves on the trees gently rustling in the light breeze a background to the quiet murmurs of his companions as they talked and smoked.

As the sun hovered, blood red, on the horizon, they were again at a border post—some fourteen hours and 450 miles after having left the previous one.

Mike parked his bike outside the *Bureau de Change* and exchanged some travellers' cheques for a supply of Escudos.

He walked out into the fading sunlight to see Geneviève and Pascale shooing away a dozen or so urchins, begging from anyone who stopped long enough for them to gather.

He was about to comment, but as if reading his mind, Geneviève spoke. "Don't be taken in Michael, they are professionals. Dirty and scruffy, they may be, but does one of them look poorly fed?"

"Well, now that you mention it..."

"There are good pickings to be had at border posts, they are after all those useless coins that you will never use again and cannot change at the banks."

"So why not?" he asked.

"We work for our income—so can they. Well, their parents, anyway."

He shrugged. "Reset your watch," he said, changing the subject as he pulled on his helmet.

"Ah, of course, we go back an hour. I had almost forgotten."

"So had I, until I saw the clock in the bank."

The road from the border to the shantytown that constituted Vilar Formoso was almost non-existent and the ruts and boulders made riding difficult, so they rode carefully, relaxing their grip on the bars to allow the bikes to make their own headway over the uneven surface.

Having negotiated it, they stopped at the café bar in Phil's itinerary and, as happened at Parthenay, the proprietor insisted that they park the bikes in his garage overnight.

Once they had removed their luggage, they rode their machines around the bar to the back of the building, towards the garage where the patron was busily reversing his car out, nearly dismounting Freddie in the process—it was only some rapid back paddling that saved his skin.

***

They spent that evening quietly enjoying the atmosphere of the Portuguese sunset—listening to the sound of cicadas and the soft murmured voices at the bar.

Portugal had a unique flavour, different to neighbouring Spain and the language had a softer sound, which contributed to the tranquillity of the experience. As she drew on a cigarette, watching the red glow against the darkening sky, Pascale Hervé reflected that the evening would remain with her for the rest of her life, not realising, that indeed, it would come to haunt her some thirty years hence. After the hectic, almost manic day that preceded it, the peace and calm of that moment was a welcome oasis.

Chapter 10

Despite his scepticism, Radfield had been as good as his word and arranged passage for Pascale on the Eurostar. She asked no questions about what strings he had pulled to allow her to pass through while armed, but didn't spend too long questioning it. Now, having disembarked at Lille, she waited for the Perpignan TGV that would take her to Montpellier.

She sat on a metal bench seat halfway down the Spartan platform designed, she thought, for function with not a nod of the head towards beauty, unlike the gothic architecture of railway stations of a bygone era. Pure utility in concrete and steel. Form followed function and how desolate and drab it was, she reflected as watched the queue for the UK bound Eurostar weaving slowly towards security. She pondered on recent events, putting the pieces together in her mind. That ride thirty years ago had been nothing more than ancient history until a few days ago. A crime committed and solved. Geneviève's death had been resolved and a man sent to gaol. Now all those certainties were uncertain. Out there, somewhere was that stolen diamond. And Rousseau, what of him?

Too many coincidences had combined now. Events that she had taken for granted and not questioned now resurfaced in her mind as incongruous upon re-examination. While she was pondering, a TGV rolled into the station. She glanced at her watch.

On time.

Shouldering her travel bag she walked down the platform to the carriage where her booked seat was located. Placing the bag in the small rack in the vestibule, she made her way down to her seat and sat, stretching her legs under the table, idly watching the to-ing and fro-ing on the platform outside as the train despatch team prepared the train to leave. Urgent whistles and waving of flags followed by a small lurch and the train moved noiselessly out of Lille and headed south.

Pascale dozed as the gentle rocking of the train lulled her, her mind churning over the events of recent days and those of decades previously. She woke with a start. Looking around her, the light appeared to have changed. The carriage seemed darker, the quality of the light was subdued despite the sunshine outside, and the temperature had dropped. On the one hand, she was surrounded by other people in the carriage, yet felt alone. Occupying the seat opposite was someone she had met before. He wore his distinctive hood pulled forward, so that all she could see in the shadows it created were the two glowing eyes.

"You again. Am I dead?"

"No more than you were the last time we met."

"Then what are you doing here?"

"Can't I look in? See how you are doing?"

Pascale stared at him, wondering what to make of this—her third encounter with Death in a matter of months. "It's not exactly usual. Can anyone else on the train see you?"

Death shook his head. "We are alone among the crowd, you and I."

Pascale looked around her. As if outside a bubble, people were talking, looking at their phones, eating and drinking. All were oblivious to her and the entity occupying the seat opposite.

"You have come a long way since I saw you last Christmas."

"You knew about this?"

"I know about everything, everywhere, all of the time. I see all things, past, present, future."

"So what do you want?"

"Want? I want nothing. I am merely looking in on an old acquaintance."

"Some might call it stalking."

"I'm hurt." Death fished in his cape and pulled out a packet of cigarettes and a Zippo. He opened the packet and pushed out a tube, putting it to his mouth and lighting the end.

"This is a railway carriage," Pascale hissed. "You can't smoke here!"

Death looked around with raised eyebrows and, again, Pascale found herself wondering how he managed to do that.

"No one is taking the slightest bit of notice," he observed. "I am a supernatural being consisting of ectoplasm. No one here other than you can see me. Look for yourself."

Pascale turned her head again. It was as if they were both alone yet surrounded by life—a bubble of fantasy surrounded by reality. Death was correct: no one was taking any notice. They were talking among themselves or peering at the screens on their mobile phones or dozing as before. No one was going to complain that a supernatural being consisting of ectoplasm was breaching railway regulations and smoking a cigarette. She sighed heavily to herself.

"What do you want?"

"Can't I drop in and see how you are? I see that you took my advice about motorcycle training. How is that going?"

"Just at this moment, it isn't."

Death looked out of the window as the flat countryside of Northern France sped by. "Yes, I see."

"Do you do this often? Drop in on unsuspecting people?"

"No. Not usually. But sometimes, there are ripples in the universe. Wrinkles if you like, that need correcting. So I, er, give them a little nudge."

He blew a plume of smoke into the air and leaned back in his seat. Looking out of the window, he said *"I thought you would be pleased to see me—our being old friends and all."*

"Not really. Most people get through life without supernatural apparitions stalking them."

Death had the grace to look wounded by the accusation.

"Stalking, indeed. As if I would." He paused as he watched the countryside speed by before continuing on another tack. *"Things haven't been the same for me since they brought in the new technology. I used to be able to predict much more accurately then. These days, I get an alert on my phone and it sends me to the wrong place or the wrong time—or both,"* he added morosely. *"The point is, there are ripples. Ripples that need a resolution."*

He took another drag at the cigarette, blowing the smoke out and watching it dissipate. *"Time is meaningless to me,"* he said, changing the subject. *"One moment you are on that journey with a stolen diamond and in the blink of an eye, you have retired from the police and wondering what it was that you missed all those years ago."*

"I think I do understand what I missed."

Death arched an eyebrow.

Pascale sighed. "I still see Geneviève."

"I told you last Christmas that you had ghosts to lay to rest."

"I was wrong. We both were. It cost her life."

"And the wrong man went to gaol. Do not forget that."

The train continued south, the flat landscape speeding past. She watched the trucks trundling along the motorway as it ran alongside the railway line, their drivers oblivious of her inner struggle and, indeed, of her companion. There was a grey overcast above, giving the landscape a bleak, desolate air that matched her mood. Regret and sadness mingled to form a cocktail of despair. Things she never said and now it was too late.

"Do not despair," Death said as if reading her mind, which he was. *"You have time to put matters right. That is your destiny."*

"If only I could go back. I'd do things differently."

"You cannot. The past is what it is, you cannot undo the mistakes you made then, nor use the knowledge you have now to fiddle with the timeline. Regrets are a waste of time and effort. All you have now is now. And now you must go back to Étienne Paccard."

She raised an eyebrow. Death remarked to himself once more how attractive that quizzical look made her. *I like this woman,* he thought to himself.

"Only Fábián Rousseau can answer your question and it is Étienne who will lead you to him."

"Because they are the same person," she said flatly.

"Just injecting a dramatic flourish…"

"Well don't. Your being here is quite dramatic enough without flourishes. I don't need flourishes."

"Okay, if you insist. No flourishes."

She cast her mind back to that day when she played poker with Étienne Paccard in Marseilles. "It's been a long time, but I last saw him in that little club he owned in the back streets of Marseille."

Death snuffed out his cigarette by pinching it between two bony digits and putting the stub somewhere in the folds of his cape.

"Don't want to litter the place, do we?" he smiled. *"He is still there,"* he said. *"In Marseille."*

Pascale started awake. The train was slowing down. Death had vanished—which he was wont to do. The train was drawing into Montpellier station, so she rose and made her way to the vestibule. The sun was shining outside although the semi-enclosed platform was cool. Once up the escalators and out into the sunlight, the blast of hot air hit her and she slipped on her sunglasses.

She took a taxi back to the flat. Guillaume wasn't around. *Must be at work,* she thought to herself. She showered and once freshened up, put on her leather jacket and jeans. The BMW rested on its side stand outside and she fired it up, heading for Marseille and the back streets where the club that Étienne Paccard ran for his less than salubrious customers existed in the shadows of a world between here and there, not quite of this world, an underground that Pascale had never quite explored. Nor was she sure that she wanted to.

Finally, she felt that a resolution was coming.

Chapter 11

The sun was streaming through the window when Pascale woke—someone had opened the shutters. *Must have been Geneviève*, she concluded sleepily. Portuguese buildings, almost without exception, were fitted with metal roller shutters on the outside of the windows—operated by webbing straps on the inside. During the heat of the day they kept the interior cool. During the night they kept the mosquitoes out. At least that's what she had supposed. Unfortunately she had several red lumps on her arms where a swarm of the beasts had partied during the night.

She glanced around, but there was no sign of Geneviève. She peered at her watch and promptly received a shock—it was half past nine. Three days' riding had taken their toll, causing her to oversleep.

She hauled herself out of bed, dressed and went in search of the others. She found them in the bar. Geneviève was dunking some bread in a cup of milky coffee. She glanced sarcastically at her watch.

"*Bonjour* Pascale."

"*Bonjour* Geneviève. I overslept." Her talent for stating the obvious could always be relied upon to never fail her, she thought wryly to herself.

"So I see," Geneviève gave a Gallic shrug. "We will arrive when we arrive," she said with passive indifference. She finished her coffee and stood. "See you in a few minutes."

Mike grinned. "Yeah."

Perhaps it is just I who worries about time, Pascale reflected. She sat down and breakfasted with Freddie and Mike who, like her, appeared to have some difficulty with mornings.

"So," she said to Freddie "What about you?"

"What about me?"

"For starters, how come you're working for a French motorcycle magazine these days? When we met the other year you were working for a British newspaper."

"I like France."

"So do I but I was born there."

He returned her gaze across his coffee cup. "I had nothing to stay in the UK for, so France seemed to be a perfect new start."

"A woman?" she said archly.

"Something like that, yes."

"And this Ted Stanshaw person that everyone seems to be concerned about?"

"Ah, Ted, I wondered when you would get around to him."

"I just did."

"Ted and I go back a long way. We knew each other at college. He went into newspaper journalism and I eventually specialised in the magazine market."

"And now you help each other out."

"You could put it that way."

"Who helps who the most, I wonder?"

He didn't answer, which was answer enough, she figured.

Due to Pascale's inadvertent oversleeping, it was late morning before they were on the road to Viseu. Freddie stayed to ride with them. Phil and Frank rode ahead with the rest of the party shortly after Pascale rose.

"We'll see you around lunchtime in Viseu," were Phil's parting words before navigating his Honda out onto the rutted road.

"There is somewhere we need to go in Viseu," Geneviève said. Mike arched an eyebrow, but she remained enigmatically silent and wouldn't be drawn.

***

The gently undulating plains of Spain gave way to a more rugged terrain once they were within the Portuguese border. Sheer drops and valleys held snaking roads and rivers that wound their tortuous path in harmony with the precipitous rock faces.

Frequently the brown and grey strata would be obscured by a blanket of dense pine forests—occasionally scorched and blackened by the regular forest fires, suffered as a consequence of the parched climate.

By about eleven o'clock, the sun was roasting the land and they could see a heat haze on the road ahead. The cool of the Spanish mountains seemed but a distant memory. Along the roadside, traders tempted the traveller with succulent fruits: nectarines, oranges and watermelons.

A new highway now supplants this old road, running from Vilar Formoso to Aveiro, on the Atlantic coast. Very much like the French 'N' roads, it consists of three lanes with the centre one being shared by both traffic flows. In the interests of progress, this road now replaces the meandering 'old' road that no longer exists. But back then, the old road was the only route available and progress was slow due to the poor road surface combined with blind bends and steep climbs. No one mentioned oversleeping, but it hung in the air nevertheless. And no one mentioned the sluggish handling that beleaguered Pascale's Harley on these tortuous roads.

***

Viseu, the capital town of its district, snuggled between the Rio Vouga and the Rio Mondego. Proud of its heritage dating back to the Roman occupation, it is still referred to as Cava de Viriato—in honour of Viriato, who was supposed to have had his last stronghold there. This legend persists, despite a lack of evidence to support it.

High above the town, on its rocky outcrop, the ornate cathedral stared disdainfully down at its lowly congregation of buildings, huddling, dominated, at the foot of its promontory.

By the time they reached Viseu it was well past one o'clock and at that time on a Saturday afternoon, the shops and offices were closed for the weekend.

The heat of the afternoon sun had driven everyone indoors for the siesta. This was the start of the swelter, when the ferocity of the heavenly eye desiccated the earth, sending the local population scurrying indoors to indolently doze until the cool of the early evening.

Having parked the bikes on the edge of the town centre, Geneviève, Mike and Freddie made their way to the centre on foot.

"You wait here," she instructed Pascale. Remain out of sight."

Pascale nodded and watched as the others walked away.

-Their footsteps echoed in the empty streets as they walked to the office in a tiny cobbled back street, tucked in amongst a row of shoe shops, fashion stores and gift emporiums.

Nothing moved in the close, searing heat of the early afternoon.

"Mad dogs and Englishmen," Mike murmured. Geneviève chuckled and stood, hands on hips, looking up at the office building, with its dark, silent windows, sandy brown stonework, bleached by decades of exposure to the violent sun, and also at the neat row of brass nameplates next to the heavy wooden door.

"Nothing we can do until Monday," she said, sharing Pascale's talent for the obvious.

"What, exactly were we expecting to find here?" Freddie asked.

"An acquaintance of mine," Geneviève said. "But it will wait, we have time."

They walked slowly, conserving their energies, along the narrow street back to the bikes.

Geneviève raised a quizzical eyebrow and Pascale responded with a brief shake of the head. Mike looked from one to the other, but as neither showed any inclination to share anything with him, he shrugged and gave up his pursuit of knowledge.

They rode west to the bus station on the edge of the town. Opposite was a car park among the shade of the trees. They parked the bikes there and went in search of lunch. Crossing the dried up riverbed via the bridge on the main street, they found a café where Phil was just finishing coffee. "You'd better hurry," he said. "They're planning to stop serving in a few minutes. What kept you, apart from oversleeping?"

"Oh, we went for a walk around the town," Pascale replied easily.

"Mm, well, if you ask me, you got your priorities wrong," Phil said.

"We didn't," Pascale replied with a smile that had all the sincerity of a cobra waiting to strike.

"So where will we be staying for the weekend?" Geneviève asked, browsing through the menu.

"It's a little place about fifteen miles from here," Phil replied, ignoring Pascale's stab. "Termas São Pedro Do Sul. You can't miss it, it's where the N16 crosses the river. The old Aveiro road."

"The spa of Saint Pedro in the sun," Pascale said.

"Yeah. The Hotel Vouga. It's right by the bridge on the roadside. Like I said, you can't miss it."

"Chips with everything," Mike mused, taking the menu from Geneviève.

After lunch, they walked out into the intense heat to the bikes. Their decision to park them in the shade of the trees had the advantage of not causing the vinyl seats to overcook. Even so, the machines shimmered in the heat haze and were hot to the touch. Lifting his Yamaha off its side stand was little effort but Mike was rewarded with a sodden brow under his helmet. Salty perspiration dripped into his eyes and he blinked it away as they followed Pascale out onto the roundabout and took the N16 toward Aveiro.

***

Termas São Pedro do Sul was a thermal spa of Roman origin, with a steaming sulphurous spring—like many to be found in northern Portugal.

The heat was by now oppressive and Pascale could feel her scalp prickling underneath her helmet.

The dusty road ahead entered the village and twisted sharply left, across the river. Once across the bridge, the road veered right, into the pine forest, on its way to Olivera de Frades.

Pascale rode the Soft tail into the village and stopped outside the smart three-star Hotel Vouga, on the corner, next to the bridge across the river from whence it took its name just as Phil described it. Once inside, their enquiries elicited rooms overlooking the slow moving river.

The car park, accessed by a steep ramp, was hidden below the level of the road by a wall and shielded from the bridge by the bulk of the hotel.

They unpacked their bags and went down to the bar. Pascale sipped at her drink. "Time for a siesta, I think," she remarked. "I am weary, now."

"I think I will sunbathe by the river for a while, then have a shower," smiled Geneviève. "This is a beautiful place. You have been here before?"

"No," Mike replied looking across at Freddie who shook his head. "I wonder how Maguire Motorcycle Tours found it?"

"By chance, I would suspect," Pascale said.

"I will go down to the river too, I think," Freddie said. "Nothing like the warmth of the sun on one's skin, eh?"

Pascale, preferring the cool of the room, lay down on the bed and closed her eyes. She heard the door close behind Geneviève as she made her way to the river. How anyone could sunbathe in that heat was beyond Pascale's understanding.

She woke with her heart thumping. Something had woken her. Her head still fuzzy, she tried to collect thoughts that were stirring like evaporating mist on a September morning. The pager. that was it, the pager. Fishing in her bag she pulled it out. She read the number on the tiny display, memorised it and cleared the message from the memory.

She left the room while the others were still out sunbathing. She made her way to the hotel lobby and found the public phone. She dialled the number.

"Yes?"

"It's me."

"Ah, good. Where are you now?"

"The hotel."

"Get away and meet me." He gave directions and hung up.

Pascale replaced the receiver and made her way back to the room.

She dressed, slipped on her jacket, jeans and her short bike boots, and walked out to where the bikes were parked. Glancing down to the small beach area, she could see the others sunbathing and talking. *Hopefully they won't notice I'm gone.*

Pascale rode out of the village towards Olivera, turning right after crossing the bridge. The road wound up into the pines, high above the valley with the river and the village nestling on its banks.

Eventually she arrived at a remote bend in the road. Behind pine trees, smelling slightly of stale burning and below, there was a sheer drop to the river, glittering green blue in the harsh light of the afternoon sun.

She parked the Harley and sat in the shade of one of the trees overlooking the gorge.

He wouldn't be long, she thought, so she sat, silently, taking in the scene below her. The world seemed to stop on its orbit in those moments as she waited.

The road from São Pedro do Sul drifted away into the pine forest, en route to Olivera de Frades and beyond. She looked at the distance wondering vaguely about where the road led as it disappeared into the pines. Somewhere she couldn't follow because she had other things to be doing that day.

Eventually she heard the sound of a car approaching from the direction of Termas São Pedro do Sul. Eventually an old Seat hove into view and pulled up alongside the Harley. Alain got out and walked over to Pascale and sat down beside her.

"This is a wonderful spot," she said at length. "There's a tranquil charm about it—even now in the height of the tourist season. The pace of life is so slow and relaxed. I think I could like Portugal."

Alain looked about him, not seeing the beauty that took Pascale's breath away, merely the job in hand.

"What have you to report?" he asked.

"No change from when we met in Vittoria."

"Have you not made contact with Lopez?"

She shook her head. "We were too late. So Monday."

"And Rousseau's people, have they been in contact?"

"No."

She lapsed into silence for a moment. Somewhere she could hear a bird calling. The screech of a bird of prey hunting in the azure sky echoed through the valley. Then silence before the scream of a small animal as it was swept into the talons of death.

"I presume they will at some point," she said at length. "For the moment, they are staying their hand."

She pulled her legs to her chest and wrapped her arms around them. A cloud passed across the sun, casting the day briefly into shadow.

"Have you heard anything about how they plan to get the contraband out of Portugal?"

"We have a source that suggests South America. For the smaller gems, we think they will be used to fund a narcotics shipment. For the Koh-I-Noor, I'm not so sure. Rousseau is an obsessive art collector. Word has it that he has a collection of stolen artefacts and works of art salted away somewhere. I think he wants that one for himself. If I am right, that will be your job."

"To take it back to France?"

Alain nodded. "I believe so. Once the exchange has occurred, you are to take the gem back to Marseille. Lead us to the rest."

"How do you know all of this?"

"Do you think that you are my only operative in the field?"

She raised an eyebrow, but Alain merely returned the quizzical expression with an enigmatic half-smile, which was no more than she expected. Who, she wondered, was the other player in the field?

"And Inspector Duval? What of her?"

"What of her?

"Do you trust her?"

Pascale turned to look him directly in the eye. "With my life."

When she arrived back at the Vouga, Geneviève was waiting with Phil. "Where've you been?" he asked irritably. "I was planning to arrange a ride out this evening."

"I went on a ride of my own," Pascale replied equably, ignoring Geneviève's interrogative expression.

132

"Yeah, well, just let me know in future," he responded, deflating slightly. "You two gonna come with us, or not, then?"

Pascale shook her head. "Some rest, then something to eat here, I think."

Chapter 12

The intense heat of the Mediterranean wafted across the sleepy city sweltering in the afternoon sun. Seagulls squawked and keened overhead, squabbling for scraps that they could find, swooping from time to time to steal from the unwary pedestrians. There was a stale seaweed smell wafting in with the tide and Pascale wrinkled her nose as she put the F800GT on its sidestand and killed the engine. As it cooled and the sounds of the city enveloped her senses, she pulled off her helmet and thought about what she was going to do next.

The alleyway had barely changed in the past twenty years. Still the litter and detritus of the modern metropolis lined the gutters, blown along by the incoming sea breeze. The gulls dived down and picked apart anything that had the potential for food. Watching them idly, she slunk off the bike and popped her helmet in the pannier, clipping it closed.

The interior of the club was gloomy being windowless and with the lights on a low setting. Somewhere a vacuum cleaner was being worked through a back room, the hum filling the air. Pascale breathed in the air intoxicated with stale alcohol fumes. No one seemed to be about.

"Hello?"

The vacuum went silent and a man walked into the bar.

"Hello, Bernard," Pascale said.

He stiffened as he recognised her. "What are you doing here?"

"Can't I look up an old friend?"

Bernard snorted. "You are no friend of mine!"

"Is Fábián about?"

"What's it to you?"

"The Koh-I-Noor."

Bernard stiffened. "What of it?"

"It's still out there somewhere and Fábián knows that doesn't he?"

"I know what?" Came a voice from a door behind the bar.

"Hello, Fábián," Pascale said more easily than she felt. As he stepped out of the shadows into the dimly lit bar, she could see how he had aged. Prison had taken its toll. The dark hair and beard were grey now and he walked with a slight stoop. This was the man she and Geneviève had chased all those years ago. How insignificant he looked now, how frail, she thought.

"You are taking a risk coming here," he said. "I could have you killed."

That thought had occurred to her, but there was something else—a feeling that she had been manipulated this far and for a reason. As she looked at him, she thought she saw another figure in the shadows. He was difficult to make out but two glowing eyes gave him away. He said nothing and did nothing, he just watched as events unfolded. She wondered if the others could see him, but they showed no evidence of doing so.

"Who killed Geneviève Duval?" she asked.

Rousseau stared at her, his eyes blank. "I spent nearly twenty years in prison…"

"For a crime you did not commit. Who did? Who are you protecting?"

Bernard stepped forward. "I think you should leave."

"Who are you protecting?"

For an answer, Bernard reached down behind the counter and pulled out a pistol. Aiming it at Pascale, he repeated his instruction. "Leave. Now!"

Pascale looked past him and Rousseau at the shadowy figure with the glowing eyes. Inside the hood she could see the barest of nods. She sighed heavily. This was a wasted trip and she had learned nothing that she had not already worked out. Somewhere there was another—another that Bernard was prepared to kill for, another that Rousseau had been prepared to spend time in gaol for. She retreated and returned to the bike. *Damn! So now what?*

She rode the bike a couple of blocks away and parked it, locking her helmet in the pannier and donning a baseball cap and sunglasses. She walked back along the Quai de Belges and followed it around to the Quai de Rive-Neuve. On the quayside, she found a bench where she could see the road leading up to Paccard's club.

Pulling the hat low so that the peak cast her face in shadow, she sat and watched.

"What do you expect to see?" Genevieve asked.

Pascale turned to look at her. "I don't know until I see it, do I?"

"Have it your way."

"I will."

They sat in silence for a moment, Pascale watching the club and Geneviève reading her book.

"Still reading that?"

"Yes, you should try it. It's a fascinating case."

Pascale frowned. "That card you are using for a bookmark?"

Geneviève handed it over and Pascale took it. It was the one that she had found in the car. It was a postcard of somewhere they had been a long time ago. "Viseu. The market by the bus station."

"Yes."

"There's a pinhole in it."

"Yes," Geneviève said, taking it back and placing it between the pages of the novel. "I kept it on my cork board, remember?"

As they talked they heard the growl of a four cylinder motorcycle engine, its four-into-one exhaust grumbling its tune through the narrow streets, reverberating and echoing as it progressed. Pascale turned her head to watch as a black Kawasaki pulled up outside the club and drew to a halt.

The rider killed the engine and the nine hundred cubic centimetres ceased their guttural growl.

"See? I was right. I've rattled their cages."

"Okay."

The rider put the stand down and alighted. He took off his helmet and hooked it over the handlebar mirror. He turned and looked their way. His gaze passed through them and out into the harbour behind. Her reaction wasn't one of surprise. She sighed. It was a sigh of disappointment, but, no, not one of surprise for she had been half expecting this. There had been too many coincidences.

"Is that the man who shot you?" she asked.

"Yes," Geneviève said, watching alongside Pascale as the assassin disappeared inside the club.

"So, *Monsieur* Assassin…"

She turned to look at Geneviève, but she wasn't there. Pascale shrugged—she was getting used to this now—and stood up. She reached into her bag and pulled out the Beretta. She held the weapon, looking at it for a moment or two and feeling the cold metal against her skin and the weight in her hand before tucking it into the belt of her jeans and pulling her jacket around her to conceal it. She then walked purposefully towards the club.

A reckoning. Resolution.

***

Termas São Pedro Do Sul, September, 1987

Pascale was growing used to the Portuguese mornings. Sunshine every day accompanied by the smell of the pine forest. She sat with Geneviève at one of the breakfast tables. Vertical blinds sliced shadows in the light streaming through the windows from the street outside. Inside, the mostly elderly clientele, sat to an indifferent breakfast. It seemed to her that the more expensive the hotel, the less effort, and money, was expended on the catering. The rest of the party shuffled in dribs and drabs as they woke to face the day. Mike was still dead to the world having spent much of the night and early hours crawling around the bars with Freddie. Geneviève poured a coffee and passed it to Pascale.

They'd spent Sunday relaxing on the small Grecian waterside patio at the back of the hotel or lounging in one of the many bars. Neither Phil Maguire nor Frank Cotter had made any attempt to speak to Pascale and she wondered why, but didn't give it much thought. They would make a move eventually, she decided.

Finally, Mike joined them as they were about to finish.

"How do you feel?" Geneviève asked.

Mike shook his head and clearly regretted the decision. "Freddie can drink," he murmured. "I need a coffee."

Pascale poured one from the stainless steel pot and eyed the ashen face beneath its light tan. "Hangover?"

He smiled weakly. "Yes, a little."

"Drink some water," she said. "You'll be dehydrated. How is Freddie?"

"Er, he is okay," he replied. "When I left him."

Pascale arched an eyebrow. "And when was that?"

"About three o' clock."

Geneviève drained her cup. "We go into Viseu this morning. I hope you recover quickly."

Mike nodded, grimaced and sipped his coffee. "I will be there." He took another gulp and grimaced as the bitter liquid coursed over his tongue. "I was speaking with Radfield last night—before I went out with Freddie," he added.

"Oh?" Geneviève said.

"Apparently, Ted Stanshawe got in touch with him. He'd been doing some digging."

"And what did he dig up?"

"Well, now, he has been doing some searches on Maguire Motorcycle Tours."

"What about them?"

"Owned by a holding company called Eurotravel based in Marseille…"

"And?"

"And, the guy who runs it has fingers in a multitude of iffy pies. Goes by the name of Rousseau."

"What sort of iffy pies?"

"Holding companies mostly—you know, companies that own companies and shift money around. In the end you can't make out what exactly they do."

"Apart from shifting money around."

"Exactly."

"So where does this money come from?"

Mike shrugged. "Exactly. Who knows? That's the point, isn't it?"

Pascale finished her coffee and stood. "Well, I guess it all happens today," she said.

"Yes," Geneviève replied. "When we arrive at Viseu, we can park outside. The car park we stopped at on Saturday will do."

"Mm, where they have the market. What, exactly are we going to do?" Mike asked.

"See an acquaintance of mine."

He raised his eyebrows. "This being the office we went to on Saturday?"

138

"Correct."

"And do you mind telling me what we will be seeing this er, acquaintance of yours for?"

"Two things. I want to see that the diamonds are recovered."

"And the other?"

"We are working on someone else's territory. It is polite to inform them."

He inclined his head. "I see."

"I'm not sure that you do." Geneviève, having decided that breakfast was now going to be extended, ignored Pascale's obvious irritation and broke into a bread roll and proceeded to spread some butter. "The offices belong to a company called Eurotravel."

"Anything to do with Maguire Motorcycle Tours?" Mike asked innocently.

She smiled. "The parent company."

"So who is your friend?"

"Someone who is not what he claims to be," she replied with a smile as Pascale gave up on leaving and pulled up a chair. She poured herself another coffee. She could wait if necessary.

***

Freddie joined them for the fifteen-mile ride to Viseu. Unlike Mike he seemed untroubled by his late night binge.

The sun was warm on their backs, burning through the denim and gently toasting them as they meandered like the Vouga on their way east to the capital town of the district. Geneviève set a steady pace through the slatted sunlight as it shone through the blackened trees with the tang of burned pine sharp in the morning air. As the road twisted, they entered deep forest and the singed air became pungent with the smell of fresh pine.

When they reached the edge of the town Geneviève turned her Ducati across the road and rested it on the sidestand in the shade of one of the many trees scattered about the car park. As they walked to the ramshackle bar in the eastern corner of the parking area the traders were setting up their stalls displaying their wares, leather belts, souvenirs, coloured tiles and plates: the tourist industry's web to capture the unwary fly. They sat at one of the tables outside the bar.

"We will walk into town from here," Geneviève said. She turned to Pascale. "If we give you about 15 minutes, by the time we arrive at the office, you should have found somewhere to wait and watch."

The waiter, a dark skinned boy barely into his teens, emerged from the dark interior of the café and blinking from the sunlight waited silently to take their order. The others ordered fizzy Portuguese beer while Pascale settled for Cola. The waiter disappeared back into the café.

"Go on," Mike said.

"Pascale will see if the diamonds are recovered from your motorcycle," Geneviève smiled.

"Uh huh," he said flatly.

The waiter returned and placed the drinks on the table, flashed a toothy smile, and retreated to the cool of the bar. Geneviève sipped at her beer. "What do you mean, 'uh huh?'"

"So that's what the charade was about on Saturday, eh?"

"Yes, but nothing happened."

"Well, what happens then? Assuming that something does happen today."

"We shall see," Geneviève said easily. "It depends on many things."

"Such as?" Freddie said sceptically while casting a surreptitious wink in Mike's direction.

Geneviève remained unruffled. "We will find out when we find out, *n'est c'est pas?*"

Freddie smiled, "A real mine of information, eh? If I didn't know different, I'd think you were up to something."

Geneviève raised her glass and returned the smile. Freddie lifted his in response.

"I try my best," she said

"Need to know, and all that," Mike said with a desert wind blowing through his voice. "And we don't."

"At the moment."

"Ta very much," he said.

"Please…"

"What?"

"Will you do something for me?"

"You mean I haven't already?"

"Mike, Freddie..."

Relenting under the direct gaze, Mike said, "Okay, go on."

"Will you do one more thing for me?"

"Depends what it is."

"I appreciate your spontaneity," Geneviève said dryly.

"A part of my inimitable charm."

Geneviève sighed heavily. "Will you?"

"Maybe."

"*Please* will you?"

"Well, seeing as you put it like that, how can I resist. Go on, you've talked me into it."

Geneviève pouted as she realised that Freddie and Mike had been playing a game with her. "Leave the talking to me," she said. "Say nothing unless I specifically ask you to? Have you got that?"

"Uh huh," Mike replied, eliciting a flash of annoyance.

"Trust me," she replied.

Freddie grinned broadly. "Now where have we heard that before?"

"I can't possibly think," Geneviève said blandly.

"What devious game are you playing?"

Pascale smirked into her drink and flashed a conspiratorial glance at Geneviève. Geneviève ignored the glance and stared directly at Mike.

"Trust me," she said. Mike continued to peer through half-closed eyes, making no attempt to disguise his scepticism.

Geneviève turned to Pascale "You've got fifteen minutes."

Pascale stood and turned to Geneviève, smiling briefly she said "*Au revoir.*" With a brief nod to Freddie and Mike she said "See you later."

Pascale walked away hips swinging loosely, weaving through the market traders and soon disappeared. Freddie, Geneviève and Mike sat, slowly sipping their drinks, Freddie occasionally glancing at his watch. After a while, he paid for the drinks and they stood. Unhurriedly they walked along the main street over the dank trickle that passed for the river, crossed the road and headed into the old quarter of the town. Although he looked, Mike could see no sign of Pascale. It appeared that she had an uncanny knack for concealing herself. He hoped vaguely that her efforts were worthwhile.

Pascale watched the others as they made their way to the centre of the town and ambled back to the bikes where she sat on one of the benches that lined the square. She glanced at her watch and waited. Before long, she was rewarded. Phil Maguire and Frank Cotter rode into the parking area and parked their Hondas. Having dismounted they walked over to Pascale. Phil sat beside her.

"Well?"

"They are in the town."

"The diamonds?"

"On the bike where you left them."

"Good." Phil nodded to Frank who then pulled off the side panel of the Yamaha and removed the packet. He brought it over to Phil who unwrapped it and studied the contents. He held the large one up to the light and whistled softly. "It's a beautiful thing, eh?"

"Ay," Frank replied before returning to the bike and placing small packages into the space vacated by the diamonds.

Phil turned to Pascale. "Do they suspect anything?

She shook her head. "No one knows anything about this nor has the slightest hint. You are perfectly safe."

"Good. I'd hate to think that you would betray us." There was a menacing tone to his voice but Pascale let it ride. She remained placid and let the threat pass by without comment.

"Had you not better be going?" she said.

Phil pocketed the gemstones and stood. "You are right. Come on, Frank, let's be off."

Pascale watched as they mounted the Hondas and rode off. She reached into her jacket and took out her cigarettes, lit one and sat smoking as she waited.

The office building cast a shadow over the narrow cobbled streets. The heavy oak door was open. Mike looked around. Several shops were opening and the alleyway began to fill with shoppers.

Inside, the entrance hall was cool and dim—the only light came from the sunshine pouring through the open doorway. They climbed the narrow stairway in single file to the office on the second floor. The hallway grew darker as they entered deeper into the building and left behind the cheerful pool of light in the entrance. Their footsteps echoed in the semi-dark silence, a slip slapping sound on the cool marble floor.

At the second floor, Geneviève paused and peered, in the half-light, at the brass label on the door of the Portuguese division of <u>Eurotravel</u>. She pushed open the door.

In dramatic contrast to the hallway, the interior was brightly lit by the sun streaming in through the window opposite the door, only partially subdued by a vertical blind. There were two people in the room. A young girl, barely out of her teens, sat absorbed at an electronic typewriter next to the window. As they entered, she looked up and smiled.

"*Bom dia Senhors, Senhora*". She rose to greet them but was ushered back into her seat by the other occupant, a middle-aged man with slim, tired features, his dark hair receding into a widow's peak.

"*Bom dia Senhorita*," Geneviève said, turning to face the man. "*Bom dia, Senhor Lopez?*"

"Yes," Lopez replied.

"Geneviève Duval, you are expecting me?"

Lopez frowned, "Ah, *Senhora*, we were expecting you before this."

"It's been a long ride. Things did not go according to plan."

"But you arrived on Saturday, no?"

Geneviève raised her eyebrows with surprise. "You are well informed *Senhor*. The office was closed when we arrived, so we carried on to our accommodation."

Lopez looked suspiciously at Freddie and Mike. "And your friends are?"

"That was one of the complications," she said. "Perhaps..."

"Of course," Lopez said, gesturing to the back office. Freddie and Mike followed Geneviève. Lopez closed the door behind us.

"This is Sergeant Lopez of the *Guarda Nacional Republicana*, the GNR," Geneviève said.

Lopez sat at the desk and gestured his guests to do likewise. "Perhaps you had better explain," he said. Geneviève told him about Parthenay.

142

Lopez said "I'm not sure..."

"We have no choice," Geneviève said.

"But can we trust..."

"I do," Geneviève said flatly.

"Mm," Lopez remained sceptical. "I have some information," he said eventually, reaching into a desk drawer, he pulled out a map of the region and spread it on the desk. "The man who owns Eurotravel is..."

"*Monsieur* Fábián Rousseau," Mike said

Geneviève arched an eyebrow and flashed an irritated look, reminding Mike silently of her instructions to remain mute.

Lopez looked quizzically at Geneviève and Mike and back again before reaching into his drawer and pulling out a map of the area. "Rousseau has a villa," he said "Near Alvarenga." His finger traced a line on the map. "We have been watching it. At the moment he is not at home."

"Do we know where he is?" Geneviève asked.

Lopez shrugged.

"Or what he looks like?"

"How do we know that this Rousseau has anything to do with the smuggling?" Mike asked.

Lopez looked up from the map thoughtfully. "We don't for certain," he said. "But as it is his company that is the mechanism by which the diamonds are moving through Europe, it is reasonable to suspect him."

Mike conceded the point; it cost him nothing and he felt largely detached from the discussion. Geneviève and Lopez discussed their arrangements for contacting each other. "We're staying at the Hotel Vouga in Termas São Pedro do Sul," she said. "We will be touring the area according to our itinerary. You may reach me there in the meantime. Was that all?"

"Yes, but I do not expect to need you unless something happens in the next day or so. If it does, I will call you via the hotel reception."

"Understood. If that's all, we'll be off then."

Lopez ran a hand irritably through his hair as a worried frown passed across his face. "I trust that you have not taken too much of a risk..." He ran a wary eye over Freddie and Mike, still unconvinced.

Geneviève smiled. "I have no choice. Pascale and I were caught in the act." She shrugged. "We must live with it, eh?"

"As you say, there is no choice, but take care, *Senhora*."

Geneviève reached for his hand and shook it. "I will, thank you."

They stepped out of the dark interior of the doorway into the glare of the sunlight and made their way back to the tree-lined car park. The bikes were where they left them, apparently undisturbed. There were a few shoppers further up the square, but no sign of Pascale. They walked unhurriedly to the bar where they sat, idly flicking the flies away as they watched the market traders selling their wares. Inside the café they could hear voices, the clink of glasses and the occasional burst of laughter. They drank as they watched and listened. Mike allowed his thoughts to drift aimlessly in the tranquil atmosphere.

Pascale came into view, striding briskly amongst the market stalls clutching a carrier bag. She waved as she caught sight of the others and Geneviève raised a hand in casual acknowledgement. Pascale flopped breathlessly into an empty chair.

"Hello."

Almost immediately the waiter materialised, ready to take her order. She ordered a cola with ice.

The waiter disappeared into the café.

"So?" Geneviève said. "How did it go?"

"Good, I think."

"You think?"

"I will show you when we have finished our drinks."

"Show me?" Geneviève asked, puzzled.

Pascale waved a dismissive hand. "I waited by a shoe stall and bought a new pair of boots." She held up the carrier bag.

"I wondered where you were," Geneviève said flatly.

"Want to see them?"

"Yeah, why not?" Mike said. Boots always interested him. *It must be something in my quirky makeup*, he thought to himself. The waiter returned with Pascale's drink and she took several thirsty gulps before reaching into the bag and withdrawing a pair of tall cowboy boots with embossed patterns, dummy spurs and high heels.

"Tidy," Mike said. "How much?"

"3,450 Escudos."

He did some rapid mental arithmetic. "Fifteen pounds, about. That's pretty good. They're well made, too."

Pascale held them up with undisguised pleasure. "I will wear them this afternoon, I think."

"So, what did you see?" Genevieve asked, bringing the conversation back to the point.

"When you were in the office, Phil retrieved the stones from your bike."

They said nothing for a moment. Freddie eventually broke the silence. Mike watched as he flicked his gaze from Geneviève to Pascale, appraising them and taking in the half lidded eyes of the dark Frenchwoman and the bland look carefully disguising the emotions hidden deep in her companion.

"You knew, didn't you?" Freddie said. They didn't deny it and that was an answer enough.

"So did I," Mike said.

Freddie stared at him, lids half concealing his dark eyes.

"I spoke to Ted Stanshawe last night," he explained. "So I knew. It wasn't such a surprise, I guess. More of a disappointment."

Freddie continued his silent interrogation.

"My friend, Karen, is in hospital," he explained. "Someone tried to kill her, got in and disconnected the life support. Ted did some digging. Got a description." He paused, remembering the shock of the discovery. "Phil is a pretty unmistakable man."

"We will look at the bike, eh?" Pascal said, draining her drink.

"Fine," Mike replied, standing, the metal chair scraping uncannily loud against the rough ground.

"I will pay," Geneviève said, disappearing into the dark of the café and returning moments later. "Let's go."

As they reached the bikes, Pascale stopped and looked along the road towards the town centre, shading her eyes with one hand.

"Take the panel off, Mike. I will keep a look out for company."

Mike crouched down and unclipped the side panel, pulling it away from the main body of the fairing. Wordlessly, he looked at the mass of small plastic packets crammed into the hollow. He prised out one of the packets and turned it over in his hands, absorbing the significance of the white powder contained in the clear polythene.

"Well?" he asked, stunned into monosyllables. Geneviève held out her hand, silently, her back to the bike, never taking her eyes from the road. He placed the packet in her open palm and she took it, prising it open and tipping a trace of the powder onto a finger. Gingerly she touched it with the tip of her tongue.

"Cocaine."

Mike turned to Pascale who watched events with a deadpan expression. "That's what you meant by "*I think*.""

She nodded. "There is more in the other panel."

Freddie sighed heavily. "So, we just moved up a league."

"Yes," Geneviève murmured.

"You didn't know, did you?" Mike said, looking across at her. "This is bad news you hadn't expected."

"I was looking for diamond thieves."

"Neat," Mike said woodenly. "Stones out, narcotics back. Bloody brilliant."

Geneviève nodded thoughtfully. "The big diamond is something else, though. Rousseau is an obsessive collector. He will want that one for himself."

"There can't be much in there," Freddie pointed out. "I wouldn't have thought it worth their while, all this way for that small bit."

"You haven't looked behind the fairing panels yet," Pascale murmured.

"Do I want to?" Mike asked warily.

"Probably not."

"But you are right," Geneviève said. "There is a piece of the puzzle missing. Why Portugal and why this way? Why not directly to wherever he hides out in France?"

"Marseille," Pascale said.

"I'm not sure I care too much," Mike replied. "I want out."

"I don't think we have any choice," Geneviève said, still looking at the road.

"So now what?"

"Put everything back and continue as before," she instructed, handing the packet back.

Mike stuffed the bag back into the space it vacated and replaced the panel. Geneviève watched as he worked, a cloud of worry flitted across her eyes.

"I am very sorry, Mike. I may have placed you in grave danger."

"Oh?" he said sarcastically. "You do surprise me."

"It may be nothing. We shall see, eh?" Pascale said, brushing the concern away.

"Perhaps we should come clean, mm?" Mike said flatly.

Pascale shrugged. "Need to know . . ."

"We've had this conversation before," he scowled at them both. "I think you need backup. Get hold of Lopez and his mob, tell them about the dope…"

"You are right," Geneviève sighed. "When we get back to the hotel."

"I would have thought the sooner the better," Mike said.

She shook her head.

Silently they donned helmets and gloves before mounting up and setting off for Termas São Pedro do Sul. The midday heat baked the road causing it to melt into a heat haze that shimmered before them as they zigzagged through the blackened pines to Termas São Pedro do Sul. Pascale turned the Harley into the car park and descended the steep slope. Once the engines died into a silence broken only by the ticking of their cooling she flicked down the sidestand and rested the machine against it and dismounted. The others did the same. Mike removed his helmet and placed it in one of the panniers.

Such was the intensity of the heat that they walked lethargically to the Hotel Vouga—weighed down by the gravity of their thoughts. They had just reached the door to the foyer when Geneviève stopped. "I have left my bag in the pannier."

Mike turned, intending to return with her to the bikes but Geneviève stopped him with a raised hand. "No, you go on up. I will be along shortly."

"Sure," he said.

Turning to retrace her steps, Geneviève said "I will join you in a minute."

Freddie pushed open the door and held it while Pascale and Mike entered the hotel.

"Why don't you both go on upstairs, I will wait for Geneviève here," Pascale said.

Freddie grinned easily. "Why don't I wait down here with you?"

Pascale shrugged indifferently, so Mike left them to their politics and made his way upstairs to the room. He entered and closed the door behind him. He had barely tossed his jacket over the back of a chair before there was a knock at the door. Thinking it was the others he said "Come in, it's open."

Phil and Frank strode into the room. "Hello Mike," Phil said genially. Frank said nothing but beamed at him cheerfully. Mike refrained from returning the greeting.

"Er, what can I do for you, gentlemen?"

Phil grinned. "We're going for a little ride, Mike."

"Um, thanks for the offer," he replied, attempting to keep his voice light and failing. "But I could do with a rest, busy morning and all that. Feel free to go without me though."

Phil remained outwardly cheerful despite Mike's obtuseness.

"I'm afraid you've no choice, old son."

Frank leered, sending a sliver of frost down Mike's spine where it did a little tap dance before returning the long way through his intestine.

"No choice, old son."

Despite his nerves playing like a tone-deaf brass band, Mike kept his voice even.

"Oh, why is that?"

Frank pulled back the flap of his jacket, revealing a large handgun. As an argument it carried more clout than reasoned debate. Mike gave in. It seemed the logical thing to do.

"A little ride, you say? You know, I was just thinking that I could fancy a little ride."

Phil's voice was smooth like the glassy surface of a deep river concealing the dark raging currents beneath, beguiling and deadly.

"Now that's more like it. I knew you would see things our way, didn't I, Frank?"

Frank lowered his jacket flap. "Yeah."

"Frank didn't believe me," Phil said conversationally.

"Should I care?" Mike said *sotto voce*.

"Sorry?"

"Nothing," he said, resigned.

"Come on, we've some way to go," Phil said, ignoring Mike's attitude.

He walked obediently between Phil and Frank down through the hotel to the sunlit street. Freddie, Geneviève and Pascale were nowhere to be seen. Outside Phil directed him to a large Mercedes. One wing was severely dented. Mike nodded to the damage.

"I like the custom job. How did you come by that?"

"Shut up and get in," Phil snarled. Mike had hit a nerve and smiled to himself, planting his tongue firmly in his cheek.

"Ah, you hit something, then."

"I said, shut up and get in the car."

"Sorry, just making conversation."

"Well don't."

"Sorry for breathing," he said flatly. In retrospect probably not the wisest thing he'd said, he thought to himself.

Frank smiled, enjoying himself. "You will be, you will be."

Phil sighed heavily. "Shut up, Frank."

They bundled Mike into the back of the Mercedes and Frank clambered in beside him, still grinning inanely. Phil slid into the driving seat and slammed the door noisily. Starting the car, he executed a rapid "U" turn with a squeal of tyres and a scrunch of gravel, nearly causing a collision with a van emerging from the bridge—resulting in a blared horn warning and a screech of brakes. The shaken driver treated Phil to an extensive repertoire of expletives but to no avail—the Mercedes was already several hundred metres away and accelerating quickly.

***

Pascale watched as the car sped out of the car park and onto the road heading for São Pedro. She went back into the foyer and walked over to Geneviève. "They've taken Mike."

"Who?"

"Phil and Frank. Heading out onto the road for São Pedro."

"I'll get the bike. You?"

"I'll make a call. More use."

"*D'Accord.* On my way."

Pascale waited until Genevieve was out of the hotel and mounting her bike before going into the back of the foyer to the telephone cubicle. She picked up the handset and dialled.

"Yes?"

"It's started."

"Good. What has happened?"

"They have taken Jenner."

"Do you know where?"

"The villa—that is the direction they are heading."

"Very good. I'll meet you there."

She hung up the handset and made her way out into the sunlight. She pulled on her helmet and straddled the Harley. She wasn't worried about catching up with Geneviève, for she knew the destination.

***

Mike looked for Geneviève as the car hurtled out of the hotel car park, but couldn't see her, Phil was driving too quickly. He pushed the gas pedal to the floor and the big car responded eagerly, punching forwards with rapid acceleration as they approached the left-hand bend at the exit of the village, his face set with determination, jaw muscles rigid, eyes staring forward at the dusty road. The Mercedes responded to gentle braking, quickly losing speed. He changed down a gear and powered through the bend. Mike glanced round and saw a bike behind them some way back.

Phil lost speed again as they entered the outskirts of São Pedro Do Sul. The cobbled road surface had subsided in places, leaving a sharp ridge on the right-hand edge, pulling the nearside wheel to the right. Phil swore under his breath as he fought the steering to keep the car out of the gutter. Mike decided not to point out that a lower speed would have the desired effect. Smart arse comments, he concluded, would be out of place. Instead he concentrated his efforts on wondering about Geneviève and whether Phil knew that she was following them. He figured that if he had seen the bike, it was unlikely that Phil had missed it.

In the centre of São Pedro, Phil turned left towards the mountains, the sharp junction forcing him almost to a standstill while his hands snaked around the steering wheel, letting it slip through his fingers with the acceleration on the exit. The road followed a sinuous path through the Serra de Arada. Barely wide enough for two cars to pass and often unmetalled where the occasional stretches of smooth tarmac came as a relief. Large though it was, the car coped with the terrain. Phil relaxed, driving swiftly but smoothly. The car was sure footed—picking its own line amongst the potholes and ridges. The Mercedes, having the advantage of four wheels, left Geneviève far behind and she was soon lost to sight.

Again they turned left, this time at Castro Daire. Phil was forced to slow in order to negotiate the narrow roads filled with pedestrians and other traffic. He leaned out of the driver's window and flung a few well-aimed curses at the milling crowd. Some stared disinterestedly at him before moving out of his path. Dark hostile eyes stared at them as they crawled through the congested streets. In the distance, Mike caught sight of Geneviève as they turned west towards Castelo de Paiva. She followed. Phil, Mike decided, must have seen her too as they were both using the same mirror. He presumed that Phil didn't care, or had plans.

The road snaked, climbing high into the Serra Montemuro. Mike could occasionally see the Rio Paiva through the trees far below to the left. To the right, the sheer rock face reached up to the heavens. The sun blazed, a boiling orb suspended in a copper-sulphate sky. Frank mopped his brow with a grubby handkerchief that had seen worse days. As the uneven road twisted and turned, Phil was forced to keep his speed down, constantly shifting gear to help the vehicle as he guided it through one hairpin bend after another, climbing ever higher into the desolate mountains. The car ground almost to a stop as Phil slowed behind a lorry trundling amidst a cloud of diesel fumes on its weary way to Porto. Again, Geneviève was in sight intermittently.

Just prior to Alvarenga, the truck carried on towards Castelo de Paiva while Phil turned the Mercedes left towards Arouca. Geneviève followed at a discreet distance. Just before the tiny village, they arrived at a villa perched on the slope at the edge of the pine forest.

The land in front of the house was barren and sloped down towards the road, where it dropped almost vertically for about two metres to the verge. To the right of the building was the edge of the pine forest. To the left, several metres of uncultivated land before yet more pines.

Phil swung the Mercedes into the driveway, stopped and killed the engine. Frank bundled Mike out of the car and along the drive to the front door of the building.

Between them Phil and Frank frog-marched him into the villa and through to the front room overlooking the road. A man sat in a chair, sipping a glass of wine. He dressed as he appeared—casual and relaxed in a white open necked pilot shirt and shorts. In the other chair Lopez sat reading a magazine. He put this down as they entered. In the middle of the room was a coffee table with a handgun lying on it.

The first man stood, beaming convivially. "Mr Jenner…"

Mike ignored the outstretched hand, leaving it dangling awkwardly until he let it hang by his side. The moment passed and he turned to Phil.

"Philip, you stay please. Frank, you can leave us."

Wordlessly Frank slipped from the room on some errand of his own. Mike wondered vaguely why he seemed uncomfortable in the company of the others.

"*Senhor* Jenner, we meet again," Lopez said. "I believe you have not met…"

"*Monsieur* Rousseau," Mike interrupted. Mike looked the man up and down. Not as old as he looked, he thought, with short cropped hair cut in a military style with a close beard and tanned skin that had seen plenty of dry hot climates, which along with the manner of dress suggested a forces background.

"Quite," Lopez said.

"No matter," Rousseau intervened. "No matter."

Mike stared from one to the other.

"What's wrong, *Senhor*, nothing to say?" Lopez goaded gently.

150

"No," Mike said flatly. "I felt that remaining silent was probably the best way of ensuring politeness."

Rousseau remained oblivious to the jibe. "May I offer you a glass of wine? It's an excellent vintage."

"I'm sure it is, but no, thank-you."

"Do I detect a sense of outrage?"

"I don't know, do you?"

Rousseau sipped the wine, rolling it around his tongue. "You really should try it, *Monsieur*, you don't know what you're missing."

"Yes I do," Mike replied brusquely.

Rousseau feigned hurt. "Dear, dear, not very sociable are we?" His voice hardened as molten lava hardens to impervious rock.

"Still, I gleaned as much from my research. You have a remarkable capacity for offensiveness, Mr Jenner. As indeed, did your friend, Miss Ross."

For a fleeting second Mike was wrong footed. He hadn't expected him to make the connection between them.

"Comes with years of practice," he replied neutrally.

Lopez started to rise, his mouth opening when Rousseau silenced him with a wave of his hand.

"I think we should come to the point, don't you?"

"There is one?"

"Oh, yes Mr Jenner," the voice, oily smooth layered over an undercurrent of dangerous menace. "And I think it is now overdue."

"If you like," Mike said flatly.

"I do like, *Monsieur*. Where are our diamonds?"

Mike frowned, genuinely puzzled. To cover his confusion, he prevaricated.

"Your diamonds? That's funny, I thought they belonged to the people you thieving bastards stole 'em from."

Phil reacted quickly, punching him viciously in the kidneys. Mike fell, gasping, at his feet, writhing in agony.

"Phil and Frank, as a matter of fact," Rousseau said conversationally, ignoring the undignified display on the floor. "Although, they had some of my people with them. Seems the police have some of them in custody. No matter, they won't talk. Now don't play games with me. I am not a humorous man and my companions are extremely upset with you for making fools of them."

"That's their problem." Mike knew it was the wrong thing to say as soon as the words slipped from his lips but his teeth weren't quick enough to catch his tongue.

"No," said Phil. "It's yours, so, if I were you, I would consider my position very carefully before giving smart arse answers."

Rousseau stared down at Mike, contempt drifting across the dark pools in his eyes—black ice.

"Oh, get up. Where are those diamonds?"

The tone in Rousseau's voice gave Mike the impetus he needed so he cautiously stood, gingerly rubbing his sore back.

"Didn't Phil take 'em off the bike? While we were in with Lopez?"

Rousseau studied him without replying immediately. Reflectively, he removed a cigarette packet from his pocket, withdrew a tube, tapped it on the packet and placed it between his lips.

"So, you're not as stupid as you look."

"Thanks a bundle."

"You're arrogant, *Monsieur*, but I didn't think you were that bright as well." He turned to Lopez. "Should've chosen one of the others, pity."

"Pity?" Mike asked, puzzled.

Rousseau fumbled around in his pocket and retrieved a lighter.

"Never mind." He lit the cigarette and sucked deeply at it, causing the end to glow bright orange. He breathed out a stream of smoke, slitting his eyes as it wafted back into his face. He gestured with the cigarette. "You don't mind, do you?"

"Bit academic really."

"Like I said, arrogant."

"We're two of a kind, then."

"Let Philip see to him..." Lopez started.

"Shut up. I'll deal with this," Rousseau interrupted. He reached for a plastic packet lying on the coffee table and held it out for Mike to see.

"These?" he asked contemptuously, pouring the contents of the packet onto the floor where they bounced in glittering profusion. Among them, a large glistering stone that he picked up and held to the light, its facets glinting in the rays streaming through the slatted blind that covered the window. The Koh-i-Noor. He studied the stone, apparently mesmerised by its beauty.

"Exquisite, isn't it?" Then he let it fall from the packet to the floor along with the cluster of smaller stones and stamped on them, crushing them underfoot.

"Paste. What have you and Madame Duval done with the originals?"

"Search me," Mike said, shrugging, realising immediately that it was the wrong thing to say.

"We might just do that yet."

Mike sighed as heavily as he convincingly could. "I don't know anything about them, so far as I knew they were the originals."

"Oh come on, *Senhor*," Lopez said. "Stop this. I've had enough of your sarcasm."

Rousseau snapped angrily. "And I've had enough of you. Now shut up. I can handle this without your help." He turned back to Mike. "Where are those diamonds?"

"Disappoint your Colombian friends, will it?" Mike hit a raw nerve. Rousseau flung him a look of pure hatred as he snatched the pistol lying on the coffee table and strode across the room, thrusting the muzzle under Mike's chin, forcing his head back. Screeching with fury, he said, "Where are those fucking diamonds?"

"I don't know."

Rousseau swung the pistol, smashing it into the side of Mike's face. Mike fell, reeling with pain, a gash welling blood across his cheek.

"I don't know," he said, choking on the pain. "I don't bloody know."

"Get up," Rousseau said flatly.

Mike shook his head drunkenly, remaining where he was. Rousseau kicked him viciously in the ribs. "Get up!"

Slowly, seeing the room in a swirl of pain Mike hauled himself onto his knees and swayed for what seemed an eternity, on all fours, before staggering upright. Rousseau stood, looking at him—the venom visible in his pale face, flared nostrils and ragged breathing. Somehow, despite the suffering in his face and kidneys, Mike's arrogant spirit remained unbowed and his tongue got the better of his teeth again.

"I was right about the Colombians, then," he said thickly.

"How did you know about the coke?" Rousseau asked dangerously.

Mike shrugged, swaying like a Saturday night reveller.

"Madame Duval?" Rousseau asked.

Mike reached gingerly for his jaw. His head was spinning and the room seemed distant—Rousseau's voice echoed from another place, another time, so remote was it.

"I said, was it Duval, *Monsieur*? Concentrate."

Mike could hear Phil's voice, low, soft, talking. He shook his head, attempting to clear the fuzziness.

"I think you overdid it Mr Rousseau."

Rousseau's brittle voice snapped back irritated. "If I need your opinion, I'll ask for it, *n'est-ce pas*?"

"Okay, you're the boss," Phil replied, shrugging.

"Good. Just remember it." He returned his attention to Mike. "Michael, Michael…" He shook him by the shoulder. Mike focused hazily on his face and concentrated on his anger.

"Mr Jenner, to you," he slurred.

Rousseau sighed. "*Monsieur*…"

Lopez rose and stood next to Rousseau. "I think Philip may be right, *Senhor*, you have overdone it…" his voice rose in panic.

Swaying drunkenly, Mike lifted his gaze to Lopez causing him to wince and shrink back into the chair as Rousseau gripped his shoulders and shook him again while turning to Lopez and snapping angrily "Silence," then to Mike, "Now, *Monsieur*, one of you switched those diamonds. And they weren't there on Saturday. So, if it wasn't you, it must have been Madame Duval, where is she? And where are the stones?" He thrust his face into Mike's.

Mike looked at the man.

That's funny. I hadn't realised that you were fuzzy around the edges before.

He passed out.

Mike was drowning, gasping through the water for air. His face was wet. Phil stood over him with an empty bowl. Gasping, Mike wiped his face with his hands, and played for time. Sitting up, he leaned forward, head hanging.

"Where is Madame Duval, *Monsieur*?

Why doesn't Phil say anything—he knows. Slowly moving his head from side to side and trying to ignore the rending in his skull, then, looking directly at Phil, Mike replied, "I would have thought you knew that."

Rousseau exchanged glances with Phil. "Well?"

"She was on the road behind us," Phil replied, "but Frank would've been back by now if he'd found her."

Rousseau returned his attention to Mike. "Where are the diamonds?"

"Search me."

Rousseau's reply was predictably unsympathetic. "As I said, we might yet. Get up."

Again, Mike lifted himself carefully to his feet. "I've told you, I don't know," he said tiredly. "How many times must I tell you?" As he spoke, his thoughts crystallised. "The Colombians, they'll kill you, won't they?"

The expression on Rousseau's face was sulphuric. "Not before I've killed you."

Mike was missing something and struggled with his dulled senses for the elusive thought before it slipped into focus like the image in a camera viewfinder. Laughing weakly, he said, "We were late. That's it, isn't it? And...you said something about them not being there on Saturday"

Even his sluggish consciousness could pick up the sharp exchange between Phil and Rousseau. He kept going, thinking aloud.

"You should've made the switch yesterday, or Saturday."

"Saturday morning," Rousseau said flatly.

"But we didn't get to Viseu until Saturday afternoon, so you couldn't make the switch." He sniggered despite himself. "And they let you have the dope without the diamonds?" he asked, disbelieving.

"I can be very persuasive. Besides, we have a long business association. The diamonds were on their way, weren't they?"

"Hell of a risk," Mike said, swaying slightly.

"So it would seem," Rousseau said dryly.

Mike shrugged.

"You knew they were on board." It was a statement, he knew.

"I found out."

"How?" Phil asked.

"I'm a light sleeper."

Phil jabbed him in the kidneys. Sobbing with agony as his knees gave way, Mike collapsed once more to the floor.

"Liar," Rousseau said dispassionately.

Whimpering with pain, Mike decided that bravado was probably not getting him anywhere. "Okay, okay, The Spanish customs found 'em."

Phil frowned. "So that's why you were so long."

For the third time, Mike lifted himself to his knees, but made no effort to stand. He just knelt where he was, leaning forward, head resting on the cool, tiled floor.

"Yeah," he whimpered.

"I did wonder," Phil mused. "You set off at seven in the morning and were still at the border at gone eight. Seemed odd at the time."

"If we could cut the reminiscences," Rousseau said. Phil shrugged. Mike did nothing.

"This raises all sorts of questions," Rousseau continued.

"It does?" Mike groaned.

"Don't get smart with me," he barked. "Why aren't you still in some Spanish prison?"

"They were fakes."

Rousseau's voice was tart. "Oh, I see. So they just decided to let you go on your way with these fake diamonds concealed on the bike, no questions asked." He reached down, grabbed Mike's hair and, thrusting his face close, snarled "what do you take me for?"

"Do you want an answer to that?"

Phil kicked him viciously in the ribs as Rousseau dropped his head. Gasping with pain, Mike decided that he probably asked for that. Ignoring his suffering, Rousseau continued the questioning. "How did you persuade the Spanish to let you go?"

"Geneviève…" Mike started.

Rousseau smiled. "Ah, now, that's more like it. Go on."

"Geneviève persuaded them."

"Just like that, eh?"

Mike lifted his head from the floor to look briefly at Rousseau before returning to his examination of the tiles. "Yeah."

Rousseau's voice changed to gravel smooth with treacle. "Now why don't I believe you?"

"She's the filth, isn't she?" Phil interrupted with startling clarity. Mike said nothing, staring at the floor, wondering where Lopez fitted into the picture. He couldn't be sure whether he was a double playing for the police, in which case Geneviève was on steady ground, or whether he was a double playing for the opposition, in which case they were in deep trouble. He knew Geneviève was <u>Sûreté</u>. As Phil didn't, *perhaps we are safe,* he thought. Rousseau was speaking.

"You're not saying anything, *Monsieur.* I am beginning to think that perhaps Philip should be allowed to persuade you to change your attitude. What you have just experienced is just a little taster of his many skills."

The door burst open and Frank stumbled into the room, propelled by Geneviève. She held him by his left arm uncomfortably twisted behind his back. To his temple she held an automatic pistol.

"Found 'er snooping around outside," Frank gasped.

"She found you, more like," Mike muttered.

"Well," Rousseau said flatly, ignoring Mike's comment. "*Madame* Duval. Perhaps you will be kind enough to enlighten us as to the whereabouts of our diamonds?"

Geneviève ignored Rousseau and turned her attention to Mike.

"Michael…"

Mike lifted his head from the floor to look at her. "Hi."

"Never mind the reunions," Rousseau snapped. "Where are the diamonds?"

Geneviève stared at Rousseau. "I believe that I have the upper hand here, don't you?"

"Is that what you believe?" Rousseau spoke softly, dangerously. "Oh, I think not, *Madame.* I have another card to play."

Geneviève smiled, sure of her ground. More sure than Mike would have been, for he could see behind her and knew what was coming next.

"What card is that *Monsieur*?"

"Me," Pascale Hervé said.

No one heard her come into the room. Mike smiled briefly, despite the gun pointing at Geneviève's head.

"Hello, Fábián," Pascale said, smiling.

Rousseau inclined his head and returned the smile. "*Madame*, please, let Frank go."

Silently Geneviève complied while treating Pascale with a look that would have killed. Frank, rubbing his arm, snatched the pistol from her grasp.

"Thanks," he said.

"Where are my diamonds?" Rousseau asked patiently.

Geneviève shrugged.

"But they were on Mike's motorcycle," Pascale said.

"Were, is the operative word," Rousseau replied. "By the time you arrived in Portugal, they had been replaced with fakes. Who knew about them?"

"Oh." Pascale shrugged. "Geneviève myself, Mike, Phil, Frank, oh, and Freddie…"

"Freddie?"

"Oh, he's just one of the punters," Phil replied.

"Just one of the punters?" Rousseau said nastily. "So how come he knows about the diamonds, eh?"

Phil squirmed awkwardly. "First I knew of it."

"Well perhaps we had better talk to this Freddie. What do you think?"

"Er, I think it's a great idea," Phil agreed hesitantly.

"So where will we find this Freddie?" Rousseau cast his question casually at Geneviève who stared dully back at him.

"Back at the hotel, I presume," Pascale said.

Rousseau turned to Frank. "Get back to the hotel and pick up this Freddie character, I think it's time we had a word. Oh and take Lopez with you." Lopez lifted himself out of the chair and wordlessly followed Frank. Rousseau returned his attention to Geneviève.

"Where did you put them?"

"Why don't you ask Pascale?"

For a brief second, Rousseau nearly fell for it. His eyes narrowed to basilisk slits causing Pascale to flinch. Something passed between them. Mike looked from one to the other and saw a moment when trust teeters. Rousseau no longer entirely trusted her. He was wondering in that second just who he could trust and Mike experienced a brief flash of sympathy, *you and me both, mate.*

Rousseau turned that blank, lifeless gaze to Mike.

"If I shoot you, *Madame* Hervé will tell me…"

"She doesn't know," Geneviève said.

Rousseau's face twisted into a sneer. "Ah, then I will shoot her and you will tell me."

"What are you waiting for?" Geneviève relied deadpan.

Mike felt the alarm rising through his arteries. "Gen!"

Geneviève ignored Mike's outburst. Rousseau ran his tongue over his lips, his eyes moving from Geneviève to Mike and then to Pascale, who still held her pistol loosely in one hand. He levelled the gun at Mike's abdomen. Mike decided that at this juncture, pleading would be in order.

"Christ, Gen!"

"It will do no good," Geneviève sighed. "I no longer have them."

Rousseau lowered the pistol, leaving it hovering somewhere about Mike's crotch—*not much better*, Mike thought—but the atmosphere eased a micron or two.

"Why should I believe you?" Rousseau asked suspiciously.

Geneviève shrugged, causing Mike's stress levels to soar once more. "Should I care if you don't?"

The dark eyes narrowed speculatively. "You are police, you would have backup, no? So, there is someone else in your team who has them?"

Geneviève shrugged again.

"Yes, I thought as much."

"But there are only the two of us..." Pascale started. "And Lopez..."

"You fool," Rousseau's words lashed like a sliced power cable causing Pascale to flinch. "She was watching you all the time—of course there is someone else, someone you won't know about."

Geneviève remained passive her face betraying nothing of her thoughts.

"I thought . . ." Phil said

"Shut up, Phil," Rousseau said.

"I . . ."

"I said, shut up." He turned to Geneviève. "Now, *Madame* Duval, where did you dispose of the diamonds? Or perhaps I should say to whom?"

"Is it me, or is this conversation going round in circles?" Mike asked. He struggled slowly to his feet. "I don't suppose the Colombians will be interested in fakes."

"No, I suppose not," Geneviève smiled.

Rousseau's knuckles whitened as he tightened his grip on the pistol, pointing it at Mike yet speaking to Geneviève and losing control of the conversation.

"Where did you put them?" He screamed.

Geneviève smiled much as a saltwater crocodile does when it welcomes someone into its domain. "I hear that the cartels can be very ruthless."

The telephone rang. At first no one made any attempt to answer it. The insistent jangling cut through the tension of the room, eventually breaking it.

"*Merde!*" Rousseau grabbed the receiver "Yes?" He listened for a few moments, grunting intermittently and glancing at his watch. "We will wait for you here. Yes, see you then." He slammed the receiver back onto its cradle and turned to Phil. "Estevez is coming here."

"What about these two?" Phil asked.

"Put them in the back room for the moment," Rousseau replied. "I need to think."

"Yes baas," Phil scowled. Rousseau glared at him but didn't respond. Estevez's imminent arrival clearly gave him plenty to think about. Mike thought a good excuse would be handy.

Phil frog-marched Mike and Geneviève out of the front room and along a corridor to the back of the house, pausing to push open the door and usher them in. As he held a gun pointing mostly in Mike's direction, they were in no hurry to argue. Once they were jostled through the door Phil locked it behind them.

Like a small time pensão, the room was a utilitarian box. In one corner a stained and cracked washbasin lurked while in another a chair tiredly slumped against the plaster wall. The window was shuttered and locked.

Mike flopped onto the bed and closed his eyes while Geneviève spent a couple of fruitless minutes trying the blind. Eventually she gave up and sat beside him on the bed. Running her fingers delicately over his injured face, she said "I'm sorry."

He opened his eyes and looked at her. "Couldn't be helped, I guess."

Geneviève stood and walked across to the basin where she wet a towel. She returned and gently placed it against his injured jaw. The cool water numbed the throbbing ache a little.

"Thanks."

"There are no broken bones."

"A tooth . . ."

"Does it hurt much?"

"What sort of question is that?"

"Sorry," she said. "I have no pain killers, they are in my bag."

Mike reached for his jacket pocket. "In here. I never go anywhere without 'em."

Geneviève took the sachet. "Let me." She walked to the sink and filled a tooth mug with water before returning. She placed an arm behind his head and lifted him forward as he took the mug and tablets from her.

"Here," she said.

Mike swallowed the tablets gratefully. Geneviève walked back to the shuttered window and shook the base of the shutter. "Locked."

"Surprise, surprise."

"You knew who they were..."

"Mm."

"Mind telling me?"

"Ted Stanshawe."

"I thought he was a journalist...the one who annoyed you."

"Even annoying little ticks have their uses," he smiled and instantly regretted it. "And no thanks to you, that maniac nearly shot me in there."

Geneviève smiled. "Bluff."

"You play poker?"

"She does. Rousseau, he owns the touring company, and was using the company as cover, no?"

"So, we knew that."

"And Pascale is working for him. Interesting, no?"

"Very," Mike replied sarcastically. "But you knew all this."

"What surprises me is that you did."

"Like I said, contacts. Rousseau and Pascale are of a kind, I reckon. Besides, if I could find out, so must you at some point."

Geneviève walked around the room trying the door and the window again to no avail. It seemed to Mike that she was trying from idle curiosity rather than from any immediate desire to escape. He watched in silence as she ran her fingers along the back of the chair, her attitude one of distraction, her eyes in a distant place where he couldn't follow.

The door was unlocked and pushed open. Phil entered carrying a tray with bread, smoked ham and two cups of coffee. He placed the tray on one of the bedside cabinets, picked up a chair—turning it around—and sat astride it with his arms resting on the back.

"Mike, Geneviève, er, look," he started awkwardly. "No hard feelings, eh? I was just doing my job."

"They said that at Nuremberg," Mike said flatly.

Phil's face flushed deep red and he started to rise. "Now look…"

Mike fingered his cheek and Phil checked his anger. "I didn't do that. I just punched you a couple of times."

"With enthusiasm," Mike replied darkly.

"Sorry, I have to make it look good."

"You do?"

"What do you want?" Geneviève asked bluntly, sitting next to Mike on the bed.

"Perhaps we could come to an arrangement."

Mike raised his eyebrows painfully. "An arrangement?"

"Rousseau doesn't intend to set you free, you know. He can't afford to, can he? Let's be fair."

"Oh, of course, we must be fair," Mike allowed the caustic to dissolve through his reply and sizzle in the atmosphere.

Geneviève jabbed him sharply in the ribs and ignoring his gasp of pain said, "I see, I suppose not. What are you proposing?"

"You tell me where the diamonds are and I'll get you out."

"But you're getting a share of the loot anyway," Mike said as reasonably as his simmering temper would allow.

"No chance," he replied. "Frank and I take all the risks. Rousseau just sits back and takes all the profits. We get treated with contempt. You saw that just now."

"I did."

"So?"

"So what?"

Phil sighed heavily at the obtuse response. "What about the diamonds?"

"Ah, quite. You want them for yourself, then?"

"That's the general idea," he said flatly.

"And the cocaine?" Geneviève asked.

Phil shrugged. "That too, why not?"

Geneviève splayed her fingers and studied them as if that were the centre of her universe. "And what about Frank?"

"Stuff Frank!"

"Oh, I see." Mike switched from caustic to nitric. "Fine mate you are. Honour amongst thieves and all that."

"Grow up," he snapped. "Look, someone's got to take the fall. Might as well be Frank. We can share the profit three ways."

"You seem to forget that Madame Duval is a police officer."

Phil glanced at Geneviève who was apparently ignoring them. "Everyone's got their price—Brigadier Hervé, Lopez, for example. Besides, your lives depend on it."

Geneviève rested her hands on her thighs and meeting Phil's gaze with her own cold blue stare replied "I think not, but thank-you for the offer."

Lightning flashed in Phil's eyes. "Dammit!"

"Is there anything else?" Geneviève asked, her voice cool as a February morning. Phil rose with the anger broiling below the surface, bubbling out in the flashes in his eyes and flushed complexion.

"No." He turned smartly on his heel and stormed out of the room, slamming the door behind him. Mike dived into the food and began to eat hungrily if a little carefully.

"Have you noticed anything?" Geneviève mused.

Wincing as he chewed, he replied "Um."

"Perhaps I should say, have you not noticed anything?"

"Um."

"The car?"

"I, ouch, never heard it…" Mike paused, his eyes widening as the significance of his comment hit home.

"No, quite."

"So…"

"So our friends Frank and Lopez haven't gone anywhere."

"Does this mean that Lopez is on the side of the angels after all?"

Geneviève nodded, smiling. "It would seem so."

"He could have been just a little less convincing."

"And be dead into the bargain."

"Mm, I suppose so. Why did you take the diamonds off the bike over the weekend?" Mike asked, switching the conversation.

"I wanted to have control over the timing, and, it interested me to see who became angry."

Mike recalled Phil's irritation and it fell into place. "He was angry with me." He thought for a moment. "And Freddie, he's in league with you, isn't he?"

Geneviève's eyes narrowed. "How long have you known?"

"I knew for certain in the other room when Rousseau talked about backup."

"He works for Radfield."

"Fat lot of good that is, though. He has no idea where we are."

Geneviève smiled. "Don't rule out Lopez just yet."

"Ah, so the cavalry are on their way…"

"They will contact Freddie."

Geneviève went back to the bed and sat down, lifting her feet in the air. "My new boots, you like them, yes?"

"Mm, they suit you. But don't we have more pressing considerations?"

"Ah, but they hide a secret." She pulled off her left boot and rolled up the leg of her jeans to reveal a small pistol taped to her calf.

The odds just shifted.

"What now?"

"We wait," she replied.

"Tell me about Pascale," Mike said.

"Brigadier Pascale Hervé is my partner and my friend. Is that all you need to know?"

Mike smiled. "Except that she's on the take and you knew all along."

"I suspected. That is not the same."

"If I didn't know better I'd say this was a scam to bring the rotten apples out of the woodwork or something."

Geneviève lapsed into a reflective silence before finally responding, her voice heavy with regret.

"Little things pointed to what I didn't want to see. You know, jobs that should have been straightforward that went inexplicably wrong. Eventually there were too many. I suspected but I did not know and I needed outside help."

"Radfield and Freddie?"

"Yes. So now I have all the evidence I require, but I need backup."

"Was it Pascale who sabotaged your bike in Parthenay?"

"I suspect so."

"Some friend..."

"We were, once."

"Well, Freddie should be with us before long. Providing Lopez comes good."

Geneviève said nothing as she turned her pistol over in her hands.

"Life's a bummer," Mike said.

"The Portuguese police will have to make the arrests."

"But first we have to get out of here."

"Mm, we must await events. And the longer we wait, the more worried Freddie will become."

Mike raised himself onto one elbow and lifted an eyebrow; promptly wishing he hadn't and winced. "You just lost me."

"I had a fall back plan."

"So?"

"So, I had made arrangements to call him by one o'clock. By now he will realise that we are in trouble."

Mike sank back onto the bed. "But you knew Phil and Frank would turn up."

"Yes."

162

"You never intended to make that call. Did you?"

Geneviève shrugged. "I raised the alarm by omission. A failsafe if we ran into trouble, eh?"

"Do you think they'll find us?"

"Not before we get out ourselves."

"Now there's confident," Mike replied, his voice arid.

Geneviève smiled. "We have the element of surprise."

"Do you think they'll kill us? Or was Phil trying to frighten us into telling him where the diamonds are?"

"What do you think?"

Mike thought about it for a moment. "He doesn't seem too concerned about casual violence."

Geneviève smiled broadly at the understatement. "Alive, we are dangerous to him. Dead, we quietly disappear. Does that answer your question?"

"But you're the fuzz. People don't just go round killing coppers and getting away with it."

Geneviève sighed. "If they think the end is worth the means, they will."

"Um," Mike said. It seemed an appropriate response in the circumstances.

Geneviève lifted her pistol and stared down the barrel as she sighted it. "So we escape and seek help," she said brightly.

"Just like that."

Geneviève stood and walked across to the shuttered window where she cocked her head and listened. "Yes, just like that."

"Great."

"I wonder why they brought the diamonds to Portugal?" she mused, listening.

"Couldn't say."

"It doesn't seem logical," she said absently. "There must be something we do not know. What do you think, Michael?"

"I dunno," he replied. Then something struck him. "Just a minute, I don't know where the real diamonds are, but you do, don't you?"

"I thought so," she ignored the question and listened still. "A car, listen."

Mike clambered off the bed and walked across the room to join her. Through the shutter they could hear the scrunch of tyres on the gravel driveway. They could make out Rousseau's voice, murmuring greetings, followed by low unintelligible replies in Spanish. Geneviève frowned as she strained to catch the words. The front door closed and she shook her head in frustration.

"Hear anything?" Mike asked.

"No, but I think we can guess who they are."

"Colombians?"

"And not best pleased, I think," she grinned.

"What do you think they'll do now?"

"Send for us, I expect," she said still smiling broadly. If he didn't know better, he'd have assumed she was enjoying herself. "They will want to present us to their guests."

Mike sat on the bed once more and reached for his jacket. Wordlessly, he gulped down two more painkillers, with a mouthful of water, from the glass on the bedside cabinet. Geneviève sat beside him, clutching her pistol. Before long the door handle rattled as the key turned in the lock and Pascale breezed in, full of self-confidence—the earlier conversations apparently forgotten.

"Right you two, *Monsieur* Rousseau wants to see you immediately. We've some visitors who want to be introduced. I hope you've got some answers for him this time."

"Oh, we have indeed," Geneviève said, raising the pistol. "Do come in and sit down."

Pascale stopped in her tracks, then twitched, reaching towards the flap of her jacket. *"Merde!"*

Geneviève tightened her grip on the gun. "I wouldn't. Mike, take the gun please."

Mike complied, treating Pascale with a disarming smile. "Thank-you so much." To which Pascale returned a furious scowl but refrained from replying. Mike admired her restraint, unsure whether he could emulate it in such circumstances.

Geneviève gestured towards the chair. "Sit, please."

Pascale obeyed wordlessly, the fury evident in her dark eyes.

"Er, what shall I do with this?" Mike asked, brandishing Pascale's pistol.

"Wave it around and look menacing," Geneviève replied.

He grinned. "Yes boss."

"Your friends," Geneviève asked Pascale, "they are Colombians?"

"What do you think?" Pascale replied sullenly.

"I think they are Colombians," Geneviève answered her own question with a self-satisfied smile. "And they are displeased. You keep disturbing company, I think. How many of them are there?"

"Piss off!"

"Tut, tut, a poor loser," Geneviève said, her voice patronising.

"I haven't lost anything," Pascale snapped angrily. "Do you seriously expect to get away? These people don't play games. And don't expect *Senhor* Lopez to help you either..."

"No," Geneviève said easily, unruffled at the reference to Lopez. "I don't suppose they do. How many of them are there?"

"I only heard two car doors open," Mike said.

"Me too. But if one of them was a rear door, we could be dealing with at least three of them, plus *Monsieur* Rousseau, Philip and Frank. And, if they have disposed of Lopez, then there's only the two of us." She ignored Pascale's triumphant sneer. "I will just have to find out for myself." Geneviève smiled sweetly at Pascale who repeated her sneer in response. "Before they wonder where our friend here has got to."

"How long will you be?" Mike asked, rising panic welling in his stomach.

"Not long."

"And what about her?"

Geneviève's voice was casual in response. "You make sure that she behaves herself."

Mike tightened his grip on Pascale's pistol. "Okay." He pointed the pistol waveringly at Pascale as Geneviève walked out of the room. Pascale smiled at him, causing worry to join panic where they danced a lambada with his digestive system. Slowly, feeling her way through the situation, Pascale stood, causing him to take a nervous step backwards.

"Stay where you are," he said tautly.

"Mike, now come on, you wouldn't shoot me. You haven't the guts."

She was right. "Don't *Mike* me. Stay still!"

Pascale took a step forward. "Mike, Mike, you know you wouldn't shoot me."

"Don't tempt your luck. I might surprise you."

Again she stepped forwards, cautiously, with both hands raised and never taking her eyes from the gun as he stepped back and readjusted his hand on the grip. Beads of sweat trickled down his forehead and he licked my lips nervously.

"Now come on, Mike," she said softly. "See sense, you'll never get away with it."

"I'm warning you . . ."

Pascale advanced another step. "Mike, look, the offer Phil made you still stands..."

"Shut up and stay still!"

"I'm not convinced, Mike. You're out of your depth. Admit it. Tempting, isn't it? Rousseau doesn't intend to let you go. You know that, don't you?"

"So you say," he replied, his voice as dry as his tongue.

"A little bike accident, there are plenty of sheer drops hereabouts. You took a bend too fast..."

"I don't take bends too fast."

"Oh," she said derisively. "So you're that bloody fantastic!"

He adjusted his grip on the pistol. "No. Just careful."

"Look," she sighed. "Phil and I can get you out of here alive. You need me."

"Geneviève . . ."

"Oh, come on," she snapped impatiently. "She's only using you. You're nothing to her. You and I can come to an arrangement, can't we?"

She stepped forwards again, causing him to retreat by the same amount. He was rapidly running out of room.

"I don't mean you any harm."

"No," he replied dismissively. "And I've the bruises to prove it. Stay still for Christ's sake or I'll pull the trigger. I mean it!"

Pascale grinned triumphantly. "You haven't even taken the safety catch off."

Mike glanced down at the weapon and she lunged, throwing him back against the wall and forcing his arms up above his head. The shock of slamming into the wall, combined with Pascale's fist ramming into his stomach, loosened his grip on the pistol. Defeated, he collapsed against the wall, retching and gasping. By the time he opened his eyes, he was staring inevitably down the wrong end of the pistol. The gaping maw of the gun barrel grabbed his attention and held it.

"Now. Let's talk diamonds, before *Madame* gets back."

"*Madame* is already back," Geneviève said from the doorway. Pascale turned her head towards the doorway but kept her gun pointing unwaveringly at Mike's head. "Tell me where the diamonds are," she snarled. "Or I'll kill him."

"Drop the gun, Pascale," Geneviève said calmly. The ice in her eyes and the steady grip with which she held her pistol matched the coldness in her voice.

"I'll kill him," Pascale replied.

"Think you can?"

"What?"

Geneviève smiled. "Think you can? Before I kill you? Fancy your chances?"

"Oh God," Mike groaned.

"You wouldn't, we're friends..."

Geneviève said nothing but the corners of her eyes narrowed slightly indicating the end of that particular friendship. In the fraction of a second and the flicker of an eyelid something died and left in its wake a deep regret. They stood there, for aeons, it seemed, in a tableau, before Pascale threw in her chips.

"*Merde*," she said as the tension in the room evaporated.

"*Tant pis.*" Geneviève said with all the sympathy of a Gestapo interrogator.

Mike retrieved the pistol from Pascale's slack grip and motioned her back to the chair. She stepped back but remained standing. Geneviève nodded to the bed.

"Mike, tear that sheet into strips."

He raised his eyebrows in interrogation.

"Tie her up," she explained, gesturing with the pistol. "My friend, sit please."

Sullenly, Pascale complied. Mike pulled the sheet from the bed and proceeded to rip it into strips. Under Geneviève's watchful eye he tied Pascale to the chair, wrapping the last strip about her mouth.

"Sorry," he said, receiving a reproachful stare in response.

"Pick up the gun," Geneviève instructed. "Time we left, I think."

They stepped into the hallway and closed the door behind them, turning the key in the lock. "Mike, I am afraid that you are very much out of your depth," Geneviève smiled.

"You were listening," he accused.

She grinned impishly.

"Sod it," he said. "How did you know she wouldn't shoot?"

"Judge of character. She is a fighter, our Pascale, but not a natural killer. *Monsieur* Rousseau now, is a different proposition. Talking of which, he and Phil are entertaining two Colombians in the front room."

"You looked?"

"Mm," she said, thinking. "Time we weren't here."

Mike turned towards the front of the house. "Suits me."

Geneviève shook her head and pointed to the back entrance. Mike frowned.

"It's this way."

"There's more risk of discovery that way," she replied. "Those Colombians have automatic weapons. I think the back will be safer."

"I really needed to know that," he said sotto voce.

Geneviève smiled. "The back is nearer and I don't want to risk taking them on if I can avoid it."

"I'm all for avoiding it," he said facetiously.

"The sooner we are out of here, the happier I will be."

"I don't wish to sound alarmist, but, where's Frank?"

"I do not know, he went out with Lopez and since then...I am worried." For once Geneviève looked concerned. Mike allowed himself a small moment of satisfaction.

"Great," he said in a stage whisper, glancing towards the back entrance. "They could be in the kitchen."

"Or by the front door."

"It's fifty-fifty, then."

"I've had worse odds."

"Ever lost?"

"Not often."

"Now why don't I find that reassuring? Let's hope your luck holds."

"Luck? Pah!"

"Perhaps we should toss a coin."

Geneviève poked her tongue out at him and turned towards the kitchen while Mike acquiesced with a shrug and followed.

Frank was sitting at the table, eating bread and cheese when Geneviève and Mike burst in. Lopez lay comatose on the floor, a dark stain from a gash on his temple spread ominously across the flagstones.

***

Pascale fumed inwardly at allowing herself to get caught out. She worked at the knots Mike Jenner had made. Fortunately, she thought to herself, he would never make a career as a seaman. She stopped for a moment to listen to their voices outside as they pondered over their escape route.

Either way they are trapped. Ah, so the kitchen it is, then.

As she wriggled her fingers, the knot eased loose. Frank had made no attempt to get Freddie, which was interesting, she thought to herself. As she worked at the bonds, she silently cursed Alain Marchant for her predicament. Geneviève was her friend and that friendship had been strained to breaking point. She grunted with satisfaction and pulled the rest of the makeshift binding away.

She stood and briefly wondered about what to do next now that she was disarmed. In a fraction of a second, she decided to follow the fugitives, then she heard it. Gunfire.

Ah, so maybe Frank didn't put up much resistance, eh?

She was on the point of following when she heard another noise. Sirens.

Damn! That's timing, eh?

She cocked her head and listened. *A helicopter. Alain, I didn't expect that.*

She changed her mind and headed back to the front room. It was all over now anyway. *No more pretences.*

***

"So, I cannot be right all the time," Geneviève said with resignation.

Frank was more surprised to see them than they were to see him. He jumped to his feet, knocking the chair backwards. Staring at Geneviève, he reached for his shoulder holster.

"Don't even think about it," she snapped.

Frank paused uncertainly as he looked from Geneviève to Mike and back again. Then he made a decision, he reached for his gun once more. Mike reacted instinctively and his foot came up sharply and his motorcycle boot connected with Frank's groin accompanied by a crunch of bone. Mike winced with sympathy as Frank whooped in pain and doubled over. Just to make sure, Mike hit him on the base of the neck with the butt of Pascale's pistol and he collapsed in an anaesthetised heap

"Sorry," he said.

Geneviève treated Mike to a pointed stare, so he liberated Frank's handgun from its holster. He reached a finger to Lopez's neck and felt a faint pulse. Looking up at Geneviève he nodded.

"This way," she said, motioning towards the kitchen door. She led the way out into the garden. Once outside, Geneviève broke into a run past the swimming pool around the house towards the front of the building. They could now hear shouts and the sound of breaking glass from a window.

"Go!" Geneviève shouted as the stutter of automatic fire rattled from the broken window. Mike needed no second encouragement. He followed her instruction, running as fast as he could in the direction of the road. Geneviève followed. The shouts and the reports of firearms echoed in his ears as the dust kicked up at his feet in a deadly line.

"They're shooting at us!" he panted.

"I noticed. Keep running, Zig zag!"

"I am, I am!"

While Mike ran, Geneviève threw herself to the ground and returned fire. As he reached the drop to the road he leaped into the air and fell, landing awkwardly and rolling in the ditch at the roadside. Seconds later a breathless Geneviève landed beside him. Without waiting to catch her breath she lifted her head above the incline and rattled off several shots, ducking back when one of the returning bullets landed too close for comfort.

"I'd help," he shouted. "But I've never used one of these before... I figure I'd be more of a danger to us than the opposition."

"Give it to me," she interrupted, taking Frank's gun from his grasp. "Here, load mine."

Mike complied, clipping the magazine into the butt of the pistol, pausing when another noise rose above the gunfire. Frowning he looked up.

"The chopper. And police sirens."

Geneviève followed his gaze. "Ah, reinforcements, they arrive, eh?"

With a swirling tornado of downdraft, the helicopter landed outside the house spewing its occupants. Freddie Mclean clambered from the machine and ambled through the battlefield to where they lay watching the Portuguese police mopping up. Behind him, Alain Marchand alighted from the aircraft and ran towards the house, returning gunfire with the occupants.

"Reckoned you might need a spot of assistance," Freddie smiled laconically.

"Reckon you do too," Mike replied looking past him.

Puzzled Freddie followed his gaze as the Mercedes crashed out of the garage with Phil at the wheel. Mike could make out Rousseau in the passenger seat and Frank in the back. Through a hail of gunfire Estevez's silver Peugeot followed them.

"Christ!" Freddie swore. "Get in the chopper, quick."

As they made their way to the helicopter, two of the Portuguese police along with Alain escorted Pascale out and he helped her into the aircraft ahead of them. Lopez smiled awkwardly, clutching one hand to his bloodied head as he came around from the back of building from the kitchen and joined the others aboard.

"Why, hello," Mike said to Pascale. Pascale treated him to a scowl.

"You tied me up!"

She acquiesced to Alain's shove into the aircraft. Geneviève and Mike followed. As Mike climbed aboard, he wondered what to do with Pascale and Frank's hardware. Shrugging, he dropped them.

"Oh well, couldn't hit a barn door with 'em anyway."

"Come on, Mike," Geneviève shouted impatiently. "We haven't got all day."

Nodding, he hauled himself into the passenger compartment. With a breath-taking whirl they were in the air and below the two cars like toys hurtled in futile flight along the narrow roads. Following them were the Portuguese police cars, lights flashing and sirens sounding. From their vantage point they watched as the pursuit descended the hill into Arouca where Phil nearly collided with an approaching car head on. They were both drifting wide on the bend. As the innocent driver swerved to avoid him, Estevez swerved wide to avoid the near collision and clipped its wing causing the driver to lose control and finish his journey facing the wrong way from the ditch at the roadside.

As they entered the town, they accelerated through the tiny cobbled streets past the Residençial on the left-hand side of the road. More cars swerved to avoid them as they tore through the square leaving a broiling mass of bent and broken metal in their wake.

"I wonder where they are going?" Geneviève asked.

"Porto, I expect," Mike replied absently.

"Why do you say that?" she said sharply.

"Rousseau's got a yacht moored there. Hasn't he, Pascale?"

Pascale said nothing but the flash in her eyes was enough confirmation.

Geneviève stared at Mike and Pascale, horrified. "Why didn't you tell me this before? How did you know?"

Mike shrugged. "Ted told me. Besides, other things kinda got in the way."

"Mike," she snapped furiously. "But that's why the diamonds came to Portugal, they planned to take them out to sea."

"But…"

"Look, the greatest risk from Rousseau's point of view was the British customs. He could never have risked them searching his yacht."

"So I was to take the risk for him," Mike said dryly.

"Both ways. With the removal of frontier controls, you were less likely to be searched travelling by road."

"Except for Spain."

"That was unusual, I admit."

"True," he said flatly.

"Once the stones are here, Rousseau can take them through the Portuguese customs at Porto only, yes?"

"Well, there is something about carrying a British Passport…"

"So, with minimal risk to himself, Rousseau switches the contraband at sea."

"Except they let him have the dope without the diamonds."

"I have a theory about that," Geneviève smiled and looked across at Pascale.

"Oh?" Mike said.

"Rousseau is merely a small part of a larger organisation. Am I not right?" she asked Pascale. Pascale grinned in return but otherwise maintained her self-imposed silence. "The cartels do not, as a rule…" Geneviève continued. "…grant credit. Rousseau is working for them, not himself."

Mike sighed. "Great. So his business empire is just a front, owned by the Colombians."

"So it would seem." She lapsed into silence as she peered out of the window to the road below.

Just beyond the square in the centre of Arouca was a crossroads where Phil turned right to Castelo de Paiva. The road wound through a circuitous route amongst the desiccated trees—often with a loose shale surface and potholes that caused the cars to weave across the road to maintain speed whilst avoiding the worst of the potholes. Further on, the road had been resurfaced and they were able to increase speed, leaving the braking as late as possible, before slicing across the bends, and accelerating away from them. As they descended into Castelo de Paiva, the Mercedes, closely followed by the Peugeot, turned right towards the Rio Douro and the Porto road. Again, the road surface deteriorated as they climbed steadily in the direction of the river.

Entre-os-Rios was a tiny hamlet on the northern bank of the Rio Douro as it turned inland; it was about half a mile wide at this point.

The road dipped steeply before entering the narrow bridge. At the southern edge of the bridge was a distribution site for a quarry situated further upstream, on the northern bank. The sand was moved by barge from the quarry, under the bridge to the distribution centre, and onto the lorries to be transported by road to Porto.

As the helicopter lifted above the last rise before the road began its descent to the bridge, they could see the cars turning onto the bridge, high above the river. Everything was drowned out by the throbbing sound of the rotors slashing the still air. Below, everything was still, apart from a couple of trucks manoeuvring in the yard—the workforce having left for the evening.

As the cars entered the northern end of the bridge, a tanker lorry entered from the southern bank, its silver tank glinting in the evening sunlight. They watched, enthralled, as the drama unfolded below them. Mike was mesmerised.

The tanker sounded its horn. Carried on the still air, the sound was tiny—muted by the distance and the helicopter's engine before it reached them. Mike thought it odd that they could hear it above the noise from the rotors. It seemed as if they were watching the final act of a play unfolding and little details jarred in the consciousness.

Phil steered the Mercedes to the right, then left. Dust kicked up from the vehicle tyres as both he and the tanker driver applied their brakes. The truck jack-knifed and slithered to a stop, punching a hole in the parapet and blocking the bridge. Phil swerved again before careening through the left parapet and hanging motionlessly for what seemed an eternity, before plummeting to the water, a hundred feet below, accompanied by chunks of masonry. As if all the other noises were drowned out by the drama they could hear the distant splash, carried on the still air, as the car hit the river and slid below the surface.

The Peugeot, too close behind Phil to manoeuvre, spun broadside and slammed into the stationary truck. It came to a halt accompanied by a rending of metal and crackling glass, finishing up with its left side jammed under the trailer. The truck's cab hung precariously over the edge, poking through the gap it had smashed in the parapet.

"Goddamn," Mike said.

The helicopter's pilot manoeuvred his aircraft towards the bridge while the police officer gabbled into the radio requesting emergency assistance. Gently, the pilot brought the chopper to a stand by the gates of the sand works. As they dismounted they could hear the distant sirens of emergency vehicles. Freddie clambered out in front of them.

"Stay here," he commanded. Geneviève and Mike ignored him and followed onto the bridge. Freddie stopped by the Peugeot and looked briefly, beckoning to the Portuguese policeman who peered disinterestedly at the Colombians. Both were dead. The passenger lay across the bonnet, half in, half out of the crazed hole in the windscreen. His ponytailed black hair was sticky with blood and his eyes stared blankly from a head twisted at an unnatural angle—the shock of his demise still evident on his features.

His companion had been crushed under the trailer of the tanker. Geneviève tried to peer into the car, but the crushed roof made investigation impossible. The engine block lying where the driver's seat was told its own story. Estevez would no longer be worried about the stolen diamonds, nor the cocaine.

They made their way to the broken barrier and looked over. The water remained still—concealing its uninvited guests.

"I wonder if they'll make it?" Geneviève mused.

"Phil's got his head screwed on," Mike replied. "If they open one of the windows and allow the car to half fill with water, the pressure will even enough for them to open one of the doors."

"What about the trucker?"

"Let's see," Freddie said. He cupped his hands about his mouth and called out. "Hello!" There was no reply. His nostrils twitched. A familiar odour hung in the still air. "Petrol," he said with alarm. "I'm gonna look."

"No," Pascale pushed past him.

"What?" Freddie started, but she was too fast. The policeman who remained with her in the helicopter ran up rubbing his jaw.

"I am sorry *Senhor*, she…"

"Never mind," Freddie replied, moving into Pascale's path. In a fraction of a second she stepped back and drop kicked him in the abdomen. Whooping, Freddie collapsed. While they were distracted, Pascale clambered over the broken parapet and edged along to the cab where she carefully climbed onto the fuel tank. The side window was open, so she reached for it with her left hand, following with her left foot to the cab step.

"Pascale! Come back here!" Alain ordered, but she ignored him.

"Careful, Pascale," Geneviève said nervously.

"Never mind me," Pascale replied. "Get back from that car, it could go up anytime."

Geneviève stepped back warily, never taking her eyes from Pascale while Mike looked on as he helped Freddie to his feet.

With her left hand gripping the window opening, Pascale let go with her right hand and reached for the door handle. The truck lurched with a sickening scraping sound causing her to lose her footing. As she grabbed the handle, the door swung open and she swung with it, crashing into the front of the cab as it reached the limit of its swing. For a moment she swung by her hands above the river.

"Damn!"

"Pascale!" Geneviève cried out reaching for the parapet.

"No," Mike left Freddie to his own devices and placed a restraining hand on her shoulder.

"I'm okay, I'm okay," Pascale panted. Hanging from the door by her fingertips. She looked down at her feet, swaying in space, high above the Rio Douro. She groaned. Straining, she hauled herself up and wrapped her left arm around the door pillar, swinging her feet in an attempt to close the door. Exhausted, she hung there.

The truck driver peered cautiously at her through the open doorway. "*Senhora*?"

Gasping for breath, Pascale asked, "You are okay?"

The driver nodded, clutching a handkerchief over a cut above his left eye. "Yes. I knocked my head, I think."

"Well, don't look down."

The driver looked down. The man's eyes widened in panic as he scrabbled away from the door opening.

The truck lurched, sending Pascale once more into the void above the river. Scrabbling with her feet she maintained a tenuous grasp on the door.

"Stay still! This thing's unstable enough as it is."

"*Senhora, Senhora*, I…"

"It's okay, just don't do anything sudden."

"There was nothing I could do, *Senhora*."

"I know," Pascale panted in reply, the fatigue draining her dark complexion. "It doesn't matter, not now, anyway."

"Pascale," Alain called out. Pascale looked across at him. Flames were licking around the Peugeot. "The car…"

The Peugeot erupted into a fireball, singeing Mike's skin and cremating its occupants. The wave of hot air blasted the truck's door outwards on its hinges and once more Pascale was thrown against the front of the cab. Freddie and Mike joined Geneviève as she ran away from the conflagration and towards the southern bank.

Alain remained close to the burning car, attempting to shield his face from the heat as he looked across at Pascale clinging to the truck door.

"Pascale, jump," he called out.

Pascale lifted her head and stared at the driver. "The way I see it, *Monsieur*, we have two choices."

"*Senhora?*"

"We can stay here and get fried…"

"Or?"

"Or we can jump and get drowned."

The driver hesitated, the fear naked in his eyes.

"Driver?"

"Yes?"

"What does this tanker carry?"

"Aviation fuel."

Pascale's eyes widened in alarm. "*Merde!*"

She reached into the cab and grasped the driver's shoulder hauling him out of the cab launching him into space and down to the cold clutches of the Douro. For a brief moment she hung there looking across to the bridge where the others stood.

"Geneviève I…" The rest was lost in the dull whump of the conflagration on the bridge as it flung the cab far out across the river. Showers of flaming debris fell about us as we dived to the ground.

Aeons later as the others dragged themselves to their feet Mike saw tears streaming down Geneviève's face.

174

"She was my friend," she said simply.

He nodded dumbly. "In the end," he said, finally finding his voice, "she proved it."

Alain patted her briefly on the shoulder. "She always was. She was one of mine." He held out his warrant card.

"She was GSIGN?"

"Yes. I'm sorry, but you could not be told. She was under strict instructions to maintain her cover at all times."

"GSIGN?" Mike asked.

"Groupement de sécurité et d'intervention de la Gendarmerie nationale. We are a specialist unit investigating organised crime. Pascale was an undercover operative. She was working as a corrupt police officer in Rousseau's pay. You are a surprise, *Monsieur,* you discovered much about the operation. Perhaps we should be more careful around you, eh?" He sighed heavily. "I have lost a good operative today."

Back at the sandworks they could hear the chugging note of a motor launch. Mike turned and watched, until it drew alongside. In the fading daylight, a GNR Sergeant reached down and secured the boat before his colleague motioned the sole survivor to step onto the shore. Phil stepped out wrapped in a blanket and escorted by the GNR sergeant as he was guided to the helicopter. The trucker followed. Phil looked up at Mike as he stumbled ashore. There was a flash of anger, but no words.

Alain looked from one to the other. "Rousseau?"

Phil shook his head, the barest of movements, before his eyes slid away and returned to their study of the ground at his feet.

"And Pascale?" Alain asked weakly, hoping vaguely that she might have survived, but believing that she hadn't. Phil looked across at the bridge and the Douro, quiet and inky in the fading light.

"No. I saw no sign."

Further up the bank, an ambulance crew were rushing down to the shore.

Pascale! Alain ran, his heart pounding, hoping that she was alive.

***

Pascale slid down into the murky waters, her head pounding from the explosion, the current caught at her feet, pulling her further into the dark depths. The cold of the water brought her to her senses and she swam upward towards the light, gasping for air as she broke the surface. She trod water for a moment as she looked back. Phil was being pulled on to the boat and no one was looking her way.

She swam steadily to the shore, where she pulled herself out of the water and collapsed on the beach. Somewhere she thought she could hear someone calling her name.

"We thought you were dead," Alain was saying.

Pascale pulled herself up and sat, shivering from the cold water and coughing it out of her lungs. She could see two paramedics dashing across. She looked up to the bridge and watched as the searchers headed back to their vehicles and the helicopter took off.

"Well, I seem to be here," she said.

Alain stood as the paramedics took over, wrapping Pascale in a foil blanket to contain her body heat.

"Get back, *Senhor*," one of them ordered. Alain backed away and watched as they worked.

"It seems to me," he said, "that you being dead might be a useful benefit for us."

Pascale looked at him. "I won't be on the pay sheet?" she grinned.

"I wasn't thinking of that," he said. "However, yes, a dead undercover agent could be very useful indeed."

***

On the opposite bank near a little inlet where the river lapped against a rocky shore, a head broke the surface. Fábián Rousseau lifted his arms and started to swim. As he made land, he twisted round and looked across at the far bank. No one was looking his way. He saw Phil being bundled out of the boat and into an ambulance. One of the police officers accompanied him. No one could see Rousseau.

"So," he murmured to himself. "They all think I am dead. That could prove very useful. Very useful indeed."

Chapter 13

Pascale crossed the street and walked into the club again, her eyes blinking as they adjusted to the low light after the glare of the sun outside. She descended the stairs to the club below.

Paccard was still at the bar cleaning glasses ready for the evening customers. The assassin was talking to him. He turned as she walked into the bar, her pistol held out at arm's length.

"Hello Freddie."

Freddie McLean stared at her and smiled. "Pascale. So, you have figured it out, eh?"

"Yes, I figured it out. Too many coincidences. You just happened to be there on the Isle of Man. But you were there all along, weren't you?"

He didn't deny it.

"At first, when I saw you I was relieved to see a familiar face —even one from so long ago. But slowly it dawned on me. Rousseau wasn't the player here, was he?" She looked across at Paccard.

Paccard returned the stare with barely disguised contempt.

"Paccard, Rousseau, either way, it was never you who ran this little show—just like that time in Portugal. It was the Columbians then. How do you think the cartels will feel knowing that you survived, eh?"

Rousseau remained silent. He stared at her with barely concealed anger suffusing his face. She thought she saw a vein pulsing on his temple. Freddie was clearly enjoying the little show. But then, she thought, he would. It was always his show.

"Alain Marchand always thought you were his other player in the field—you were supposedly working for Radfield. But you weren't, were you? You never were."

Freddie smiled. "A costly mistake for him."

Pascale nodded. Alain's death had always gone unexplained. Now, at least, she knew.

"Why did you play along that time in Portugal?"

He shrugged, it cost nothing to satisfy her curiosity. "The game was up. The diamonds were gone—I assumed that your partner had got them back to the UK police. So showing my hand made no sense. I could carry on playing the undercover cop for a while. Meantime, I was building my little empire. When Fábián turned up out of the blue a short while later, I took him back on and set him up here as the boss. I prefer the shadows myself. You lot all believed that he was in charge, so no one ever looked my way. Until now."

Pascale smiled. "Yes, it took me a while, eh? I should have realised earlier, Rousseau never had the *cojones* to kill the way that you do, Freddie.

He was happy enough to indulge in some physical violence, but you have a coldness in you that he just doesn't have. That's why he went to gaol for Geneviève's murder for you. That was what I always thought so out of place. It took me years to work it out. He is a coward. He always was."

Rousseau snapped then. He reached down to the bar and pulled out a gun from under the counter and started to lift it, but Freddie reached out and pushed it down, slapping it to the bar top with a loud snap.

"No! We need her alive."

Pascale gripped the handle of the pistol a little more tightly. The bones in her trigger finger were white pressing against the skin. The tension in the air was as stifling as the heat outside. Then she lowered the muzzle again.

"Why?"

"Because we need you to find the Koh-I-Noor. And the rest of the stones," Freddie said easily. "Paccard here—well, Rousseau—would still like it in his collection, wouldn't you, old son?"

Rousseau nodded. "I spent years of my life inside thinking that stone was back in the tower and it was out there all along. I want it now. I've earned it."

"Really? Earned it? How? By having Geneviève killed?"

"That was her own fault," he said. "She was warned to stay away, but she just couldn't resist."

Freddie waved a hand. "Much as this reminiscing is fascinating, the point here is that we want what is ours and you have the key as it were."

Pascale shook her head. "But I have no idea. She did not tell me. All I know is that the Koh-I-Noor is still a fake. Beyond that, I know no more than you do."

Freddie leaned against the bar and turned to Rousseau. "Could you get me a whisky, old bean?"

Rousseau nodded and reached for the optics. Freddie scowled. "Oh, please! The real stuff if you don't mind."

Rousseau smiled and reached under the bar, withdrawing a single malt. He poured the amber liquid into a tumbler and pushed it across to Freddie who lifted the glass to the light, admiring the drink before taking a sip and nodding appreciatively.

"I was rather hoping that you would lead us to the loot," he said. "That was the whole point of setting this little trail for you."

"I said I have no idea where they are," she repeated. As she spoke, Pascale could see a shadowy figure behind Rousseau, lurking in the half-light, somewhere between this world and the next.

Good God! Will he never stop stalking me?

Death watched the proceedings, smoking one of his foul-smelling cigarettes.

"Stalking? Do you think so?"

Yes, she snapped silently at him. *Now go away.*

178

Death tried to look hurt, failed dismally, and shrugged as he took another drag at the cigarette and watched the proceedings unfold as if it was entertainment that demanded his attention. Which, he thought to himself, in a way, it was.

"Ah, but…" Freddie was saying, "you have the means to find out. After all, your erstwhile partner knew where they were. We had assumed that she returned them to Radfield and he got them back to their original owners. Now it appears not. So, what did she do with them, eh?"

"I have no idea, I told you."

"But you can work it out."

"Why should I?"

Freddie took another sip at the whisky and sighed. "Because, sweetheart, sooner or later, I will come for you."

"How do I know you won't do that anyway?"

"You don't."

Pascale lowered her gun slightly. "How? How am I supposed to know this?"

Freddie smiled. "I'm sure you will work it out."

"Geneviève has been telling you."

She took a sharp intake of breath. "How…?"

Freddie caught her gaze and turned to the mirror, but saw nothing. "What?"

She shook her head, "Nothing."

"Well, just go. Go on, find the loot."

Death grinned from behind the mirror. *"Just search your mind. It's all there. It always has been."*

Pascale stepped back and lifted the pistol again seeing only the two faces grinning back at her. She looked across to the shadows behind Rousseau. Death was nonchalantly sharpening his scythe with a whetstone, apparently unconcerned. He looked up at her and winked as if there was a shared knowledge between them.

"Search your mind."

For a moment or two, she looked from one to the other, before lowering the pistol and flipping the safety catch back on.

"Go on," Freddie said. "Go and find the loot."

"I will come back for you. Our business is not finished."

As she reached the door leading to the stairway, something occurred to her. She turned back. "Just one thing…"

"Aye?"

"It was you who tried to sabotage Geneviève's bike in France?"

Freddie nodded. "Of course. You were supposedly on our side. She was the only threat. Mike could have been dealt with easily enough. But you spoiled it." He shrugged and sipped the whisky. "Water under the bridge now, anyway."

Feeling stunned by the exchange, she walked out of the club, up the stairs, and into the searing light of the Mediterranean sun. Still dazed, she made her way across the street to where she had parked the bike.

Genevieve has been telling you. Just search your mind. It's all there. It always has been.

What had she been missing? What had Geneviève been telling her?

She mounted the BMW and started it up. The twin cylinder engine fired into life with a satisfying grumble. She selected first gear with the typical BMW "clunk" and released the clutch as she joined the traffic flowing through the city. She headed out onto the road to Arles, from where turned west onto the smaller roads that traversed the Camargue towards Montpellier. While these roads were slower, on a bike they were more satisfying and she let the rhythm of the ride settle her mind. The synchronicity between machine and rider allowed her mind to wander through the past, seeking whatever it was Freddie was so convinced that she had missed.

On this back route she had the road to herself. As she rode, a flamboyance of flamingos rose up from the flats, taking flight. She pulled over and stopped to watch as they lifted themselves into the air, their long necks stretched out before them and their great wings flapping lazily as their squawking carried on the still air, the pink of their feathers stark against the blue-vitriol sky. And Pascale watched, awe-struck, despite having seen it so many times before. Sometimes the majesty of nature was so magnificent that all she could do was stop and stare. And in that moment of transcendental beauty came clarity.

"It really is quite marvellous, isn't it"? Death said.

Pascale turned to look at him. She hadn't noticed the Ducati pull up alongside her, so absorbed was she in the moment.

"Yes."

Death turned his eyes skywards after the departing birds. *"The world is a magnificent place, so full of wonder."* He sighed heavily. *"And yet also so full of heartaches."*

Pascale looked at him, seeing something that she hadn't before. A lost soul.

"You know what you are looking for now, don't you?"

"Yes," she said. "I know now."

***

The flat was empty when she arrived home. There was no sign of Guillaume. She assumed that he was out on some errand, so went through to the office and started searching through the drawers of paperwork until she found what she was looking for.

"It took you long enough," Geneviève said.

Pascale held up the postcard and looked at it. "A pin to see the peepshow," she said.

"Yes."

Pascale studied the card. It must have been thirty years old, now, she thought to herself. But she recognised the place. It was as if no time had passed at all. That sunlit square thirty years ago. So that's where they were—and Geneviève had marked the spot.

She looked up, but Geneviève had gone, like a passing beam of light that vanishes when the sun goes behind a cloud. She sighed and turned to walk out, slipping the postcard into her pocket. She had just finished packing a few things for the journey and shouldered the pannier bags when she heard the door open.

"Guillaume."

He turned and looked in her direction.

"Pascale?"

"Yes, my dear. I have to go away for a few days, but I'll be back soon."

She kissed him lightly on the cheek and went out.

Guillaume reached up and touched his cheek where her kiss had landed and looked back at the closed door as it closed behind his evanescent wife.

Once outside, she slipped the pannier bags into the panniers and rode west heading along the coast road that eventually turned northwards to Toulouse. Rather than crossing into Spain, she stayed north of the Pyrenees, passing through Carcassonne, stopping overnight in Pau.

Early next morning she carried on riding west until she reached the Atlantic coast, turning south to cross into Spain at Hendaye. Unlike thirty years previously, the crossing point was deserted. She wondered vaguely what had happened to the two border guards they had met that day, but presumed that, by now, they would have both been retired for several years.

Once out of San Sebastian, she picked up the road that runs across the Spanish plain. This time, though, the single carriageway road with its indifferent surface carrying convoys of trucks was a smooth dual carriageway road, making passing those trucks much simpler and the progress much easier. By late afternoon she was on the border at Vilar Formoso. The guesthouse they had stayed at in 1987 no longer existed, but she found another and rested after the long ride.

That evening, she sat listening to the sound of the cicadas and relaxing with a cool drink, remembering another such evening three decades earlier and the company she shared it with.

"Hasn't changed much," Geneviève said.

Pascale took a sip of her drink and nodded towards the derelict hotel across the road. "That was a three-star hotel back then. Look at it now."

Geneviève followed her gaze. In the fading light, the once smart hotel was now crumbling. Earlier in the evening, Pascale had walked over to it and looked through the windows. Inside, everything was as it had been left—tables laid for breakfast now coated in dust. The windows likewise were dusty and some of the panes cracked. A desolate place that stood in testament to its past glory, like a land-bound Mary Celeste.

"A bit like us, eh?" Geneviève said.

"Pah!"

Pascale finished her drink and retired for the night. It had been a long day and she was weary. Tomorrow she would finally lay her ghost to rest.

The following day was bright and clear. Pascale rose early feeling refreshed. There was no sign of Geneviève, but she had long since given up worrying about whether she would see her or not. Likewise Death didn't seem to want to put in an appearance for which she was mildly relieved.

The old N16 road that wound a circuitous route through the hills no longer existed, having been replaced by a motorway. Now the A25 bypassed Guarda and the little towns and villages along the way. Speed had replaced the essence of the journey. Although, on this occasion, Pascale was less concerned about the journey than she was about the destination.

***

Viseu, August 2018

It was late morning by the time Pascale arrived in Viseu. The market place car park was much as she recalled, although the rough surface was now paved. She pulled the bike into a bay and switched off the engine. She walked across to a bench and sat down. She fished the postcard out of her pocket and looked at it. A typical tourist picture of the market square intended to provide the best possible view of the town, while at the same time being bland and evenly lit. And at the base of one of the trees lining the square was a pinhole.

"So, here we are," she said to herself. She walked back to the bike and opened one of the panniers, taking out a small hand trowel.

Then she went to the foot of the tree and started to dig among the roots. Puzzled, she worked around the roots, but each time there was nothing there. Something must be wrong. Had she made a mistake? Had she got it completely wrong and made this journey for nothing? Frantically, she dug, searching for the bounty that clearly wasn't there.

"It must be here. It must be!"

"It isn't. It never was."

She looked up. "I wondered when you would show up. "Geneviève left me clues."

Death shook his head. *"No, that was all you."*

"What?"

"It was always you."

"I don't understand."

Death sighed. *No, I don't suppose that you do. So we must go back to where this all started."* He lifted his hand and snapped two bony fingers together.

***

Pascale felt the cold dark waters of the Douro drawing her down, the current below the surface dragged her deeper and deeper. She tried to shake her head, but it felt heavy. She tried to breathe but her lungs filled with water and she coughed it up and her head felt light. She pushed down with her arms, fighting her way to the surface.

Eventually she found herself on the shore. She lifted her head, coughing river water from her lungs. She could see a figure standing over her.

"Alain?"

"No. Alain is still on the bridge."

"But…"

Death leaned down and reached out a hand. She pushed herself up and took it standing beside him. She turned and looked back.

"No!"

"Yes, I am afraid so."

Alain was running down the shore having seen her from the bridge. Two paramedics had arrived before him. One looked up and shook his head. Alain put his hands to his head and crouched down beside the inert form.

"But the last thirty years," she said.

Death sighed. *"Thirty years. Thirty years or thirty minutes. Could have been thirty seconds… You see, my dear, time is meaningless here. But you have spent that time building a world somewhere between life and death in which you were chasing the answer to a problem that had already been solved. You had a ghost to lay to rest."*

"Geneviève?"

He shook his head.

"It was me all along, wasn't it?"

"Yes."

"But… Why… I asked you last Christmas if I was dead and you said…"

"I told you that you weren't ready to come with me. Which you weren't. You had not accepted the reality. You were living in a world of your own creation somewhere between this world and the next. I had no option but to let things play out until you found out for yourself. Creative of you, I must say. You even had off-stage events to fill the narrative. That was impressive. I've not come across that before."

She looked at him. "I don't understand."

"That little thing with the assassin and Frank. Frank died here, the same day as you, but you could not have known that. Hence the elaborate story. As with Phil's murder."

"Frank died here? What about the others?"

Death sighed again. It was one of those sighs that could be felt across the ages, where the ripples of time meet the outer edges of space and the stardust swirls in time. *"Frank died here. Phil was killed a few years later in a prison fight. Rousseau died in prison as well, while serving time for Geneviève's murder."*

"And Freddie? The assassin?"

Freddie wasn't an assassin. He was exactly what he said he was. You needed a villain and you manufactured him. But did it not occur to you that it was all a little too convenient, his finding you on the Isle of Man? You created that. He was never there. Everything that has happened since this moment has been a product that you created. None of it was real. Sometimes your world touched the real world and people sensed your presence and you were able to see them."

"And the stones? The Koh-I-Noor? They were fakes."

"Genevieve swapped them that night in Parthenay. She got them back to Radfield and they were returned to their rightful owners. There was no trail, no hidden gems, and no pin to see the peepshow. It was all you. No one else. Your McGuffin if you like."

Something occurred to her then that filled her with overwhelming sadness. "Guillaume?"

Ah, yes, Guillaume. That is one place where you have been touching the real world. You have haunted him for thirty years. He has sensed your presence. Remember when you kissed him and he touched his cheek? He has felt you beside him as if you had never gone, but he was alone."

She stood there, a tear running down her cheek as she mourned for everything that she had lost. "Guillaume...."

"Is it not time to let him go? So that he can let you go?"

He reached out a bony hand. Pascale looked back at Alain as he stood watching the paramedics zipping up the body bag. She reached out and took the proffered hand. It seemed oddly soft and gentle.

"Come," he said hurriedly, lest she change her mind. *"Time to go. Geneviève is waiting."*

She started to follow, but something made her stop. "No. Wait."

Death turned. *"What?"*

"Something's not right here, is it? You're in far too much of a hurry. You've been lying to me."

For just a brief second he hesitated. It was the barest flicker, but enough. Enough for her to realise that she was right. Death swore softly to himself. His elaborate plan was unravelling before his eyes.

"Oh, my God! I'm right, aren't I? This isn't what is supposed to happen."

Death had the grace to look sheepish and he shuffled as he looked at her. *"Actually, this is precisely what was supposed to happen."*

"Then I wasn't supposed to live?"

He sighed. *"For thirty years, I've been trying to right this wrong. Waiting for the moment to correct it. Now, can we please...?"*

"How?"

Death fished in his cape and pulled out a smartphone.

"This!" he spat derisively. *"Ever since the IT guys took over it's all gadgetry and apps. And can you get anyone to fix it when it goes wrong?"*

Pascale frowned. "But they hadn't been invented in 1987."

"I do not exist in linear time as you do," Death replied dismissively. *"I am a supernatural being. I told you one that I can do as I please with time. Helpful in a job like this. Anyway, the phone app sent me to the wrong time. I arrived after Alain had found you alive."*

"And this charade? These visitations? These clues? They were all meant to bring me back here? To this moment in time at this place? So that you could put right your cock-up of thirty years ago?"

Death didn't deny it. *"The universe is what it is. I cannot afford to upset the timeline. And it wasn't my cock-up, I'll have you know."*

"But you have upset the timeline. And has anything drastic happened as a consequence?"

Death hesitated again.

"It didn't, did it?"

He shook his head. *"Fortunately, this time, no. Subtle ones that may be noticed if I do not correct them. So you must now come with me."*

Pascale stood her ground. "No. I don't think so, do you?"

"I have to think about the timeline."

"Stuff the timeline. I've lived this past thirty years. I've had a career, married... Saved lives, remember?"

"And I'm sorry."

"And you think that you can just put it all right and that's all okay?" Something else occurred to her.

"The diamonds. Geneviève didn't send them back? Did she? And all that stuff about me being dead all this time and creating a parallel existence? All bullshit!"

Death looked at the ground and shuffled his feet. *"Bang to rights, I guess. But it changes nothing. You still need to come with me. You were supposed to die here, now. In this moment."*

"What did you do with them? Where are they?"

Death fished in the folds of his cavernous cape and pulled out the packet that had been the cause of so much trouble.

"I dug them up before you got there. Sorry." His shoulders slumped as he lifted his arms in a gesture of submission. *"I need to correct my mistake—well, strictly speaking, the IT Guys' mistake. You need to die here, today, in this place. It is the way of the universe."*

Pascale shook her head. "The universe has been just dandy for this past thirty years. So, you being an all-powerful supernatural being, you can put it right and let me live."

He made a mistake. He hesitated once more.

"You can!"

He nodded and she was sure there was a hint of dejection. *"I can, but I will not. You should have died here thirty years ago—in this moment. I need…"*

"I think not." She folded her arms and stared at him and he recognised that pugnacious stare, one that would not be brooked.

"We appear to be at a stalemate."

Then something occurred to her. "I'll give you a chance."

Death raised an eyebrow—one that he did not have. He wondered what game she was playing.

Pascale sat on the sandy beach and gestured him to do likewise. Puzzled, he slumped down beside her and crossed his bony legs, grunting with the effort.

"What game are you playing?"

"Poker." She fished in a jacket pocket and withdrew a pack of cards. She shuffled them and instructed him to divide the diamonds equally between them.

"What about the big one?"

"I'll have that."

He raised his eyebrows.

"I have more to lose."

Death could not deny her logic.

"So, we play. Winner takes all. I win, I get my life back. You win, I go with you. Yes?"

He nodded as she cut the pack. Then something occurred to her. "If I get my life back, I can make changes… Geneviève…"

"No! Absolutely not. If you win, the past thirty years will exist as you now recall them, but you will be unable to change anything. That is my only condition."

Pascale thought about it for a moment. Then she nodded. "Okay, I agree. Five card hand, Ace high." She turned over the half pack to reveal the King of Hearts. Death drew a deuce.

"My deal," she said.

She dealt the cards and they played. Steadily she lost as Death's pile of diamonds grew larger and hers grew smaller. Death smiled. This was going to be easy.

186

Eventually, she was left with only the Koh-I-Noor. She tossed it onto the pile. "Call."

Death turned over his cards with a triumphant grin. At last he could set the universe straight.

"Straight Flush." He stood and lifted his scythe. *"Well, my dear, amusing though it has been, it is time…"*

"Not so fast."

He stopped and his heart sank.

She turned over her hand.

Chapter 14

It was late morning by the time Pascale arrived in Viseu. The market place car park was much as she recalled. She pulled the bike into a bay and switched off the engine. She walked across to a bench and sat down. She fished the postcard out of her pocket and looked at it. A typical tourist picture of the market square intended to provide the best possible view of the town, while at the same time being bland and evenly lit. And at the base of one of the trees lining the square was a pinhole.

"So, here we are," she said to herself.

"Quite so," Genevieve replied.

Pascale looked across at her as she sat at the opposite end of the bench. "You led me here."

"I was beginning to wonder, but eventually you got there."

"A pin to see the peepshow was a bit obscure, don't you think?"

"Pascale, my old friend, you are a detective. Besides, I enjoyed the game."

"Pah! Why here? Why so long?"

"At the time, it was simply to secure them where they would not be found. Then things got in the way. We thought you had been killed and I just never had the time to get back here and retrieve them. By the time you came back to life after your stint with the GIGN, it no longer seemed to matter. I felt there was enough blood on them, so best left here."

"You could have told Radfield."

Geneviève shrugged. "The originals had been replaced with fakes. No one seemed too concerned about recovering them. As I said, life just got in the way."

"Not to mention death."

"That, too."

Pascale rose and walked back to the bike and opened one of the panniers, taking out a small hand trowel.

Then she went to the foot of the tree and started to dig. Eventually she found it. Still hidden underneath one of the roots, where Geneviève had stashed it thirty years previously she found the little package that they had taken from Mike's Yamaha that night in Parthenay.

She opened the packet and looked at the stones, their facets shining in the sunlight for the first time in three decades. She lifted the large stone to the light.

"This is what it was all about, eh? This is what Rousseau so desired."

Geneviève stood beside her and looked down at the find. "What will you do now?"

"Return them. But first one last thing to do."

Geneviève sighed and then she was gone. Pascale knew that she would see her no more. Her ghost was finally at peace.

To no one in particular, but to someone who she once met, she said, "My ghost is finally laid to rest."

***

The club was as dingy as when she last saw it. Rousseau looked up as she walked in.

"You have the diamonds?" he asked.

"Where is Freddie?"

"I'm here," Freddie said, walking out from the office behind the bar. "Let's see them."

Pascale fished in a pocket and took out the packet, dropping it onto the bar. Freddie snatched it up and opened it pouring the contents out onto the bar top.

"Finally. After all these years." He picked up the Koh-I-Noor and handed it to Rousseau. "Yours, I believe?"

Rousseau greedily grabbed the gem and held it up to the light, admiring the facets as they reflected the little light there was in the room. While they pored over the stolen loot, Pascale reached behind her and carefully withdrew the Beretta from her waistband, allowing her hand to drop to her side, loosely gripping the pistol.

Freddie looked at his business partner with barely disguised contempt.

"The problem with you, Fábián, is that you are weak. You always were. Time, I think, to end our business relationship. You have outlived your usefulness, my old friend."

Rousseau detected the menace in his voice and turned to Freddie who took a pistol out of his shoulder holster.

"No!" There was a moment when he looked about him frantically for an escape or a weapon, but it was futile.

"I'm sorry, but time to move on and I'd rather like to have that for myself."

Freddie pulled the trigger and Rousseau fell back, collapsing on the floor. He twitched briefly then lay still.

"Ah," Freddie remarked casually. "The end of a beautiful friendship."

Freddie turned then to Pascale. "Well, much as it's been a pleasure doing business and all that, it's time we went our separate ways as well. I'll spare you the pain that Frank went through. Clean and quick. I liked you, I really did."

Pascale smiled, then sighed. "Freddie, *really*? You are so predictable."

She heard footsteps coming down the corridor behind the bar and a door burst open and Bernard came into the room, his gun held up ready to shoot.

190

Freddie hesitated then. Her smile unnerved him momentarily and momentarily was all she needed. She lifted her Beretta and pulled the trigger. There was a brief moment of surprise on Freddie's face as the bullet plunged into his forehead and he went back against the glass mirror that ran along the back of the bar and slumped lifeless to the floor. She looked beyond him into the mirror and nodded at the shady apparition lurking in its shadowy half-world. Death lifted a bony finger in salute and faded away. She thought that she would not see him again in this world. She was sure in that moment as he faded from view that she could hear an echo of his voice *"You hustled me…"*

She turned the gun on Bernard. "Put the gun down, *Monsieur.*"

Bernard hesitated for a fraction of a second as he thought about his options, limited though they were, given that he was staring at the barrel of a handgun. Then he heard it. The sound of sirens. The game was up.

"Do you think I am so stupid to either trust any of you or to come here without planned backup?"

Bernard slumped his shoulders and complied. A moment later, Patrice Laurent came into the bar accompanied by heavily armed GIGN officers.

"Well?" He looked around him at Freddie and Rousseau slumped dead on the floor and Bernard with his hands in the air and the recovered diamonds on the bar top.

"You have everything under control, I see." He nodded to the officers who lowered their automatic weapons and retreated upstairs.

Pascale nodded and smiled. "I see you arrived in time to clear up."

Patrice grinned. "I expected nothing less. So, this retirement thing? How is that working out?"

Epilogue

Blaenau Ffestiniog, Wales, May 2019

The sky, what could be seen of it, was as grey as the slate tips that surrounded the village and the station. Rain came in gusts, soaking the dull, grey landscape.

Pascale and Guillaume pulled up their bikes outside the small station building and leaned them on the sidestands. Pascale slipped off the BMW and looked across at her companion. Like her, he was wearing lightweight waterproofs over his leathers. He dismounted the Yamaha Tracer and grimaced. He lifted the front of his helmet and water ran down his face, dripping off his three-day stubble.

"My boots leak," he said miserably.

For an answer, Pascale pulled off her gloves and turned them upside down and watched as the water streamed out of them. She sighed. This wasn't quite how she had planned things.

Guillaume looked across at the station building. "Shall we get something to drink?" he asked, nodding towards the café.

"Yes," she replied. "Good idea."

They locked the bikes and made their way through the pouring rain to the shelter of the café.

"Find a seat, I'll get some drinks," Guillaume said.

Pascale made her way to a window table and peeled off her wet waterproofs and sat. She stared out of the window at the railway line that disappeared into the murky, misty, rain-sodden mountains. Above, the sky was obscured by low cloud that clung to the top of the mountain. The rain lashed the platform, bounding in the air, drenching the atmosphere.

"Here," Guillaume said, placing a steaming mug before her. He took a sip of his own before divesting his own waterproofs. He pulled a face.

"English coffee," he muttered.

"Welsh," she corrected absently.

"Welsh, English, no matter, it is disgusting. How dare they call it coffee. It resembles dishwater."

She laughed at his contempt for the British version of the drink. She turned her gaze to the platform again.

"Why are we here, remind me?" he asked.

"Someone I met once. Said I should come. Look at the trains."

"Anyone I know?"

She shook her head. "I thought I would come anyway."

As she watched a train pulled up into the station, all burnished brass and bright red paintwork, hissing steam and smelling of oil and coal as it came to a stand. The doors of the carriages opened and the passengers made a dash for shelter, splashing their way across the platform to the café.

She frowned. She was sure… She blinked. There was a shadowy figure standing beside the train, sharpening his scythe with a whetstone. He looked up at the café and caught her eye. He lifted a hand to his brow before boarding the train.

"Pascale."

"Mmm?"

"Pascale, sweetheart, you were miles away."

"Sorry. What?"

"I was saying… The next time you decide that we should go on a bike trip, maybe let me decide the destination, eh?"

About the Author

Mark Ellott is a freelance trainer and assessor having worked in the rail industry delivering track safety training and assessment as well as providing consultancy services in competence management. He is also a motorcycle instructor, delivering training for students who require compulsory basic training and direct access courses and recently joined with a colleague to buy a motorcycle training school, which is now taking up most of his time.

He writes fiction in his spare time. Mostly, his fiction consists of short stories crossing a range of genres and he has published collections of stories in "Blackjack" and "Sinistré, the Morning Cloud Chronicles". His first novel, "Ransom" was published in March 2017. "Rebellion" followed soon after and "Resolution" is his third novel.

Ransom - A novel set in modern Bristol.

It's been several weeks since Stephanie Ross' partner went missing and she is worried. Was he just on another of his drunken benders or was there something more sinister going on?

Then people start turning up dead on the local railway line.

As she worries about the whereabouts of Roddy Schaeffer, a nasty ransom virus is threatening not only her business but that of her clients. And who is Louis J Madison and what does he want?

During a few sultry weeks in July, Stephanie finds herself fighting not only to keep her computer support business and her clients... but also her life.

Rebellion – A novel set within the Jacobite Rebellion

It is May 1745 and the British army is licking its wounds following defeat at the hands of the French at Fontenay. Meanwhile, there is a stirring in the north as the restless clans are gathering to the standard of the House of Stuart where Prince Charles Edward Stuart, the Young Pretender, is forming an army ready to invade England and reclaim the thrones of England and Scotland for his father, James III.

Captain Ewan McLeod of the Royal Scots waits by the roadside in Northern France for a carriage. A carriage that carries the man who will send him on his next mission. Perhaps the most dangerous mission he has undertaken, for he is to be sent home to the highlands of his youth and to his estranged family in the service of the crown.

As the Jacobites march south, so too do Ewan McLeod and his comrade Fiona Ross as the Hanoverian government struggles to respond to the threat they had underestimated. And who is betraying Ewan and Fiona? Not only must they keep their spymasters informed of developments, they also seek to discover the identity of the traitor in their midst before one or both of them dies.

Blackjack

A collection of short stories spanning a range of genres.

Some of these appeared previously in the first four books of the Underdog Anthologies (listed overleaf)

Sinistré (The Morning Cloud Chronicles)

The collected tales of a half-breed female gunslinger in the Wild West. The life of Sinistré is told in a series of stand-alone short stories, with illustrations by the author.

LEG IRON BOOKS

Also available from Leg Iron Books:

Fiction:
    'The Underdog Anthology, volume 1'
    'Tales the Hollow Bunnies Tell' (anthology II)
    'Treeskull Stories' (anthology III)
    'The Good, the Bad and Santa' (anthology IV)
    'Six in Five in Four' (anthology V)
    'The Gallows stone' (anthology VI)
    'Christmas Lights… and Darks' (anthology VII)
    'Transgenre Dreams' (anthology VIII)
        All edited by H.K. Hillman and Roo B. Doo.

    'The Goddess of Protruding Ears' by Justin Sanebridge.
    'De Godin van de Flaporen' by Justin Sanebridge (in Dutch)
    'Ransom', by Mark Ellott
    'Rebellion' by Mark Ellott
    'Blackjack' a collection of short stories by Mark Ellott.
    'Sinistré (The Morning Cloud Chronicles)' by Mark Ellott
    'The Mark' by Margo Jackson
    'You'll be Fine' by Lee Bidgood
    'Feesten onder de Drinkboom' by Dirk Vleugels (in Dutch)
    'Es-Tu là, Allah?' by Dirk Vleugels (in French)
    'Jessica's Trap' by H.K. Hillman
    'Samuel's Girl' by H.K. Hillman
    'Norman's House' by H. K. Hillman
    'The Articles of Dume' by H.K. Hillman
    'Fears of the Old and the New' short stories by H.K. Hillman
    'Dark Thoughts and Demons' short stories by H.K. Hillman

Non-fiction:
    'Ghosthunting for the Sensible Investigator' first and second editions, by Romulus Crowe.

Biography:
    'Han Snel' by Dirk Vleugels (in Dutch).

Printed in Great Britain
by Amazon